Betray your lover
Dirty your family name
Violate all you call holy
Help murder your brother . . .

These were only the first steps in the education of Danny Andradi, promising young attorney, in the ways of his new calling.

For Danny was soon to become Don Andradi of the Brotherhood, a ruling power in the most incredible criminal organization of all time.

Here is the story of Danny's bloody rise to power in the hierarchy of crime, of the men he crushed and of the forbidden woman he loved.

But even stranger and more chilling is the third face of Danny Andradi, agent for the strangest secret agency ever known, the handful of trained counter-assassins known only as FANG.

Empire of Evil

Sterling Noel

WILDSIDE PRESS

ONE

From the old Carroll Mansion in South Flatbush, on the outer fringe of Brooklyn's Little Italy, to the high-walled villa of Lupi Mazzarini in the hills behind Palermo are some 6,000 miles and two hundred years. It is a voyage I embarked upon in November of 1957, and it may be said that I covered much of the time as well as the distance, for a necessary part of this traveling was to associate myself with an ancient and evil tradition of Western Sicily.

The beginning of this voyaging was an unanticipated incident which came at the end of a birthday *festa* of an old Sicilian by the name of Salvatore Turrini, irrascible and lovable Uncle Sal, who raised my brother Tony and me following the death of our mother, who was his sister, when I was six and Tony eight.

This was November 13, a day that had started like any other and had progressed to late afternoon with no unusual occurence. For me there had been the interminable rewriting, paragraph by paragraph, of a brief in the case of *Coley Prentiss et al* vs. *Chatham Trust Co.*, a legal matter of little general interest. At 5:30 I was in my apartment on East 50th Street rewrapping my purchase of a couple of bottles of Misilmeri, a strong, heavy-bodied Sicilian wine unloved by Americans, when Tony arrived.

Tony was carrying a package wrapped in silver paper. He said, "Where'd you get the Misilmeri, Dando?"

"Castelli had a couple of bottles for his own use," I said. "I talked him out of them. For Uncle Sal he'd do it."

"Good boy. I found some Zucco up in the Bronx that will take the varnish off a dining-room table. . . . Can I borrow one of your shirts?"

"Sure." I pointed to the open bedroom door. "Help yourself."

Tony was like a Jesuit I knew; he would seize every opportunity to divest himself of his clerical collar and appear among the multitudes as a civilian. I never asked him why; I suppose some priests are just that way.

I stood in the bedroom doorway and said, "Uncle Sal's going to think you've been excommunicated."

5

Tony laughed. "I want to keep Uncle Sal off the Church's back tonight. Without my collar, maybe he'll forget that I'm personally responsible for the omissions of his favorite saints."

"He put Saint Filippo in the fish pond last month when it wouldn't stop raining."

"That's what I mean," said Tony. "He's liable to dunk me in the fish pond because it hasn't rained since."

We left the apartment together, carrying our packages, and got a cab on Third Avenue. I gave the driver Uncle Sal's address and we drew up in front of the rococo mansion at a few minutes before seven.

The Carroll Mansion is one of those turn-of-the-century eyesores with turrets and gingerbread and big bay windows. It is two-stories high, a rambling structure amidst a half-acre of garden. The modern apartment houses that crowd around it make it doubly obsolete. The interior matches the outside, with heavy, mahogany and plush chairs and sofas, tapestries, religious pictures, oriental rugs, and a truly wondrous collection of gimcracks from Sicily and America—the accumulation of a long lifetime.

There was nothing in this house that was not familiar to me and held in great affection, for it was within these rooms that I had grown up. I had bounced upon all of the sofas and the chairs, I had played upon the rugs and slid upon the parquet floors and had spent many fascinating hours with the coins in their glass case, the row of brightly-colored china saints, the souvenirs from Palermo and Niagara Falls and Siracusa and Atlantic City, the collection of knives and pistols, and the pottery and bronzes that were said to have come from the graves of the Greeks.

It was a wonder-house for a boy. And for both Tony and myself it was home, a sanctuary where none of the world's evils could reach us. Guarding this sanctuary was the tall, dynamic figure of our Uncle Sal, now stooped with age but nevertheless still a giant among men, who commanded the deepest respect from all who knew him.

Uncle Sal had come to America in 1927 to escape what was described as the persecution of one of Mussolini's minions, Ceasare Mori. Today I know that this Mori was Il Duce's police chief in Palermo and that he was sent there to wipe out the Sicilian secret society, the Mafia, and I suspect it was prosecution rather than persecution that brought Uncle Sal across the sea, but I know also that Uncle Sal was never an active *mafioso*—that he was accepted and assisted by the evil Brotherhood out of reverence for our family. There are several such families in Western Sicily, and the Turrinis are one of them, as are the Andradis, which is my father's family.

We are referred to, aften with malice, as *padroni dei fondi*, which means literally lords of the land, although the land we Andradis were the lords of had been reduced a hundred years ago to a few very unattractive acres behind the fishing village of Castellammare, west of Palermo. B'ut tradition is strong in this island society of tribal formalism, so even the dreaded Mafia bowed down to the names that had once been great.

Tony and I entered the front door without ringing, as one would in his own home, and we found Uncle Sal in the big parlor off the main hall, holding court with various Turrinis and Andradis and other callers from nearby Little Italy. The *festa* was well under way, the wine was flowing, and from a hi-fi against a far wall boomed the duet from *La Forza del Destino*, sung as it never has been since by Scotti and Caruso.

Our welcome was noisy and emotional, as only Sicilians know how to make a welcome, and after uncles and aunts and nieces and nephews and cousins and friends had been embraced and toasts had been drunk and our presents placed in the hands of Uncle Sal, old Pietro, the finest Sicilian cook west of the *paese bellissimo*, announced dinner.

We trooped to the huge dining room. The great board was set for thirty-odd and its three brass candelabra cast a warm glow over the white linen, the silver, and the steaming plates of minestrone.

Tony sat on Uncle Sal's right and I on his left. Uncle Sal said, "Tony, why do you not appear tonight as a priest?"

"I am a priest," replied Tony. "The collar—the vestments can make me no more so."

"No," said Uncle Sal, "you appear like this—this lawyer." He motioned towards me and his voice had in it all of the scorn with which he regarded my profession.

Tony laughed. "The law has its temples, too," he said.

"The law is not for honest Sicilians," said Uncle Sal with conviction. "Say grace for us, Tony, and we will begin our banquet."

The dinner was served by Pietro's Marie, and a half-dozen of their relatives of various sizes and ages, and was one of the finest of the score or more November 13 banquets I remember. All of the dishes were Sicilian, as usual, with the national fish, the sardine, playing a big part. The wines were also Sicilian, with the best of these a dry Marsala that was a delight. Uncle Sal drank the first toast in this wine— an old Sicilian toast to the *vendemmia*, the grape harvest.

"Travagghia la vinnigna, t'insigna, ti springa, t'alligna e ti spigna." (The work of the vineyard instructs thee, delights thee, reinvigorates thee and lifts thy debts.)

7

Following the minestrone, there were steaming casseroles of *maccaroni con sarde*, followed by the delicious *sarde beccafico*, prepared with infinite patience and affection by Pietro. Then there were the usual roasts, followed by a *falsamagra* which I hadn't tasted for years, a meat roll stuffed with herbs and cheese. The deserts were *cannoli* and *cassata*, then the cheese and the fruit and the strong Zucco wine that is like a liqueur, and the coffee.

I had seldom seen Uncle Sal in such good spirits, for his habitual face to the world varied between gruff impatience and a sort of regal indifference. As the banquet progressed and the arguments and discussions swept up and down and across the board, Uncle Sal said, "My two boys have returned to their home and so this old man is happy."

I said, "I was here last week and the week before that, and so was Tony."

"But tonight is different," he said. "Tonight we are a family again." He gestured down the table. "Milo and Bianca and Armando and Sido and Veronica—these are the ones who are close to my heart. And you and Tony, my sons. It is a night to be truly sentimental."

Tony said, "You talk as though you were lonely, Uncle Sal."

He shook his head. "No, not lonely, but I do miss those who are not here—your father Rocco and my sister Tresca. They would have so enjoyed this *festa*. . . . And when I think of Tresca I wonder if she would approve of how I have brought up her two boys. You, Tony, I am not worried about, for I know she always wanted a son in the Church. But Danny—I don't know. What would she have thought of the law?"

I said, "Mother would not have disapproved, as you do. She was not too fond of these out-moded Sicilian traditions."

Uncle Sal laughed. "No, Tresca was a modern one!" he exclaimed. "Have I told you how she insisted upon going to college—an American college—and the troubles we had with all of her airs when she was admitted to Barnard?"

It was a story we had heard a hundred times, but we listened again to this recitation of affection and family revolt. Uncle Sal had been very proud of his baby sister and her lone defiance of the old customs. "I have kept my promise to her," he concluded. "I have seen that her sons were educated—that they have taken positions of importance in the world. Some day, Danny, you will become a great judge, a man of prominence, and even I will overlook the degrading aspects of your chosen work."

8

"I'll spend my time on the bench putting Turrinis in jail," I said.

"It's more likely you'll put an Andradi in jail," said Tony.

Uncle Sal nodded. "Your brother Rocco is a bad one," he said. "The rotten apple."

"You've heard from him?" I asked.

Uncle Sal shrugged. "There is always trouble when I do. Now these gangsters insist that I take them into my business so that they can deal with disreputable firms in Palermo—a group of cutthroats that I know well."

"You have refused?" asked Tony.

"Of course I have refused. I have an honest business. I will have nothing to do with their smuggling and their extortion and their rackets!"

Tony asked, "Do you want me to talk to Rocco?"

"No," replied Uncle Sal. "Talking will do no good. You know that."

"I'll see him, then," I said. "And not to talk."

"No, I will handle this," said Uncle Sal. "I know these people. They will listen to me—even your brother Rocco. This is an evil I know about."

"What evil?" I asked.

"The Mafia," said Uncle Sal. "The Brotherhood."

"Don't tell me that we have the Mafia with us in twentieth-century America!" I said.

Tony looked across the table at me and held up a finger. "For a lawyer, you are very naive," he said. "Don't you read anything but law books?"

Uncle Sal spoke in the Sicilian dialect, *"Tra la legge e la Mafia, la piu temibile non e la legge."* (Between the law and the Mafia, the law is not the most to be feared.)

Tony laughed. He said, "Not as represented by my baby brother!"

Uncle Sal leaned over and put an arm across my shoulder. He said, "I think that only in America will the Mafia find out some day that this is not true. Tonight, Dando, I will say for the first time that I accept you as a lawyer. You were more knowing than I, for it is the law that we honest Sicilians need."

This was quite a speech from Uncle Sal, and one that I have had good reason to remember. Later when the relatives and guests had taken their noisy and emotional departures, and we three were alone together in the small library for a final glass of wine, Tony brought up the Mafia once more. He asked, "Uncle Sal, have you spoken about this matter to the police?"

The old man nodded. "I have talked to my friend Orsini,

but there is nothing he can do. It is now just a vague threat. We must hope nothing will come of it."

As we were finishing our wine the distant sound of the doorbell came to our ears and presently Pietro brought two late guests to the library, a pair of hard-faced Sicilians, sharply dressed in the manner of successful hoodlums. Uncle Sal knew them and introduced them—Sam Scalisi and Joe Venturi—and I could see that Tony felt as uncomfortable and as depressed as I at the intrusion.

Venturi said, "We wanted to talk to you alone, Don Turrini."

"These are my family," said Uncle Sal. "They will hear what you have to say."

Venturi looked at me and shrugged. "We have been told to come back once more to ask you about the partnership," he said.

"You pick a very inconvenient hour," said Uncle Sal.

"We didn't pick no hour," said Venturi. "We were told. There is a meeting tomorrow and this matter will have to be settled by then, so there isn't much time. We are to tell you that you will have to agree, now."

"I will agree to nothing," said Uncle Sal in a quiet voice.

"Then we will take back our import company," said Venturi.

"Your import company!" exclaimed Uncle Sal angrily. "I myself have built up this business, from nothing! It belongs to no gangsters! It is mine so long as I live. That was the agreement."

Venturi said, "I'm just telling you what I was told to tell you."

Tony said, "I think you two had better leave. We have had enough of this discussion."

Venturi bowed to him, but there was a sneer on his face. "I know you—Tony the Priest. You better start saying some prayers for Uncle Salvatore."

Tony was white-faced with anger. "There will be no prayers for you, Mr. Venturi."

I said, "Come along, boys, I'll show you the way out."

TWO

On NOVEMBER 14, YOU MAY RECALL, A MEETING WAS held at Apalachin, New York, of the sixty-three Dons of the Mafia. For the first time I found myself reading the crime news in the daily press with careful interest. I must admit that the idea of a Sicilian secret society controlling the underworld in modern America seemed too fantastic to accept, and yet here was evidence, presented day by day in reputable newspapers, that the old moustache Petes of the Black Hand had evolved into a streamlined organization of crime. These were not the illiterate *contadini*; these were now the masters.

On Friday I finished the first draft of the brief on Prentiss-Chatham Trust and late in the afternoon Judge Alfredi, senior partner of Alfredi, Collins & Campbell, dropped by my cubby-hole office to smoke a cigar. His black, Italian cheroots had been forbidden by his doctor and his secretary, Emma Fenton, was by nature an enforcer, so he had to bootleg them down the hall. He lit his cigar, put his feet up on my desk, and sighed with satisfaction.

"That's a good brief, boy," he said. "If we win that case against those robbers, you're going to be a junior partner. That's the carrot I'm holding out in front of the ass's nose."

The Judge was one of my favorite human beings—a great bulk of wisdom and humor with a militant honesty that shone forth like a sun in a profession often noted for devious ethics. It was the Judge himself who had picked me from my class at Columbia Law and had installed me in his firm as man of all work and understudy to one of the most fabulous memories in jurisprudence. He was another Uncle Sal in many ways—a good, solid third father.

"We'll win it if there's any justice," I said.

"That's an unworthy notion, Danny," he said. "The only justice is what we lawyers manufacture with our briefs . . . I had an inquiry about you today by one William Orsini. You getting into trouble with the police?"

"The police? Certainly not."

"This Orsini is a Deputy Police Commissioner—used to know him when I was a boy down on Bleeker Street."

"I've heard my Uncle Sal mention him," I said. "I've never met him. What did he want to know?"

"Oh, general things—your character, what we thought of you."

"I wonder why?" I said.

The Judge blew a smoke ring and regarded it critically as it wafted upward. "He might want to steal you away from us," he said.

"Not me! I've got my career, right here."

"That's what I told him," said the Judge. He put his feet on the floor, crushed out his cigar, and stood up. "I'm going home. You want a ride uptown?"

"No thanks, Judge. I've got a couple of hours more digging."

He pointed to the newspaper open in front of me on my desk. "You won't find anything on trusts in there."

"I've been reading about Apalachin," I said.

He came back and stood over me. "That is a very distressing thing," he said. "It reflects discredit upon all of us of Italian descent—particularly Sicilians. The newspapers call these people the crime overlords of America, and it must be so. It frightens me, to realize that such people have acquired such power. I have never underestimated the underworld, but if the information we are getting about this Apalachin meeting is true, then its menace is ten-fold, and it is time we did something about it."

"Our F.B.I. and our police agencies can handle it," I said.

He shook his head. "I'm afraid not. No, this will take more than police. Even our criminal codes are not designed to deal with such nation-wide organization."

"What would you suggest?" I asked.

He ran his fingers through his mane of iron-gray hair. "It is a matter requiring much thought," he said. Then he bade me good-night and left.

It was around 8:00 P.M. that I finished the last of my research of cases bearing upon trust agreement violations and I found at least two more that would go into my brief on its final draft. I suddenly realized that I was hungry and I had just put on my coat and picked up my hat when my phone rang.

It was Tony, speaking so low that I could barely make out his words. "Dando?"

"Yes. Hello, Tony."

"Come over to Brooklyn right away. Uncle Sal is dead."

"What! Uncle Sal!"

"Hurry, Dando."

There were three police cars and an ambulance in front of the Carroll Mansion when the cab pulled up. There were twenty or thirty people standing around, drawn there by mob curiosity, and a cop was in front of the closed iron gate, his nightstick dangling on its cord from his right hand. I paid the cab driver and walked across the sidewalk to him, pushing past a couple of eager teen-agers.

"I'm Daniel Andradi," I said.

He looked at me stonily, unmoving. A photographer lifted his camera and the unexpected flash of the bulb startled and angered me.

"I live here," I said. "I'm going in."

He stepped out of the way so I could enter the gate. The front door opened and two white-coated men came out, one carrying a basket-stretcher under his arm. There were two reporters on the stoop, press cards in their hats, and they walked with the ambulance men, plying them with questions. One of the reporters spotted me as I approached and came over and put a hand on my arm.

"Who are you?" he demanded.

I pushed past him, giving him a small football hip-block and ran up the steps. The door was still open and I could see the blue uniform of a policeman in the hall. Then behind him I saw Tony, his face drawn as though in pain, his hair rumpled. He saw me as I got to the door and came quickly, putting an arm around my shoulder.

There were bloodstains on his collar and on the right shoulder of his black coat. His arm held me firmly and when he spoke his voice was steady, but anger was close to the surface.

"Uncle Sal was shot while he was walking Bello, down at the corner," he said. "I was just crossing the street—I'd come from the subway. There were two men in a new car, a black Cadillac. They had stopped and one of them got out. Then the shots—three of them in quick succession—and the man jumped in the car and it sped away. I ran and I found Uncle Sal lying on the sidewalk dead. Bello was standing over him, growling, and he tried to bite me when I picked up Uncle Sal and brought him home. . . . Danny, I'm sick. I'm sick at heart. A thing like this can't happen to us!"

"Where is he?" I asked.

Tony led me across the hall to the wide stairway and we climbed slowly, side by side. There was another policeman in the upper hall just outside the door to Uncle Sal's big bedroom. He opened the door for us and we went in.

There was a policeman just inside writing in a notebook with a frayed black cover. A plain clothesman was sitting

13

at Uncle Sal's mahogany desk, filling out a printed form. There were two men in civilian clothes standing by one of the windows and they turned to look at us. One was in his thirties with a hard, Irish face. The other was a much older man, nearing sixty, and was about my height but twenty pounds heavier. His hair was gray at the temples which gave him a distinguished look, but the set of his mouth and the attitude of his body gave the impression, too, that he was a fighter; that he was no one to cross.

I stopped just inside the door and looked at the huge four-poster bed. In the center of the blue-silk spread was a huddled form covered with a sheet.

Tony went to the bed and drew the sheet back. I moved to his side and looked down upon the face of an old Sicilian man. There was a blackened wound high on his forehead. There were two blackened holes in his throat. There was a stubble of gray beard on his chin and his mouth was set in a severe line, as though he were admonishing Tony and me for some infraction.

Tony stood holding the edge of the sheet. "There he is," he said.

I picked up one of his cold, lifeless hands, then dropped to my knees beside the bed. Tony joined me and we prayed silently. Then Tony said three "Our Fathers." We got to our feet and the older man who had been by the window came over to us. He put an arm on Tony's shoulder.

"I'm Bill Orsini," he said to me. "You're Danny?"

I nodded and took his proffered hand. I said, "You're the police, aren't you?"

"Yes," he replied.

"You let this happen?"

"All the police in New York couldn't have stopped it," he said in a tired voice.

"That's a damnable admission," I retorted.

He nodded. "It is. Whether we know it or not, the underworld rules the world."

"Only because you permit it," I said.

"No, son, it is not a matter of permission." He looked at me hard for a moment. "In the usual course of events, nobody would testify against these killers, even if we found them. Witnesses who were so foolish would not live twenty-four hours."

"You find them," I said.

Tony shook his head at me. "No, Dando. There is nothing you can do. There is nothing any one man can do."

"Somebody's got to do something," I insisted.

"Somebody will," said Orsini. "Just remember that, son, somebody will."

For two days there was the wake for Uncle Sal. The old mansion was thronged with relatives, friends, and neighbors from Little Italy who came to pay their last respects. Pietro and his Marie worked day and night in the kitchen to prepare the food for the mourners. It was another *festa* for Uncle Sal. The last *festa*.

Tony and I stayed in the house, in the rooms we had occupied for so many years. I envied him his church and his faith, for they gave to him a strength which I lacked, and needed so much. His church was my church, but there is a great difference between the religious and mere worshippers. They have a conviction and understanding which is beyond us, and the secret things about death do not frighten them.

I saw Orsini on Saturday and again on Sunday evening when he came to my room with Tony. I can't say that I didn't resent him, for there was the strong feeling that the police had failed; that it was Orsini who was somehow to blame.

I said, "I don't suppose you've come to report that the killers have been arrested."

"There are some things you've got to try to understand," said Tony. "This is not a time for bitterness."

"What is it a time for?" I demanded.

Orsini took out a cigar and punctured the end. He said, "Fifty years ago we had a man on the force by the name of Joseph Petrosino who became interested in the Sicilian Black Hand society, the Mafia. He went after these extortionists with vigor and he became a legendary figure in the Little Italy of those days, around Mulberry Street. He sent some 500 *mafiosi* back to Sicily and Italy. He knew more about the Mafia than any man in America. He became interested in its origins and the roots of its control, so he went to Sicily to study it at first hand. On a street in Palermo on March 12, 1909, amidst a throng of people, he was shot to death. He was getting too close to the source."

Orsini lit his cigar and puffed on it slowly.

"Why would the Mafia kill Uncle Sal?" I demanded.

"They killed Salvatore because he was in their way—because he would not co-operate with them," he replied.

"What do the police do while such things are going on?"

"Perhaps it is not entirely a matter for the police," Tony said.

I replied, "I can find the two men who were here after

15

the *festa*—Scalisi and Venturi—and kill them. Is that what you have in mind?"

"No," said Tony. "Such vengeance would be stupid and you know it. Scalisi and Venturi didn't kill Uncle Sal, nor did they order him killed."

Orsini said, "We believe the order was given at the Apalachin meeting of the Dons. . . . It is something to think about, when the underworld is so well organized that its leaders hold conferences and decide who must die."

I said, "You're the police. You think about it."

Tony said, "Let's all think about it, Dando. When you have stopped being angry, you will be able to see more clearly the problems that have to be solved."

On Monday morning there was the funeral for Uncle Sal, and that was the end of that *festa*. It was the end of a lot of other things, too, but not of my anger.

When we were walking from the graveside back to our car, Tony said, "There is a proverb in the argot of the Mafia, *Bell' arti parrari picca*—'To speak little is a fine art.' As your brother, the little I want to say to you is that the death of Uncle Sal should be avenged—but in the right way. . . . As a churchman, of course, I should not say any of this."

I said, "Do you want to be more specific?"

He shook his head. "In time you will learn about it."

Two men came into my office in the middle of December. I had moved two doors up the hall from my small cubbyhole, now a junior partner in the firm of Alfredi, Collins & Campbell as the result of an unexpectedly quick verdict in the Chatham Trust case. There was a broad desk and visitors' chairs and my own bookcase, and I had three clients of my own, counting the two new arrivals.

These two were unprepossessing. One was about six feet tall, quite thin, with a large nose and pale blue, watery eyes. He carried a paper sack under his arm tied with white string. His companion was several inches shorter, a little plumper, and had sparse and unkempt gray hair. The tall one was McFarland, the shorter Bayliss, and they had apparently talked to George Campbell before being passed on to me.

McFarland said, "We want you to represent a friend of ours. He's out of the country just now, but he'll come back and give himself up when we say the word. It's embezzling."

"We don't handle criminal cases," I said. "Didn't Mr. Campbell tell you that?"

"Yeah, he told us, and he said you could handle it for us if you wanted to, sort of on your own."

"I have no interest in criminal law," I said. "Why in the world did you come to this firm?"

"We got to have a respectable lawyer," McFarland said. "We don't want no shysters. . . . There's real dough in it, Mr. Andradi."

I shook my head. "It's not a question of the fee, Mr. McFarland."

"Look," he said earnestly, leaning forward in his chair and slapping his hand on my desk, "the money means nothing to us. We can't spend it, but you could make it legitimate. You're a big lawyer and nobody would question where it came from. There's ten grand in it for you if you play along with us. Ten grand all tax free, Mr. Andradi."

He put the paper bag on my desk and snapped the string. It was filled with packages of banknotes and they spilled out—a very pretty sight to a three-day-old junior partner.

Bayliss spoke up for the first time, echoing my thought. "Ain't that pretty?" he said.

I said, "I don't know what you expect to buy, but you've come to the wrong store. Embezzlement doesn't interest me."

"We could make it fifteen grand," said McFarland.

I shook my head at him. "Why me?"

Bayliss said, "Maybe he's too sharp, Joe. Maybe we come to the wrong place."

"All right," said McFarland. "What's the percentage?"

"The percentage?"

"Yeah. How much do you figure you're worth?"

I said, "Will you two gentlemen kindly get the hell out of here?"

Bayliss said, "We'll go as high as forty per cent. No more. Not one cent more."

"That would be eighty grand," added McFarland. "But you'd have to handle the whole stake. You'll have to clean it all up for us."

I got up. I picked up the bag of money and stuffed the packages into it. I walked around the desk and put the bag against McFarland's chest, hard. I said, "I've asked you to leave. Now I'm going to insist upon it."

They got up and backed to the door. Bayliss said, "He's nuts. Come on, Joe."

McFarland said, "I guess we made a mistake."

I clo d the door after them.

THREE

Two days later, on December 18, there was a phone call from a man with a cultured voice who said, "We are ready to discuss the death of your uncle, Salvatore Turrini, with you. Will you meet us?"

"Where?" I asked.

"Someone will pick you up on your way home tonight."

"Just like that?" I asked.

"Just like that."

He hung up and I was left with a dead phone in my hand and some unanswered questions. Was this the Mafia and the underworld, or was it the unnamed something both Tony and Bill Orsini had hinted at? Was somebody after me now? And if so, was it good or bad? I admit I was apprehensive.

I wasted the two hours left until 5:30, then walked to the Wall Street station of the East Side subway, as was my custom. The subway platform was thronged as usual and I fought my way into the first train, getting wedged in the vestibule against the far door by a large, granite-faced woman in a camel's hair coat and a small, clerkish man with spectacles and a Homburg. I looked over the heads of my fellow-travelers but saw no one I recognized. So maybe it was the granite-faced woman or Homburg Hat. I smiled at each of them, tentatively, and collected a couple of scowls. In New York you don't go passing out smiles to strangers.

I fought my way out of the car at Grand Central and changed to a local. Granite Face got off, too, and hurried on down the platform, ignoring me. I lost track of Homburg Hat. The local was only half-full. I rode to Fifty-first Street and got off. Nobody accosted me. Then I saw the granite-faced dame coming along the platform from a rear car. I waited for her just inside the turnstile and she sailed past me without a look. I followed her up the stairs to the street and right at the top of the stairs she turned and glared at me, her hands on her hips.

"Are you following me?" she demanded.

"No, ma'am," I said.

She pointed a finger at my nose. "Well, don't."

A crowd was beginning to collect, as one will for no reason at all. Those behind me on the stairs pushed closer and several on their way down stopped to look.

"This is a public stairway," I said. "I'm free to use it."

She addressed the crowd. "He followed me all the way from Wall Street."

"That's absurd!" I protested. "I come home this way every night!"

She turned suddenly and was gone, down Lexington Avenue. Several people were muttering at me and I heard one woman say, "Probably a sex maniac." I hurried away from there as fast as I could without running, going east on Fifty-first. I slowed down in the middle of the block and looked back. No one was chasing me.

I stopped for the light at Third Avenue, intending to cross, and there was a tap on my arm. I admit I jumped. I turned quickly, ready to slug someone, and looked into the face of another granite-faced dame, very much like the first. This one had on a black overcoat trimmed with fur and a black, inverted-lampshade hat. She said, "Would you mind getting a cab for me, young man?"

I looked at her a moment, relieved, but I refrained from smiling. "Sure," I said.

I stepped out in the street and flagged down a green and white Ford. Then when it had stopped and I was opening the door, I wondered why she hadn't waved for it herself. Or was it unladylike to wave at cabs? She came up beside me and I helped her in. Then she said, "Get in, Mr. Andradi."

"What?" I said.

"Come, come," she said, "Don't keep the man waiting."

I climbed in beside her. She told the driver, "Four ninety-five East Fifty-second Street."

It was two long blocks and two short ones away. I leaned back on the cushions. If there was going to be any conversation, it was her problem.

As we crossed First Avenue she said, "You go up to Apartment 21 A."

"Is that all?" I asked.

"Yes, that's all."

I got out in front of this huge apartment building facing the river and she stayed in the cab. The doorman closed the door and followed me into the lobby.

"You're going to 21 A?" he asked.

I looked at him. He had a tired old face with great bags under his eyes. I said, "You know everything, huh?"

He nodded solemnly. "Sure."

I followed him to an elevator on the left of the lobby

and he handed me in with a courtly gesture. "Twenty-one," he said to the operator.

The door of 21 A was open and standing there was a brisk, immaculate man in his late forties. He held out a hand as I approached and said, "Mr. Andradi?"

"Yes," I replied. He grasped my hand firmly and moved me into the apartment, closing the door behind me.

"I'm Mr. Smith," he said.

(I will not use the name of this man or the names of his associates, for these men are still active and their identities must be guarded. Needless to say, the address I have given does not exist and I have carefully omitted or disguised other details so that there may be no clues to identities and locales.)

Smith led me into a large, high-ceilinged living room with a row of windows overlooking the river and the island. There was a fireplace large enough to roast an ox, with great divans on each side of it and a square coffee table between them. It was a baronial room, unexpected in modern New York.

There were two other men in this room, whom I shall call Jones and Clark. They both got up as we entered and Smith introduced me.

Jones was a warm and friendly man of enormous girth—he must have weighed close to 300 pounds—and he shook my hand with enthusiasm. His voice boomed from his great chest and he made me feel unaccountably welcome and at ease. Clark was his opposite physically—a small, anonymous man with gold-rimmed spectacles and a head as bald as a zucchini. But his greeting, too, was warm and his handshake hearty.

I sat on the divan next to Smith and the two sat across from us, Jones in the very center and Clark wedged into a corner as though he were withdrawing from the proceedings.

There was an array of bottles and a large ice bucket on the coffee table and Smith mixed me a scotch and soda, then leaned back and looked at me. "It is very good to see you here, Mr. Andradi," he said. "We have been anticipating this meeting for several weeks."

I nodded at him. "You were going to talk about the death of my uncle, Salvatore Turrini?"

"Yes," he replied, "but there are other things we wish to discuss first in this general connection. We are serious men —one could call us dedicated. We are of Italian descent, as you may have surmised, and the problem we seek to solve is close to the hearts of all men who are related to Italy.

Our aim is to destroy the effectiveness of the Sicilian Secret Brotherhood, the Mafia."

He fell silent and I looked up to find the three of them regarding me intently. I said, "I assumed it would be the Mafia, if anything at all was to be destroyed."

Jones smiled across at me. "Bill Orsini has told you a little about the Brotherhood," he said. "Tonight we will tell you the rest of it."

"I'm confused," I said. "Whom do you represent, you three?"

"We will tell you that in due course," said Smith. "I can assure you that we are moral men with a just cause. In one sense, I suppose, we could be called outlaws—or superlegal might be a more accurate definition—for our methods are not conventional. Our organization is a large one and potentially powerful, but it has not yet gone into action. We still lack one or two key personnel. That is why we have had you up here, Mr. Andradi."

I said, "This is very flattering, of course, but I am well situated and I am not contemplating a change."

"We thought that the execution of Salvatore Turrini by the Mafia might influence you," said Jones.

I didn't have anything to say to that. I sipped my drink and waited. Then Clark spoke up from his corner:

"I knew your uncle very well, Mr. Andradi. You may have heard him speak of me. He was killed because he was an honest man; he was killed because he refused to co-operate with the Mafia and the underworld. Doesn't that mean anything to you?"

"Yes," I replied, "it does."

"It must be obvious to you, Mr. Andradi, that the existing law agencies are not sufficient to deal with the Mafia."

"No sir," I said, "it is not. I admit that the New York Police Department was not able to prevent my uncle's murder, but I believe that the F.B.I. and the Congressional Committees and the Federal judiciary can handle this problem."

"They can't," said Jones, "and I'll tell you why. These agencies must operate within our code of laws. This code has grown over the centuries to protect the innocent and to prevent seizure of power by ambitious men. Guilt must be proved; accusation and suspicion are not sufficient as evidence; the law remains supreme regardless of a man's professed immorality.

"The Mafia is itself a highly organized secret government, with its own code and its own ruling hierarchy. It is a disciplined, tribal oligarchy, dedicated to crime, ruled by a council of seniors who have the power of life and death over all Brothers. Their code is called *omertà*. It requires specifically that all *mafiosi* must violate the laws of our country and adopt instead their rules of immorality, under pain of death. It provides that the only loyalty is to the Mafia.

"This is a peril that is beyond the control of our laws. The present power and immunity of the underworld prove it. We do not plead the law for mad dogs, Mr. Andradi. Mad men such as these deserve no more."

I said, "Put that way, I can see your point. But if this Mafia super-government is as strong as you say, you'll never wipe it out in our lifetime."

"We do not expect to wipe it out entirely," said Smith. "Crime and the underworld will always exist. What we will do is to destory its national and international organization. It is this organization that the Mafia has contributed to the underworld. Without it the activities of our criminal elements can be contained by ordinary police methods."

"It is an ambitious plan," I said. "If your methods are sound, you may succeed."

"Our methods," said Clark, "are the Mafia's own—secrecy, terror, murder. The Mafia has proved them sound and so shall we. This is not a Sunday-school picnic, Mr. Andradi."

I looked around at the three and tried to reconcile this dire pronouncement with their accoutrements of civilzation. Could this suave, intellectual Smith commit murder? Or the fat, jolly Jones or mousy, retiring Clark? It did not seem possible, yet in wartime such men as these—conventional, successful householders—had killed and been killed. The veneer of civilization was only so thick.

I said, "Where would a struggling young lawyer fit into your plans?"

Jones sighed as though he had been waiting too long for this question. "You are unique, Mr. Andradi," he said. "You possess the priceless combination of background, honesty, and ability to perform the most critical function of our Anti-Mafia. Your family origin in Castellammare, and its tradition, make you eligible for membership in the Mafia. You have a brother Rocco who is one of the most important Mafia Dons in the East, and he would sponsor you, under the right conditions. You could bring to the Mafia all of the fine intelligence that promises to make you outstanding in jurisprudence, and in a very short time you could become a *capo mafioso*. You would work from the inside, Mr. Andradi. Nowhere in America have we found anyone who could do this as you could."

I said, "There were a couple of men who came to my office the other day—McFarland and Bayliss. They were from your organization?"

"Yes," said Smith. "Those are our men."

"They were very good," I said.

Smith smiled at me. "So were you," he said.

"What we offer you is not very enticing," said Jones. "I will admit it. You would have to become one of them—a hoodlum. You would be publicly disgraced. You would be disbarred. And you would be at all times in a most dangerous position. The compensation would be adequate from a material point of view, but I doubt that there ever would be enough money to pay you for the self-respect and the career you would have to sacrifice. . . . You would be serving your country and your Italian ancestors, as well as all honest Italians. Financially, we would give you a drawing account of all the money you would need for the rest of your life."

I finished my drink and Smith mixed me a fresh one. I don't remember now exactly what thoughts went through my mind, but I suppose I was weighing the material benefits against my law career. I was not thinking on a clearly conscious level—just vaguely and generally about these men and their Idea and my relation to them.

Clark said, "We don't think we made a mistake about you, Mr. Andradi. We believe that you are as interested as we are in controlling this murderous conspiracy. Your uncle's death has given you more personal motives than ours, but our aim is not a narrow vengeance, and we know yours is not. We are simply seeking to make our country a more decent place in which to live."

The discussion continued for many hours and the gray dawn had lighted the East windows before any decision was reached. For me, it was the most momentous decision of my life, and I did not arrive at it easily. Even now, I cannot tell you why I decided as I did, but I strongly suspect that pride of race and love of my father's people must have been overwhelming factors, for one does not thoughtlessly throw away a life's dream and the years of work it takes to support it.

And, of course, there was Uncle Sal and his violent death at the hands of my natural enemies. From that personal standpoint, it was war, and I was joining an army to fight this war.

At 6:35 A.M. I said, "All right, what do you want me to do next?"

FOUR

THE CONTROLLING ORGANIZATION OF ANTI-MAFIA, IS THE SO-called FAN-Group, a name derived from the initials of its three founders and known to us simply as FANG. Despite a wide-spread belief to the contrary, FANG is not, nor was it ever, a government agency, nor was I ever a government employee. In fact, I must insist that I never represented the government in any way and that my activities were never officially sanctioned. I know this may appear confusing, in view of the co-operation we were given from time to time which led to the commonly accepted fallacy that we were a federal agency. But since most of the confusion was within the Mafia itself, no real harm was done.

The first sacrifice I made for the Anti-Mafia was Francia Fortune, a dark-eyed, serious girl who had been in my life for a year. I very nearly chucked the whole thing when I was told that I must give her up, and I well might have if there had not been still the smouldering anger over Uncle Sal's murder.

The day following my meeting at East Fifty-second Street, I went to the Park Avenue office of a Dr. Harley Owens during the late afternoon. I was continuing my connection with Alfredi, Collins & Campbell and my FANG appointments were arranged not to interfere with my law work. Dr. Owens was a short, round man in his late forties, as neat and antiseptic in his white gown as his examination room. He and a plump, hot-eyed nurse put me through a thorough physical examination, then he took me into his office, closed the door, and started probing into the rest of me.

When he got to Francia, he questioned me closely—where I had met her and when, what our relationship had developed into, and exactly why I thought I might marry her and why she wanted to marry me.

Then he said, "It's no good, Dan. This girl is too close to you. She knows too much about you."

I said, "I'm willing to postpone the wedding, if that's what you want. As a matter of fact, she's been talking about it herself. She wants to give this industrial psychology business a whirl before she settles down to become a housewife."

"That's not what I mean," said Owens. "You'll have to give her up. Break with her. You're not going to fool any woman you've been intimate with—who loves you enough to go away on weekends with you. Especially not a psychology major at Smith. She'll see through you like a window."

"Now wait a minute! I'm not going to break with Francie!"

"I'm afraid you are. Break with her, Dan. Make up a good story and make it final. Don't leave any residue so you'll ever see each other again. That's an order."

I said, "You can't be serious! You've given me no reason! Why, I can't walk out on her—just like that!"

He smiled at me and shook his head. "How many times have you been in love, Dan?"

"Several times."

"Yes. Now think back. Did you love any of these others as much as you love Francia?"

I thought. I considered my first love, back in high school. Marie Cassell, another dark-eyed nymph like Francie—prettier, perhaps, but without Francie's mental equipment. I had loved her through months of misery and longing and frustration. Maybe I had loved her more than anyone I had loved since, for I had been unable to eat or study or conduct myself in any normal way. Then her parents had moved West and that was the end of that.

After Marie there had been fair Doris and then fair Marcia. . . . Marcia was the hedonist who introduced me to the mysteries of sex and she surely would have been my wife if she had been willing to tailor her ambitions to a law student with doubtful propsects. Marcia was my great regret.

"I probably loved a couple of them more," I replied, "but that's not the point. I don't want to miss the boat again."

"Ah, youth!" exclaimed Owens. "Always impatient, always in a hurry. You'll meet a dozen Francias a year, if you'll give yourself a chance. I don't mean to disparage her, Dan, but at your age the world is full of availible sweethearts and, if you're inclined, wives. I've given you a sufficient reason for my order, whether you want to agree with me or not. Any girl with whom you've been intimate knows too much about the inside of you to be safe for our organization. She knows how you think and why you think as you do. She knows how you feel, which is more important and more dangerous. She knows the emotional Dan Andradi, and the instant you change your emotional patterns she will be aware of it. . . . Do you honestly think that Andradi the lawyer could become Andradi the hoodlum without this Francia finding out why?"

25

"Perhaps not," I replied, "but I don't see that emotion has anything to do with it. This has not been an emotional step on my part."

"No?" he said. "Are you quite certain you're coming with the Anti-Mafia as the result of an intellectual process?"

I thought about that question. Then I said, "I'm seeing Francie tonight. I'll arrange something."

"Make it final," he said.

Francia Fortune was home from Smith for the holidays and would not return to Northampton until the week after the New Year. I picked her up at her apartment on Gracie Square at 7:30 that Wednesday evening. Her mother was home, and as usual she was unpleasant and unfriendly. Clara Fortune was an over-weight Irish woman who talked incessantly, with pride in the sharpness of her tongue. A favorite subject when I came to call was the inferiority of Italians. I listened to her for an interminable ten minutes while Francie put on the final gilding, then got out as quickly as possible.

Francie had always been amused by my inability to cope with her mother and this had never been a problem between us. But it could become a problem if I would say the right thing—or the wrong thing.

"Your mother is not always well mannered," I said.

Francie replied, "That's a disagreeable thing to say, Danny, even if it's true!"

We got a cab in front of her building and I told the driver to take us to the Stork Club. Francie said, "Aren't you spreading yourself? What's the matter with Nino's?"

"You don't want to go to the Stork?"

She leaned back on the cushions and regarded me for a moment. "You're being quarrelsome," she said. "What's the trouble, Danny? Are you getting involved with someone?"

I was startled by her question. It seemed that Dr. Owens had been right—that she certainly did know me too well. I said, "Nothing's happened that a night with you won't cure."

She shook her head. "There is something. If you're not going to tell me, you're not. But I wish you wouldn't try to be subtle about it. I can't stand big, clumsy, subtle men."

We dined well and danced often and talked little. I felt ill at ease and Francie knew it. I looked at her looking at me and what I saw of myself I didn't like.

We left the Stork at 1:00 A.M. and Francie suggested we ride around the park. She vetoed going to my apartment and that gave me the opening I'd been waiting for. I said,

"You don't maintain a very high level of interest in men, do you, darling?"

She said, "What do you mean by that?"

"Well, we haven't seen each other since Easter and I don't notice you rushing into my arms. . . . It's fine to be aloof and civilized, but it doesn't fit in very well with my Latin impulses."

"Is that what's been bothering you tonight? . . . My poor lamb!"

"Don't dissemble, sweetie. I've placed a proposition before the house. Let's have a frank statement."

"I'm not going to your apartment, if that's what you want to know."

"That's what I want to know. Thank you for being precise."

"Mother's right about one thing—you Latins will go tomcatting with anyone. Just so it's a girl."

"Your cotton-picking mother! Don't quote her to me!"

"You stop that, Dan. I will not have my mother insulted."

"That woman is beneath insulting. What concerns me are the cockeyed ideas you pick up from her and relay to me. I'm damned if I'm interested in what she thinks about anything. I thought you were more intelligent than to ape her."

"I think you'd better take me home right now."

"Right. I'll take you home."

We rode back to Gracie Square in silence. As the cab slowed down for her apartment I said, "You might tell your mother that the last girl I was tomcatting with was her daughter. That ought to jam her throttle."

She glared at me. "I never realized you were so vulgar. . . . Don't bother to get out. I'd rather go in alone."

"Good-bye, then," I said.

She slammed the cab door. It was a loud, final period to Francie.

My formal training to become a *mafioso* and a member of the Anti-Mafia began the end of February after a couple of months of nightly meetings with FANG agents designed to ease my way into association with hoodlums of various ilk and to establish the beginnings of a reputation for sharp practice and double-dealing.

I frequented the night clubs operated by the so-called Syndicate, gambling rooms and floating crap games, and quiet, private bars where the more conservative *mafiosi* gathered. I drank too much and I was often in the company of the women of this half-world. It is a period I don't like to write about, for it represented to me the abandonment of

27

all the ideals I had acquired in my twenty-seven years.

I saw myself losing the regard and respect of my former associates and particularly of those with whom I worked. I had many distressing conversations with Judge Alfredi, as well as with the very proper George Campbell, and I was made to feel that my position with the law firm was not at all secure; that I was in a period of probation and that I would have to mend my ways.

My most constant companions on these nightly sorties were a suave, polished operator by the name of Finley Goodrich, a man of unusual gambling skills who introduced me to the jargon of the crap and poker tables, and a svelte, iron-hard blonde who called herself Connie Masters and was known in every saloon, plush and otherwise, from the Village to Yorkville. This Connie was a walking Who's Who on the underworld and she pointed out patiently, night after night, those whom I should know and know about. She taught me particularly how to recognize the Ivy League hoodlums, how to approach them, and what attitudes I must assume to be accepted.

"Your position is that the law is lucrative if one is smart. Don't be afraid to use that word. From now on, that's what you are—smart. You spend freely, buy lots of rounds of drinks, bet heavily and don't mind losing, and they'll know you are—that your particular racket is law. It's very simple when you do it that way."

One night early in February, I was in El Morocco with Connie and Francia came in with a short, blond man about my own age. Francie nodded to me distantly as they passed our table, to sit across the room from us.

Connie said, "That's the one, eh?"

"The ex," I replied. "How did you know?"

"You almost jumped out of your chair. You've got to learn to control that, Dan. Especially with women. Never jump."

I looked at Francie, engaged in intimate conversation with her man, and I tried to analyze my feelings. I couldn't. I didn't even feel depressed. Then Connie poked me in the side with her elbow.

"There's someone you'll meet," she said.

I followed her gaze to a couple coming in, a stocky, gray-haired man in a beautifully cut suit and a long-legged girl in a gray sheath dress with the most sensational figure I'd ever seen. I couldn't take my eyes from her. She had neat, golden curls and when she turned her face towards me as she sat down a couple of tables away, my heart did a somersault.

"Not the girl," said Connie, "and stop staring. That's not for you—that's Trina Templer, the singer. The guy she's with is Frank Magardi, Don Magardi, who is the biggest operator in the East. He's got Diamond Records and a dozen legitimate businesses. Nationally, he's the Jukebox King and pulls all the strings in the truckers' union."

I heard what she said but I wasn't listening. I was comparing this Trina Templer with little Francia across the room, which was a mean thing to do.

I said, "Why would a girl like that go out with a hoodlum?"

"She doesn't go out with hoodlums. She's out with the guy who owns Diamond, that's all. She sings for Diamond. She's Corrine Templer, Back-Bay Boston social, and her family's got more loot than even Magardi."

"That's the girl for me," I said.

"Forget it," said Connie. "You're away over your head, Danny-boy. You're drowning."

On February 16, I took a leave of absence from Alfredi, Collins & Campbell. The buildup had been ill health, which I had been feigning for a week, and the report from Dr. Owens said I was on the verge of a nervous breakdown. I went to a farm in the back-country of Connecticut, a few miles outside of Higganum, and began my serious studies to become a hoodlum.

The farm was operated by Forest Wiley and his wife Doris and had been used for several years as the training school for FANG agents. Wiley, in his fifties, was a former F.B.I. special agent, and he conducted courses in gunnery, judo, and various police methods. Doris Wiley, an M.D. and psychologist, was one of the foremost specialists in the country on memory and recall, and on my first day she started a complete and systematic reorganizing of my mind so that I would remember the mass of data that was to be stuffed into it. She was the most remarkable of my many teachers, and she remains to this day a close friend.

The staff comprised a dozen other experts, including a chemist who trained me in analysis and dilution of various narcotics; several men who taught me honest and crooked gambling and card handling; an ancient Sicilian who taught me the Sicilian dialect and particularly *il gergo mafioso*, the variable slang in which the *mafiosi* converse when giving orders or information; another Sicilian who schooled me in all of the traditions and apothegms of the Mafia, and a code expert who taught me how to converse with my own FANG group and how to identify myself.

There were courses dealing with the various machines

used and misused by the underworld—jukeboxes, slot machines, coin venders, etc.; there was instruction in sabotage of many sorts; there was a course in business administration, one in corporate law (a pipe for me), and another in organization and operation of labor unions. Each day there was an hour or more of identification, wherein moving pictures, still pictures and voice recordings of scores of Mafia Dons and other underworld characters would be studied.

There was nothing left to chance, insofar as these geniuses of FANG could anticipate. I was as thoroughly trained in all aspects of my new profession as could be devised by men of intelligence and perception. When they turned me loose upon the world I would represent the very acme in gangster erudition.

One of my teachers was a tall, skinny man with theatrical clothes and too much hair who suggested I call him Doctor, or Doc if I preferred, but who was otherwise as unfriendly as a coyote and as impatient as a post-office clerk. His speciality was arithmetic. It was his job to make me a mathematical whiz-kid. He taught me more about numbers and their relationships than Isaac Newton suspected, and by the time he was through with me I could add a column of figures at a glance, I could tell you all the odds in a ten-horse race according to the amounts wagered as fast as a pari-mutuel machine, and I could tell you how to bet a poker hand or a throw of the dice or a roulette wheel.

I sat for hours at a poker table and threw dice until my arm was sore. Along with this went instruction in the basic viewpoint of the gambler and I soon found myself, once a citizen of the most conventional honesty, accepting as normal a number of attitudes of surprising deviousness. What counted was the winning; what paid off was the dough, no matter how you got it. Only the suckers played by the rules—the smart boys made their own rules. And there was always the percentage. You never bucked the percentage. You always got on the percentage side and you'd let the suckers pay you. After all, there were only two kinds of people: wise boys and suckers. You were never a sucker.

Physically, I became as trained down as I had been when I played in the backfield at Columbia. I became a passable judo player and succeeded in taking falls now and then from my instructor, holder of a brown belt. But mostly I learned all of the dirty holds, barred from the game, and I learned how to defend myself under the most adverse circumstances.

Along with the judo went a course in knife-fighting and defenses against the knife. We were bundled up in heavily padded clothing and masks for this, but otherwise it was

30

more real than pleasant. I learned a lot but I never liked the knife and I was glad when this part of the instruction was over.

I preferred the gun, and I quickly became a fair shot at both moving and still targets. My instructor was one of the FANG front-line troops, a former F.B.I. man by the name of Carter Hills, who had won the National Pistol Shoot three years in succession and the International twice. He was the fastest man on the draw I have ever seen. He would give you a gun and tell you to aim at a target. Then at a signal you would fire and he would draw and fire. He would beat you every time, and he would usually get a better score than you. But I was pretty close to his speed before I was through.

The last four weeks at the farm were devoted largely to a unique code-language for FANG communications under adverse circumstances. I was given a vocabulary of some 200 words in common use and to each was ascribed an additional arbitrary meaning, these meanings to be determined by the position of the word in a sentence or the tense of a verb. I have no idea what genius devised this gobbledegook, but it was remarkable how simply information could be conveyed or help requested or a warning sent out.

Then I was given a list of a hundred or so telephone numbers, covering the entire country, and I was told to memorize them and use them for all contacts not otherwise arranged. The numbers had been selected in several single sequences, so this was not as difficult as it would appear.

What I have omitted from all of this lore is the method we FANG agents used for identification. I am not permitted to describe it, so I will say only that we used numbers, and that the numbers were always different according to the time of day or day of the week or month. Today, as I write this, at 2:25 P.M., the identification number I would give would be 135. That's about all I can tell you.

FIVE

O~~N~~ WEDNESDAY, JULY 3, I WROTE TWO LETTERS, ONE TO Judge Alfredi resigning from his law firm, and the other to my hoodlum brother Rocco asking for help. On Friday, July 5, I was indicted by the New York County grand jury on a charge of bribery.

Neither Tony nor I had seen Rocco for years and our parents had not seen him since he was first sentenced to prison. You have probably heard of him under his adopted name of Rocky Montana, overlord of the Brooklyn waterfront, King of the Stevedores, prominent suspect in every murder from Bay Ridge to Greenpoint. Don Montana, unsmiling, shrewd, strong, who didn't need anybody in the world except possibly his harem of whores.

Both Tony and I had made brotherly overtures to him when he had come out of prison in 1947, but we had been unable to reach him in any way. There was no communication, no understanding, no shared emotion. All we had before us was his unsmiling face and his hooded eyes, and if there was anything underneath it never showed through.

My note to him said: "I am out on a limb in a jury-fixing case. Conviction appears unavoidable, which will mean disbarment. Have you any influence, and if so will you spare some for me? What I need is a judge who will give me a suspended sentence. I can take care of a fine. I'll be back in New York in a few days and I'll phone you. Leave a number with Tony where I can reach you."

I got back to New York on a hot Sunday afternoon and phoned Tony from Grand Central. He was pastor at St. Mary's on Fordham Road in the Bronx and I got him at the parish house.

"Did you hear from Rocco, Tony?" I asked.

"Dando! Where have you been? What's this about your being indicted? What in the world is happening to you?"

"I can't talk to you, Tony," I said. "Just give me the phone number."

He gave it to me—a Manhattan number. Then he said, "When are you going to tell me the story, Dando?"

"One of these days," I said. "Not now."

32

"Everything's all right, then?"

"Yes."

"If you need any help, you know where to find me."

I went out to Lexington Avenue and got a cab. I told the driver to go east on Fiftieth Street, swing around Beekman Place, then come back west. There was a cop standing in front of my building, swinging his billy. He might have been the beat cop taking the air or he might have been waiting for me. On the West Side, just off Times Square, I checked into a hotel. I bought some magazines and a couple of paper-back reprints I'd wanted to read and settled into my room until Monday. At around midnight I called the number Tony had given me.

A girl with a low, sultry voice answered. After a couple of minutes Rocky came on.

"Yeah?"

"This is Danny, Rocky."

"Well! Little Danny-boy! So you're up to your ass in it, eh? You got yourself indicted!"

I said, "Yeah. You got my letter, didn't you?"

"You call me Monday night at this same number. Around this time. I always thought you were a stuffed-shirt bastard. Maybe you're not, eh Danny-boy?"

"I'll call you," I said, and hung up.

On Monday at 10:00 A.M. I got a cab to the D.A.'s office on Foley Square to present myself for detention and bail. I walked into the office of Mike Healey, an assistant D.A. and a Columbia Law School classmate.

I said, "O.K., Mike, you've got me. I surrender."

He looked at me sourly and shook his head. There wasn't anything light about this to Mike. "For crissake, Danny, what happened to you?" he demanded. "You're the last guy in the world this could have happened to."

"I'm just a throwback to my bandit ancestors," I said. "Trouble is, I got caught."

"It doesn't add up," he said. "You know it and I know it. You want to play it like a B-movie gangster with your cheap wisecracks, it's O.K. by me. What the hell are you trying to prove?"

I got hold of myself and held on tight. I'd had no idea it would be this bad, this difficult. I said, "You want to be my defense attorney or you want to prosecute, as they pay you to do?"

He got up. "Have it your way. We'll go see a judge. You got dough for bail?"

"Plenty," I said. "They pay real good for jury fixing."

33

"If I was six inches taller and thirty pounds heavier, I'd beat the hell out of you. Come on."

We took a cab to the midtown magistrate's court on West Fifty-fourth and we sneaked in ahead of a long line of drunks, whores, and disorderly conducts to have a huddle at the side of Judge Benny Coleman's bench.

Judge Benny said, "What the hell happened to you, Danny?"

I said, "Everybody asks me that, Judge. I got caught, that's all."

He stopped being friendly suddenly, as though someone had cut it off with a knife. You don't wisecrack about crime in a courtroom. "You plead guilty or not guilty, Andradi?"

"Not guilty, Your Honor."

He turned to Mike. "How much bail do you want?"

"The usual," said Mike. "A thousand ought to be enough on this charge."

"One thousand dollars bail," said the Judge. "Held for trail in Special Sessions—ah, let me see—Part Two next Monday. That's the fifteenth. Be there at 9:30 A.M. You got an attorney, Andradi?"

"I'll have one," I said.

He turned away in disgust. "Next case!"

I peeled off ten 100-dollar bills and gave them to the clerk and got a receipt. When I looked around for Mike, he was gone.

It hadn't taken him long. I was poison.

What difference does it make how I felt? My ambitions, my years of study, my dreams for juristic distinction, these are the things I had traded for something that, now, I can't even characterize. Perhaps, it, too, was a dream. . . . Well, you make your choice and then, if you've got any sense at all, you try not to regret it. You swap one dream for another.

I walked back to the hotel and checked out. I got a cab to my apartment and I phoned a FANG contact. I said, "This is one-sixty-two. I'm back home. Bail was $1,000 and the trial is the fifteenth. What's the scoop?"

"There is a fix," said the man. "You'll plead guilty and get an S.S. Then we'll bounce this judge right off the bench. Keep in touch. It's a fine beginning."

"For you," I said. "For me, it's grim."

"I'll come over and hold your hand."

"Nuts."

I didn't want to be alone. I didn't want to think that much. I could do these things if they were off the top of my head, but I needed more time to get used to them before I could think about them. I called the ice-blonde Connie Masters.

"You busy?" I asked.

"Yes."

"Come on over. I need somebody to talk to."

There was a moment of silence. "I shouldn't. I should make the rounds."

"This is more important. Bring something for lunch and I'll let you cook it."

"Oh thanks!"

She came in about 1:30 carrying a big bag of groceries. I had a shaker of martinis mixed and we sat in my small modern living room sipping and looking at each other gloomily. I liked this Connie, but in a way different from any girl I'd ever met. She was, I suppose, a real sex-charge to most men, and she did have a delightful figure and pretty legs, but there was a peculiar something else that had passed between us when we had first met that transcended the physical. It was a deep knowing, an empathy that can bring two people much closer together than sexual attraction. And I knew that she felt it as strongly as I.

"You having a rough time, Danny?" she asked.

I nodded. "This is the worst part, I guess, getting used to being this hoodlum Danny-boy, as my brother calls me. In court, the bottom just dropped out. I felt like a female with the vapors."

"Drink your medicine. I'll hot up a chop."

She got up and went into the kitchen and I stood in the doorway and watched her.

"It's a lousy business, no matter how you look at it," she said. "And it's especially lousy for a girl, I can tell you that. You think you have troubles!"

"How did you get roped into it?" I asked.

"I did it all by myself, Danny. Nobody roped me."

"You get any satisfaction out of it?"

She shook her head. "At first there was excitement fighting this underworld. . . . Now I don't know. A woman was made to raise a family, not to go adventuring in back-alleys and trading her possessions for—what, ideals? Let me find the right man and I'll chuck it all in one minute flat."

I said, "I hope you find him, Connie. I hope we both live long enough to find what we want."

"Don't say that, Danny! We've got to live long enough!"

At 12:15 A.M. after Connie had left to keep a late date at Twenty-one, I picked up my phone and called the number with the sultry voice and Rocky at the other end. This time Rocky answered.

"Yeah?"

"This is Danny, Rocky. Any news?"

"Oh yeah, Danny-boy. You call a guy by the name of Overell. Wait a minute, I got it written down. . . . Steve Overell, Plaza 2-0131. You got that? Call him tomorrow morning. He'll tell you what to do."

"It's all set then?"

"Sure. You think I couldn't fix that? Where are you staying?"

"I've got an apartment on Fiftieth Street. Four eighty-one East."

"Wait'll I write it down. What's your phone number?"

I gave it to him and then he said, "I'll be up to see you tomorrow night. You be in."

"O.K.," I said.

I wasted another twenty-two hours feeling sorry for myself. I called this Steve Overell in the morning and a feminine voice said, "McNally, Fitts and Overell. Good morning."

Then I knew who he was. G. Stephen Overell, eminent partner in an eminent law firm and a hell of a man in a courtroom. With that kind of representation I was in the big leagues.

"May I speak to Mr. Overell, please?"

Two secretaries later I got him.

"I've been expecting your call Mr. Andradi," he said in a purring, expensive voice. "Can you come to my office this afternoon?"

"There's no particular point in it, is there?" I said. "The case has been set for Special Sessions, Part Two, at 9:30 A.M. on Monday next."

There was a full minute of silence and I thought I had lost him. Then he said, "I'll see you in court at 9:30 on Monday, Mr. Andradi."

That was that. With everything arranged, nobody had to prepare any case. Nobody even had to know what the case was about—who had done what to whom. That was one way to practice law.

At 9:45 P.M. Rocky himself knocked on my door and came striding into my living room. The ten years since I had seen him at the Sing Sing prison gate had changed him dramatically. He was still relatively slim and moved with catlike grace, but his hair had turned gray and his features had blunted to coarseness. I had remembered him particularly as the handsome one of the family but now that was gone.

He sat down on my sofa and took a cigarette out of a

36

gold case, lighting it with a gold lighter. He said, "Cozy hideout you've got here, Danny. Good place to bring dames. . . . You call this Overell?"

"I called him. You want a drink?"

He shook his head. "I got work to do tonight."

He sat there and smoked, apparently not impelled to talk. Then I realized with sudden surprise that we now had complete communication once again, as we had had when we were children together, and that it wasn't necessary to put thoughts into words. He understood me and I understood him, and I have no remote idea how it had come about.

Finally he said, "What are you planning to do now?"

I shrugged. "Nothing."

He nodded. He liked that. Nothing meant that I was through with conventional employment and paychecks and a nine-to-five life.

"You come with us?"

"O.K.," I said.

"I need somebody with brains," he said. Then he laughed and got up. "I can get you here?"

"I'll be here," I replied.

He poked my shoulder with a finger as we stood by the door. "You're O.K.," he said. "You're an Andradi."

He turned and walked out and I closed the door after him.

That's how I became a member of the Mafia.

At 8:50 on Monday morning, July 15, a dapper little man by the name of Luke Veccio, smoking a new cigar and flashing a diamond on his little finger, came ringing my bell. I was just finishing my coffee and I asked him if he would have a cup. He assented and he drank it standing up, leaning forward so that he would not stain his immaculate beige suit.

"We got to get started," he said, handing me the half-finished cup. "We don't want to keep the judges waiting."

I put on a linen jacket and we went out. We got a cab at Forty-ninth and First and rode downtown to the Criminal Courts Building. In the corridor outside Special Sessions Veccio introduced me to G. Stephen Overell.

Overell was a big, loose-jointed man with faded blue eyes, rimless glasses, sparse sandy hair, and a paunch. He had a cigarette in his mouth and as he talked it waggled up and down, spilling ashes down the front of his vest, all the way to his Phi Beta Kappa key. His voice was low and nicely modulated and there was about him an air of great confidence.

"I will plead you guilty," he said. "There should be no difficulties. A fine, probably, and a suspended jail sentence

37

at worst. . . . I've talked to the assistant D.A., a young fellow by the name of Healey, and he is prepared for our plea. He'll go along with this. . . . You know Healey, don't you?"

"We were classmates at Columbia," I said.

Overell shook his head. "A shame," he said. "You'll be disbarred, of course."

"Of course," I said.

He took my arm and we went into the courtroom. We sat in the rear for half an hour, then the bailiff intoned:

"The State versus Daniel Andradi. Andradi, is he here?"

We stood up and were recognized. We walked down the aisle side by side and I followed Overell through the wooden gate into the arena before the bench. Healey joined us, not looking at me, and we three stood and faced the judges of Special Sessions. The presiding judge, Walter Bayfield, read the charge and asked me how I pleaded. Overell said, "Guilty, Your Honor."

The three judges went into a brief huddle and came out of it with the answer. Judge Bayfield read me off a lecture on my immorality, on the dishonor I had brought to my profession, on the sacred trust that I, an officer of the court, had violated, and then got down to the meat of it. I was holding my breath and my fists were clenched at my side. It was an awful moment.

". . . . a fine of $1,000 and one year in State's prison, the prison term to be suspended and the prisoner to be paroled in the custody of this court. . . ."

Then I stood before the clerk and signed over my $1,000 bail for the fine. Overell waited for me. We walked together back up the aisle and past Luke Veccio. He followed us out into the corridor.

Overell shook my hand. "Good-bye, son," he said.

"I'll be seeing you," I replied.

Veccio tapped me on the arm. "It was a breeze, like I told you. I'll go uptown with you."

We found a cab in front of the courthouse and started up Centre Street. Veccio was proud of himself and wanted to talk about his success. "I never had one easier," he said. "This Bayfield is a good pal but usually he comes high. This time it cost us peanuts."

I said, "That's all it was worth. Peanuts."

He looked at me with surprise. "What you got to be sore about?" he demanded.

"I'm not sore," I said. "I'm very happy."

SIX

IN THE MAFIA THERE ARE NO PRESCRIBED RULES OF procedure, as you would find either in a business organization, which it is, or a fraternal order, which it is. You seldom get a job with routine duties and an understanding of your status. What authority you get, among *alta mafiosi*, is usually by assumption, with the tacit approval of your superiors. There is no initiation, no formal introduction to brothers, no membership meetings. Social evenings there are plenty of, however, in the Syndicate night clubs and the better restaurants.

There is a period of probation which may last for months, when the initiate is under the closest scrutiny at times and ignored at others; when he is subject to a sort of sadistic hazing from any *alta mafioso* seeking relaxation, ranging from mild practical jokes to painful assaults upon his dignity.

The practical joke is the only form of fraternal ceremony. Success of these activities is judged by the degree of embarrassment produced. Embarrassment, pain, and finally death are all-important components of the ancient customs of the Brotherhood.

As the brother of Rocky Montana, one of the most important Dons of the Northeast, I was able to short-cut much of the hazing and its embarrassments. There is also the fact that I was bigger, stronger, faster, and in better shape than most of the Brothers, and that if I mussed them up as a result of a gag that misfired, they had no redress.

One such experience seemed to be enough for the *mafiosi*. Several of the Dons set a couple of their "workmen" on me one night to mug me and lift my wallet with a considerable sum won at a crap table. The money would have been returned, amidst hilarious laughter and an endless repetition of how foolish I had looked while being robbed. But I had not known that at the time. I had so mishandled the "workmen" that they had required medical treatment.

Rocky's method of introducing me into the Brotherhood was through a series of dinners at the best restaurants and night clubs, during which I would sit with several silent, watchful Sicilian Dons, eating the finest food, regaled by the best entertainers, and giving or receiving no communication whatever.

Two of the most important of the Mafia apothegms are, *L'omu chi parra assai, nun dicti nenti* ("The man who talks enough says nothing"), and *L'omu chi parra picca e sapienti,* ("The man who talks little is wise"). The only talking I permitted myself was the shortest possible answer to any direct question. And when I parted from these men at the end of our silent evenings, I always said, *"Baccio le mani"* ("I kiss your hands") which was not, under the circumstances, servile but merely the acme of politeness.

I met at these dinners Dons Joey DiMassi and Charles Giosa, who shared with Rocky the territorial subdivisions of Brooklyn, Queens, and Nassau; Don Leo Gamma, who had most of Bergen County, New Jersey; Don Stephano (Steve the Waiter) Fischetti, who had Hudson County and other sections of New Jersey; Don Nino Stalaci, who shared some Bergen and Hudson County activities, particularly the waterfronts, with Fischetti and Gamma, and last but not least Don Frankie Magardi, the Jukebox King, who had once squired the unforgettable Trina Templer.

As I list these Mafia Dons and their territories, you must understand that most of my knowledge of them was acquired much later. The whole purpose of my assignment within the Brotherhood was to discover the Mafia organization itself and to determine the exact position each Don held and his relative importance in the ruling hierarchy.

The Anti-Mafia could not hope to launch any effective campaign against the Brotherhood unless they knew the composition of this hierarchy and the order of succession. My briefings on these points had been woefully vague and gave ample proof of the effectiveness of *omertà*, the conspiracy of silence. The facts of the Mafia were just not known to anyone on the outside, and not to most of those on the inside. Was my brother Rocky bigger than Magardi? Were Giosa and Fischetti above or below them? And could any of them be classified among the rulers? These were the questions I would have to answer, one day.

In the public conception of the Mafia, as promoted in the press and by the hearings of the various Congressional rackets committees, such figures as Frankie Costello, Joe Adonis, Vito Genovese, and even the non-*mafioso* Longy Zwillman, were touted as the overlords. I don't mean to low-rate any of them because they are all important underworld figures, but they were not the men FANG was hunting for. They were not the key hoodlums who exercised control—whose sudden assassination by an Anti-Mafia would create effective consternation and, we hoped, disintegration.

Magardi was the one of these I was the most interested in, not only because he could lead me to Trina Templer but, more practically, because he seemed to fit in with our conception of a possible ruler. He appeared to have greater authority and to use it with more accustomed ease. He lapsed into the Sicilian Mafia slang more often than the others and there was about him a more constant awareness of his surroundings. Here was an underworld figure who was always conscious of those things which differentiated him from society in general. You could not be with him more than a few minutes without becoming aware of these differences.

I checked on him with FANG after my dinner with him and Stalaci and Rocky at the plush Algiers, which was the chief Mafia night club in New York.

My FANG contact was Clark and we met early in the morning—before the *alta mafiosi* were up and about—in the swimming pool at the Kenworth Hotel in Brooklyn.

I gave him a full report on all of the Dons I had met and then I asked him, "Can you find out anything for me on Magardi? He's the one most likely to be in the upper council."

"Magardi, eh? Bigger than Costello?"

"Undoubtedly. I'd say he's above Costello and Adonis and all those we know about. I haven't much to go on—his manner, his assumption of authority with the others, the unusual deference he gets from them and the respect he got at the Algiers—things like that."

"We'll get his background for you," he said, "but I don't think that's going to be much help. You're the only one who can track him down. . . . What exactly did you have in mind?"

"What'll help me most right now, I think, is his connection with Diamond Records. I'd like to know that full set-up and just how much he has to do with it. I've got a hunch I may be able to get to him through some legitimate enterprise, where he might be able to use a bright young man."

"A good thought. . . . Anything else on your mind?"

"Nothing. How are the over-all plans progressing?"

"Fair. We're onto a good thing down in Cuba. Batista is hungry for money and we're trying to induce your brother to move in there. If we can engineer that, a lot of Dons should be knocked off. It'll be a good starter for the Anti-Mafia."

I was with Rocco for several hours every night and I met more than a score of his organization—hoodlums and near-hoodlums who were his business and underworld lieutenants.

41

I met a few of his girls as well, for the social position of a *capo mafioso* is related directly to the number of girls he keeps, without any particular regard to quality. Rocky was up near the social top.

These social evenings were my only contact with the Brotherhood until the end of August. The Mafia, by this time, was beginning to receive prominent attention as a result of the Apalachin meeting, and pressure was closing in on the Dons from several sides. Many of them were subpoenaed for hearings by Congressional Committees as well as by State investigations, and the usefulness of the Dons so exposed to public knowledge was greatly impaired. The Brotherhood met this crisis by the simple expedient of reshuffling its commands and replacing the Dons in the limelight by unknown *capo mafiosi*. It was an ideal time for an apprentice by the name of Danny Andradi to rise in the councils of the Brotherhood.

But opportunity was necessary, too, and this came unexpectedly the August midnight the longshoremen of New York Harbor went on strike.

The strike had been building up for two months while wage negotiations with the shipowners, presided over by a Federal mediator went on. The contract had long since expired and a strike vote had been taken the first week of the negotiations, but action had been held off while the talks progressed.

It soon became apparent that the shipowners were not going to give in on any of the points at issue, but the union was in no position for a prolonged strike either. Some $2,000,000 of union funds had unaccountably disappeared and the war-chest contained funds for less than two weeks of strike benefits. This was not generally known, of course. Rocky told me about it the morning after the strike had begun when he phoned me at my apartment.

"We got to end this fast or we're in trouble," he said. "You're a smart boy. You tell us how."

This was typical not only of the kind of challenge one might expect from an older brother, but also of the attitude of the Mafia towards educated brethren. It was a challenge usually given by the Mafia with a sneer and seldom expected to be taken up.

I said, "Maybe I will."

"I'll pick you up in half an hour," he said.

It was the day the Appellate Division formally voted my disbarment, so I remember it well. I was waiting on the sidewalk when Rocky came by in his chauffeur-driven Cadillac. I greeted his driver, stocky Sammy Corsi, then got in the back.

We drove downtown at a leisurely pace, across Brooklyn Bridge, and down to a pier below Brooklyn Heights. There were a dozen pickets marching in a rough circle in front of the pier, carrying large placards on sticks, and fifty or more longshoremen were lounging across the street. There were two uniformed cops standing with a customs officer at the pier entrance and a couple more on the corner across the street. There were two police radio cars in sight down the block. Otherwise the waterfront had a Sunday calm.

All eyes turned towards us as we got out of the car. There was a sudden rumble of voices from the crowd across the street and from the pickets. Hands were raised in salute. "Hi, Rocky! Hey, Boss, when do we eat! Atta boy, Rocky! How ya doin', Rocky! Let's kill the bastards, Rocky!"

What was it a sign of? Affection? Rocky waved at them and walked quickly to a door to the left of the pier entrance which led to a wooden stairway. I followed him.

"They're all bums," he said. "You got to watch out for them."

We climbed to the second floor of the pier and went through glass doors upon which were lettered "Apex Stevedoring Company" and "S. & M. Trucking Company." There was a personable blonde, a year or two past the bloom of youth, sitting at a desk just inside the door and typing on a printed form. Beyond her was a low counter and behind it a half-dozen men and women. The atmosphere was relaxed; very little seemed to be going on. Several greeted Rocky respectfully as "Mr. Montana" as we walked to the end of the counter and went through a door leading to a small office.

There were two men in this office playing gin rummy and they jumped to their feet as we entered. Rocky introduced them as Lou and Jake. They were the *bassa mafiosi*, the workmen of the Brotherhood. Members of the Mafia fall generally into two classes, the high and the low—the *alta* and the *bassa*. The upper class *mafiosi* rarely stoop to vulgar crimes; they are the masters who give orders to the lower classes. Only when a crime requires particular delicacy or specialization will it be performed by an *alta mafioso*.

Rocky said, "This is my brother Danny and when he's around here you do what he says."

Lou had a pock-marked face and a mouthful of gold teeth which glittered when he smiled. Jake had a tremendous nose and a scar that started at the middle of his chin and went down across his throat. They were both of medium height and broad and the muscles stood out under the cloth of their white shirts.

"New boss?" asked Lou.

43

"That's right," said Rocky. "Keep everybody out. We're having a conference."

We went through a door into a large room in the corner of the building, softly carpeted and air-conditioned, with good mahogany furniture and a portable bar against one wall. Windows looked out on the street and the spider-web Brooklyn Bridge.

Rocky took off his coat and put it on a hanger in a closet behind his desk. He motioned me into a chair and sat, putting his feet up on the desktop and leaning back in his chair.

He said, "I know a guy with all the dough in the world who wears shoes with holes in the soles, so when he puts his feet up on his desk like this, you can see he's real humble. That's a lot of crap. . . . How do you like my office?"

"It's fine," I said. "You do all your business here?"

He shook his head. "Just some of it. We run the stevedores and the trucking companies and some of the local bookies and loan sharks out of this office. Now I got another business coming up that makes all this penny-ante, so I got to have someone take over for me. Somebody I can trust, who won't rob me blind. . . . Well, let's talk about the strike."

"You run these longshoremen?" I asked.

"*We* run the longshoremen. I just got the Brooklyn locals."

"What's the strike for?"

"What's it for! You got a soft head? We got to strike every couple of years to keep the boys in line, to let 'em know who runs things and who looks after 'em."

"You always win these strikes?"

"Sure we win. But it takes time and dough, and right now we got neither."

"What happened to the dough?"

"I needed it. . . . Look, Danny-boy, stop asking foolish questions. We got a hot problem."

I said, "You can win a strike two ways. You can accept a compromise that gives you some of the things you want, or you can get your own terms by hurting the employers enough to make them give in. . . . I take it you don't want a compromise."

"No," said Rocky, "we can't. The sore-heads will say we let 'em down and the first thing you know we'll have that bum Bridges in here. . . . What I want to know is, have you got any ideas?"

I said, "I've got one. It ought to work. You've got to bring pressure on the shipping men. The way you do that is to spread the strike, tie up the whole city, the food, the transportation, the laundries, the stores—everything."

Rocky put his feet down on the floor and leaned forward.

He said, "That's a big idea. But the longshoremen are poison to every other union. You know that, don't you?"

"It doesn't make any difference," I replied. "It's how you do it. . . . First, you call out the truckers. The organization controls all the locals in the East, and we strike 'em all. Then we go after the rest of them—the milk drivers, the laundry men, the bakers, the subway men, the store clerks. We tie this town up tighter than a January blizzard. The ship men will settle within twenty-four hours."

A dreamy look came into Rocky's eyes as he considered this, and much of the tenseness went out of his face. He put his feet back up on the desk.

"How are we with Taft-Hartley?" he asked.

"In the clear. They haven't got any law against sympathy strikes, if you do it right."

He picked up a telephone and dialed a number. In a moment he said, "Vito? . . . I think we got it licked." Then he spoke rapidly in Sicilian, in the Mafia dialect. He outlined the proposal for the general strike and said furthermore that I would handle it all, that it was my idea.

He listened for a minute, then said, "O.K., boss," and hung up. He said to me, "We do it. You get to work on it right now. Just tell me what you need."

On September 1, the truckmen struck. This took no doing except a few phone calls by Rocky. I had prepared full page advertisements for all of the newspapers, meanwhile, and they started running that day over the signature of the various truckers' locals. They read, "We are loyal Union men. We support the principles of the Longshoremen's Union of Greater New York. We have gone on strike against the anti-American, Fascist tactics of some shipping owners who are opposed to the rights of Organized Labor. We beg the public to bear with the inconvenience that this strike will cause. We cannot do otherwise than fight those who seek to destroy our Unions."

One hour after the truckers went out, I was closeted with the president of the bakery drivers' union, a tough old organizer by the name of George Fallon. He said:

"You trying to make a crusade out of this, young feller?"

I nodded. "We've got to, Mr. Fallon. We can't afford a prolonged strike. If you come in with us, we can cut it down by weeks. You know that."

He shook his head. "I try to run an honest union. That isn't honest and you know it."

I said, "It's expedient. We'll pay for full page ads, like

this, to run over your signature. . . . It won't hurt you a bit in labor circles."

"I'm not interested," he said.

"I'd not like to go back and tell Rocky Montana that you said that," I replied. "Let's put it right on the line, Mr. Fallon. Either you come with us or we fight you. We fight you Rocky's way."

"That goon! That damned racketeer!"

I said, "Right, Mr. Fallon. He kills people, too."

Suddenly he seemed to collapse in his chair. He bowed his head on his chest and rubbed an ear with a nervous hand. When he spoke his voice was tired and defeated. "All right, Mr. Andradi, we'll go out at 9:00 A.M. tomorrow."

I got up and put my hand on his shoulder. He looked up at me, surprised. I suddenly pushed him away from his desk, his swivel chair groaning in protest. I pulled out the top left-hand drawer and revealed the tape recorder, the two large spools spinning slowly. I pressed the stop button, took off one of the reels and snapped the tape. I put the reel inside my belt and started for the door.

Fallon said, "You son of a bitch!"

I said, "Nine o'clock tomorrow, Mr. Fallon."

James Benton, head of the subway motormen, was another honest man. He didn't have a tape recorder but he had two cops sitting in the next office, and with the partition as thin as it was, they may as well have been sitting in my lap. Benton sneered at all of my arguments and wanted to know what threats I had used to get Fallon to join the strike.

I said, "You have a rather big mouth for such a little man, Mr. Benton. However, you've got some law muscle in the next room, so we'll let it go for the present."

Then I took two photographs from my pocket—two postcard size snapshots. One was of a girl in her twenties, an earnest, plain-faced girl sitting on a dock at a resort lake. The other was a boy-child of two and a half, wearing diapers and standing grinning at the camera. I put the photographs on the desk in front of him and started for the door.

"Hey, wait a minute! Where did you get these?"

I stopped and turned. "A friend of mine took them. I thought you'd want them."

He sat there staring at them. Sweat broke out on his forehead. He took out a soiled handkerchief and wiped his brow, then leaned back in his chair. His face was white.

"I'm going to call those cops," he said.

"You do that, Mr. Benton."

46

Then he leaned forward. hitting the desk softly with a clenched fist. Finally he said, "All right, Mr. Andradi. You got the organization. I'm no hero. We go on strike at midnight tonight. That O.K.?"

"That's fine, Mr. Benton," I said.

There were two women representing the Department Store Sales and Office Workers locals of Brooklyn and Manhattan, and a man representing Queens. We met in the union offices on Lexington Avenue and it was all very formal, with a secretary taking notes.

I said, "Just a couple more unions and we'll have New York's first general strike. The subways will be off at midnight. The buses will stop at 10:00 A.M. tomorrow. As you know, we have all of the truckmen, the bakery drivers, the milk drivers and the laundry men out already. We would like to close the stores. I can assure you it will be for a very short time. I understand that the pressure is becoming unbearable for the shipping people."

The older of the women. a Miss Fenway, said, "Your people have such an unsavory reputation, Mr. Andradi. That is what we don't like about this."

I said, "We are fighting for a principle, Miss Fenway, and the principle is clean, no matter how soiled are our workmen."

The other one, a Mary Wiswell, said, "We have principles, too. Mr. Andradi."

I said. "I'm sure you have, Miss Wiswell. Do you want to tell your secretary to stop taking notes? I am going to talk about a bookmaker—Bennie the Bookie."

"How dare you!" demanded Miss Wiswell.

"Well, he works for us and you owe him two grand," I said.

Miss Wiswell dissolved into tears—an apt if old-fashioned expression because she did it in a manner reminiscent of the Victorians. And then Miss Fenway was standing over her, masculine and defending, and I suddenly got it. A couple of Lesbians.

I said to the man, who hadn't yet opened his mouth, "You arrange it for tomorrow. I've got to go."

Sammy Carboni, a *paisan,* headed the taxi drivers' union. He was from Eastern Sicily and not a *mafioso,* but he was a thief at heart. He said, "Sure, Danny, we go out tonight, only you tell your boys not to slash tires on scab taxis. I got to operate my fleet or I don't make the finance payments."

The building service employees—principally the elevator

47

operators—were the icing on the cake. Without elevators New York was dead. You could get uptown or downtown somehow; you could eat and you could sleep and you could wash, with or without milk, bread, and laundry, but you couldn't walk up and down ten and twenty and thirty and forty flights of steps. This union was run by one Aristotle Goulandris. All he wanted to know was how much. I gave him five g's in tens and twenties.

The truckmen struck on Monday and by Wednesday the only thing moving in the city were private cars, a few pedestrians and the newspapers. We had left the newspapers alone because we needed them. Now their big, black headlines proclaimed:

GENERAL STRIKE PARALYZES CITY

The mayor and the Board of Estimate declared a state of emergency. The governor was issuing proclamations and appointing committees. The President sent a blistering wire to the shipowners and the Communists held a mass-meeting in Union Square. Wherever you looked there was a picket line and grim-faced cops, always in groups with their nightsticks clutched in their hands.

By late afternoon the anger of New York's millions had crystalized on the shipping men. No doubt was left in any minds as to who was responsible for the general strike. I had set up a press office at the Brooklyn pier, run by a smart press agent by the name of Rollo Roberts, who had been loaned to me by Don Magardi's office. We issued half-hourly bulletins on the progress of the union negotiations to all the newsapers, radio and television stations. We set up television interviews with the heads of various longshoremen's locals and of other unions, and in each case the statements were carefully prepared by Roberts and his staff.

We left nothing to chance.

At 8:05 P.M. on Wednesday the shipowners signed a two-year contract with the longshoremen meeting all demands and the general strike ended.

It is said that nobody wins a strike, but in this case the winner was Danny Andradi, who had dreamed it all up.

SEVEN

T HE DINNER THAT ROCKY GAVE TO CELEBRATE THE END
of the general strike and the victory of his longshoremen was
elaborate even by Mafia standards. The entire Frascini
Brothers restaurant off Borough Hall was taken over, two
bands played alternately in the main dining room, and entertainers, mostly girls, were brought in from two Broadway
shows and several night clubs, and a strip-teaser who called
herself Peach Peel was imported all the way from Baltimore to show the New Yorkers how they did it on The Block.
Champagne was the principal tipple, whether the *mafiosi*
liked it or not, and there was more caviar wasted than eaten.
. . . This was not strictly an *alta mafiosi* affair, as had been my
dinners with the Dons, for Rocky invited all of his lieutenants
who ran his unions, his trucking and labor businesses, his
bookmaking and loan-shark rackets, his alky cooking, and his
various smuggling enterprises. This was Rocky's *cosca* of the
New York *cacocciula*—the leaf of the artichoke.

On the second floor of the restaurant a room had been set
aside for a crap game, and this went on continuously until
closing and preoccupied the less social of the hoodlums. On
the main floor, at a large round table on the edge of the
dance floor, sat Rocky and his guests of honor. This table had
three waiters of its own and was kept well supplied with
food, wines, and liquors. Sitting at the tables immediately
surrounding it were a dozen workmen who took no part in
the festivities but kept a close watch on the table of honor
and all who approached it. If a Brother was deemed too
drunk or too loud or too enthusiastic, he was expertly
shunted away, always with careful consideration for his feelings and decorum.

At this table with Rocky were Frankie Magardi, Joey Di-
Massi, Charley Giosa, Steve Fischetti, and three others who
impressed me more than any of the Dons I had met so far,
outside of Magardi. They were quiet men, dressed in beautifully tailored suits, abstemious, polite, aloof. Their names were
Vito Nicosa, Lou Caruso, and Vincent Carmi. I had never
heard of them; FANG had never heard of them. But there
was little question in my mind, after sitting with them through

49

the evening, that I was in contact with some of the real brass of Mafia leadership.

I sat between Magardi and Carmi. I was duly impressed by this august company, of which I was certainly the least. Even as Rocky's brother I would not have been permitted among them had I not distinguished myself in Mafia eyes by my maneuvers in the general strike. Rocky had made that plain. "They want to look you over," he had told me. "I guess you got the big boys interested."

However, nobody spoke to me for the first hour. The conversations went on around me and over me and behind me, but not one at that table addressed a word to Danny Andradi.

Then Vito Nicosa, a dark-eyed, gray-haired man of about sixty, with a bland face devoid of expression, yet giving the impression of great strength, said to me, "You appear to have good ideas, Mr. Andradi." He was sitting on the other side of Carmi and he leaned forward to address me.

"Thank you, Don Nicosa," I said.

This seemed to break the ice—to get me out of the limbo of untouchables. Carmi said, "That general strike was a sound notion, Andradi."

I nodded at him. "It seemed logical."

"It was," said Magardi, from my other side. "Without that, we'd have the longshoremen around our necks for months."

"We need people with ideas," said Nicosa to no one in particular.

"How old are you?" Carmi asked.

"Twenty-seven, Don Carmi."

He was a dapper little man with the air of a pedagogue and I learned later that he actually had been an assistant professor of psychology at Vassar and was generally called the "Professor" in the Brotherhood.

Magardi said, "I could certainly use a bright young man."

Rocky, on the other side of Magardi, said, "Don't go trying to steal my kid brother from me, Don Magardi. I need him."

I decided to climb out on a limb. I said to Magardi, "If that's an offer I'd like to consider it—if Trina Templer goes with the job."

They all laughed, briefly and with a minimum of humor. Carmi said, "You aim high, young feller."

Magardi said, "She's not for you, boy. Not that one."

Rocky said, "He's got Connie Masters already. What more does he want?"

Carmi tapped my arm. "Connie Masters?" he asked.

I nodded. "Yes, I know her."

He lowered his voice. "That girl is bad news. She's got some sort of tie-up with the feds."

50

Magardi leaned closer on the other side. He said, "You watch your step, Danny. We've lost two men who knew her. Both of 'em will be deported."

I said, "How could that be?"

"It is," said the Professor. "There's no other way to account for it. It's taken us a long while to tape her. Now we're fairly sure."

At 2:00 A.M. Nicosa got up. "It's time an old man went to bed," he said. "But don't let me break up your party. It's been a wonderful night, Rocky."

He shook hands around and he said to me, "I'll see you uptown. You'll hear from me."

"O.K.," I said.

The Professor and two of the workmen left with him.

When we sat down again Magardi said to me, "You should get to know the Professor, Danny. He's the brain on the other side of the river."

My FANG contact was once again mousy little Clark. The meeting place was a U.N. bus stop on First Avenue. It was 8:00 A.M. and I'd had less than four hours' sleep. I followed Clark into the lobby of the modernistic meeting house on the East River. Only the cleaning women were there with their mops and pails and they ignored us as we mounted the open-work stairway to the balcony of the assembly room. The huge auditorium was empty and dimly lit, tomblike in its silence.

We took a couple of seats in the last row in sight of the doors. Clark said, "What's the crisis?"

"It's Connie," I said. "I was at Rocky's dinner last night and two Dons told me she was tied up with the Federals."

"What two, Dan?"

"One named Vincent Carmi and Frankie Magardi."

His face was serious, worried. "How did they make the tie-up?"

I shook my head. "I don't know. Magardi told me two men who knew her are being deported. That's all that was said."

He nodded slowly. "That would be Bartolo and Gentile. Connie gave the Department of Justice the tip-off on them. . . . It was a mistake, of course. The mistake of trying to be legal."

I said, "You going to look after her?"

"Of course. She's got to go down to Cuba for us first, then we'll take care of her."

"Won't that be too late?"

51

"Not at all. . . . This Cuba operation is shaping up well, Dan. We've got your brother hooked on it and he should involve several others. Then we'll sit back and watch the Dons kill each other off."

"Rocky won't survive?" I asked.

"Probably not," he said. "He's on the wrong side. You have anything else?"

"No, just Connie."

I left alone and went back to my apartment. At 11:00 A.M. there was a ring at my bell and Rocky came trudging up the stairs. His face was tired and his forehead was perspiring.

"You got to get a place with an elevator," he said. He looked around the living room. "You ain't got a dame here?"

I shook my head. "Not at the moment."

"You shouldn't have left so early. I had that stripper up to her hotel and there were a couple more of those dames ready to swing. . . . Well, the hell with that. I came up here for something important, Danny-boy. Something big."

I said, "You name it."

"Right now Cuba is for sale. We can buy that whole damn island for cash on the line. I get this from a very good source—in fact, they come especially to me. This Batista is real hungry and will sell everything he's got."

I said, "What's he got, Rocky?"

"What's he got! Gambling, Danny-boy. He's got more gambling than Las Vegas. Already I've bought two places from him—big, fancy layouts. Now he's got a new hotel ready to open with the biggest damn casino outside of Monte Carlo. He'll sell it to me."

"You got that kind of dough?" I asked.

"I got a syndicate—Giosa and Fischetti are in and Joey DiMassi will come along. Maybe Leo Gamma. Yes, I got the dough. I got the contacts. Now I need somebody to close the deal. . . . I can't go down there, Danny-boy. Too many people know me and it would blow the lid off. The same with Giosa and Fischetti. It's got to be handled real smart and on the q.t. You get what I mean?"

I said, "Sure. You're going into competition."

He got up and took off his jacket. Then he started to pace between the kitchen and the door. "We got to keep this tight. Those two bums down there—Joey Palermo and Vince Bottolino! They act like it's their territory! Like they own it! To hell with them!"

"You're not crossing your own Brothers, are you Rocky?"

Suddenly he was enraged. He smashed me across the

side of the face before I could duck away. "You crumb!" he yelled at me. "Who you think you're talking to about crossing?"

"Take it easy," I said. "What are you blowing your top at me for?"

"What do you know about this business?" he demanded. Then as suddenly as it had come on, the storm passed. He sank down on the sofa again and took a cigarette from his gold case. "I shouldn't have smacked you," he said. "But that gets me sore—those two thieves! I brought them up in this racket and now they're big shots! Claiming their own territory! Palermo and Bottolino are nothing but lousy pier bosses and they'll never be anything else. I'll run 'em right off the island!"

I said, "First you've got to get on it yourself."

"You always were a fresh bastard," he said. He dug into his pants pocket and pulled out two packages of bills and tossed them on the coffee table. "There's two hundred grand, which is enough for the down payment on this place, the El Capitan. Here's a couple of the contacts—" He handed me a slip of paper—"and either one of 'em will take you to Batista's man. . . . You got to negotiate, Danny-boy. You got to play it smart. I've talked to a couple of their guys here and I still don't know exactly what we're buying—what guarantees we'll get and for how long. Find out about Palermo and Bottolino—just what they own and how much we'll cut in on them. Tell 'em to send some guy who can talk English up here to New York to see me. . . . Well, you handle it. Don't give 'em the dough unless you know what we're getting—that's the main thing."

I picked up one of the packages of bills and looked at it. They were all of $1,000 denomination. I said, "You know this Batista's got a revolution on his hands—some guy back in the hills by the name of Fidel Castro? Maybe he's trying to sell you a dead horse."

"Don't you worry about that angle," he replied. "Castro's strictly for the birds. You just see what Batista has to sell, and if it's what we want, you buy it."

"How about the price?"

"That's set. That's the only thing that is set. They get fifteen million in cash delivered here in New York"

"O.K., Rocky. When do I go down?"

"My office is getting you a reservation and they'll call you, probably this afternoon. . . . You keep your lip buttoned about this, Danny-boy."

"Sure," I said.

I flew to Cuba on September 8, which was a Tuesday. FANG sent Connie Masters down on the same plane, and I was suprised to see her at Idlewild, checking her ticket and baggage. She was pert and elegant in a biege shantung suit and she wore a small, red beany, red shoes and carried a red suede bag. She turned her cheek to be kissed and she said, "I was hoping you'd be on this one, Danny. They told me you were going down today."

I took her arm and led her into a nearby restaurant. I said, "You know the boys are on to you?"

She nodded gravely. "This'll be my last assignment. I've got a date with Joey Palermo. I've got a lot of things to tell him."

We ordered coffee. I asked her, "You going to tell him about me?"

"Of course. . . . You and Rocky and all the rest."

"Then what?"

She sighed and took out a cigarette. I lit it for her. "I'm still hunting," she said.

"For your man, huh?"

She nodded. The coffee came and we drank it in silence. The flight was announced and we walked to the gate and out to the ramp. We were following a couple, the man a huge, swarthy workman type who might have been Italian and who looked like a heavyweight wrestler, and the girl a fancy redhead done up in varicolored silks and beads and gold bracelets—the kind who would call herself a model when picked up by the vice squad.

Connie inclined her head towards them and said, "I'm getting a headache, Danny."

This meant, in our code, "That's the enemy. Be careful."

We got seats over the left wing and I noticed that the swarthy man and the redhead had separated, she to sit in the rear and he taking the aisle seat just behind us. I said to Connie, "I'll try to get you an aspirin."

I got up and went to the rear and talked to the stewardess and she promised to take care of Connie as soon as we were under way. Then I went into the washroom and I wrote a note, for I hadn't yet told Connie where I'd be staying. The note said, "I'll be at the Nacional. Call me tonight late and every night, without fail."

I returned to my seat and slipped the note to her. She read it, then squeezed my hand. Presently we were taxiing and the stewardess brought her aspirin and water. When we were airborne we both put our seats back and dozed. If you couldn't talk, there wasn't much else to do. Connie woke me

54

up with a hand on my forehead. "You were groaning," she said.

I looked out the window and saw that we were back on the ground. "Miami?" I asked her.

She nodded. "You certainly do sleep, Mr. Andradi. You wouldn't do at all as a husband for me."

"That's what I figured," I said. "How's your headache?"

"The same."

Some of the passengers left and some new ones got on, leaving several vacant seats on the other side of the aisle. I was almost dozing again. I opened my eyes for an instant and got a quick flash of a pair of the most beautiful legs I'd ever seen, standing in my line of vision. I looked at the rest of her as she moved to get into the seat and everything stopped. Just like that.

It was Trina Templer!

I don't suppose it is given to man more than once in a lifetime to encounter the one and absolutely only woman. That is, from the standpoint of eye-appeal. You'll go along for years maybe, seeing thousands of females of all shapes and sizes and degrees of beauty, and some of them will be truly breath-taking. But then, suddenly, one golden, unforgettable instant of one day, you'll see The Girl. Your whole spirit will leap, the blood will pound through your head, your knees will grow weak and the palms of your hands will get wet. . . . That's what happened with this Trina—for the second time now. She wasn't what many would call beautiful. She had freckles, and upon careful analysis, her nose was too small and her mouth was too wide. But her construction and over-all presentation were truly sensational, and those could account for her impact upon me.

Connie said, "Stop jittering. You've seen girls before."

"Yeah—but that one!"

"I've told you about her, Danny."

"I wasn't listening," I said. I got up. "Well, here goes nothing—and everything."

I went across the aisle and I said, "Miss Templer?"

"Yes?" It was a very cold "yes" and with it went a level gaze out of green eyes that sent chills up my spine.

"May I join you?" I asked. "I'm Dan Andradi, a friend of Mr. Magardi."

She continued to look. A long time passed. Then she said, "Do sit down, if you wish."

I sat. I said, "I've never seen anyone who has so completely overwhelmed me as you have, Miss Templer. I probably sound like an idiot, but that's your fault. That's what you do to me."

55

She nodded gravely. She said, "You have a rather amusing line, Mr., ah—Andradi? Not very original but complimentary."

"This is no line. Why do you have to assume that I'm insincere? Does that make you feel better?"

She frowned at me. She touched my arm with a finger. She said, "You may leave, Mr. Andradi. You may rejoin your girl friend."

"Just like that, eh? You don't want to know anything about me? You're not interested?"

"Now I've injured your male vanity, haven't I?"

I shook my head. "No, Miss Templer, this isn't vanity. I meant what I said about you and what you do to me. I'm another one of your victims. If you wish to be sarcastic or scornful, there's nothing I can do about it except to regret it."

The engines were started up in succession and we fastened our seat belts. She was silent and aloof. She looked out the window as we began to taxi, then back to me.

"I saw you staring at me one night at El Morocco," she said. "You were with that same girl."

"That's Connie Masters," I said. "Connie is a friend and I would do anything for her, but that's all she is."

"But you do, in fact, go around with cheap girls like that, don't you Mr. Andradi?"

I didn't say anything. I looked down at the floor and listened to the roar of the engines as they were revved up. Then we taxied to the end of the runway and took off. I unfastened my seat belt and started to get up.

She put a hand on my arm. She said, "I'm sorry, Mr. Andradi. That was very bitchy—absolutely uncalled for. I apologize."

I sat down again. "You are a very nice person, Miss Templer, just as I thought you would be."

"Thank you," she said in a low voice.

"May I see you in Havana?"

"I'll be singing for two weeks at El Chico. But I will spend most of my time with my brother. He's an attaché at our Embassy."

"Dinner tomorrow night?" I asked. "Where shall I pick you up?"

She looked straight at me and her green eyes smiled. "I'll be at the Continental," she said. "But I'm going to see my brother tomorrow for dinner."

"What do you suggest, Miss Templer?"

"You could take me swimming in the morning," she said. "Say about eleven?"

56

"I will meet you at my peril," I said. "I've no idea how I'll react to you in a bathing suit."

"Do you always talk in hyperbole, Mr. Andradi? Gracious, you must be in the music business."

"I'm not," I said, "but I mean to be."

EIGHT

I WALKED WITH CONNIE INTO THE CUSTOMS ROOM AT THE airport. Ahead of us was Trina walking with a tall man in a good Panama—her brother—and behind us were the workman and his redhead. Connie whispered to me, "What did she say?"

"We're going swimming tomorrow at eleven."

"I've got to hand it to you. Maybe there's something about you I overlooked."

"She is Fate," I said. "You are not."

"I still think you're away over your head."

We arrived at the circular counter as the first of the baggage was being brought in from the plane. Connie went to the "M" section and I moved up to the "A". The workman and his girl stopped beside Connie. I looked around to the "T's" and saw Trina, standing tall and cool and talking to her brother. She was wearing a Summer cotton print and low-heeled sandals and she looked about eighteen. She raised her eyes and saw me looking at her. She waved a finger at me, and just this small act of recognition was all I'd ever wanted. Nothing could touch me now.

Then something touched me on my shoulder. I closed the hatch to my dream-world and looked into a couple of mean, black eyes. The eyes were attached to a stony face with a body to match. A hard-as-rock little guy who didn't come much beyond my shoulder, but plenty wide enough to make up for it. Also, if that weren't enough, he had on a uniform with Sam Browne belt and pistol in a holster.

"Andradi?" he said.

I nodded. "Something?"

"Get your bag and come with me," he said.

A porter was just placing my bag on the counter. I picked it up and walked with him. He kept a hand on my arm and he steered me down a passageway between rows of tall lockers and out a back door to the street. A Cadillac was at the curb and another hard guy was at the wheel. I was ushered into the rear seat and my escort climbed in beside me. The car took off.

We drove for about an hour, with no conversation. We

pulled up beside a gate through a high wall, in the Spanish manner, and my seat companion got out. It was a residential section and I looked around for a street sign or a number. Neither was in evidence.

My uniformed guide escorted me through the gate. We were in a lush garden, with a planting of beautiful camellia bushes. We walked along a flagstone path and up a pair of steps to a great iron-and-glass door. It was opened at our approach by a white-coated Cuban boy and I was led into a long, cool room stuffed with hand-carved Florentine furniture. There was a very fine oriental rug on the floor and good tapestries on the walls. A divan, a huge, square coffee table and deep, comfortable chairs were arranged in the center of the room. On the divan and in the chairs was the reception committee.

I was introduced to two Cubans and two others. The others were Joey Palermo and Vince Bottolino. Palermo was the suave, Ivy-League type of hoodlum. Bottolino was a tall, droopy character in a rumpled linen suit, with a cadaverous face and big hamlike hands.

Palermo said, "You're Rocky Montana's brother, right?"

"Right," I said.

"Rocky used to be a reasonable guy," he said. "Now he's crazy. Won't you sit down, Mr. Andradi? Can I get you a drink?"

"Thank you," I said, sitting on the end of the divan next to one of the Cubans. "Something tall with rum or gin would be fine."

Bottolino spoke up. His voice was harsh and gravelly. "You know Cuba belongs to us, don't you Andradi?"

"I've heard it said," I replied.

"Then what are you doing here?"

"I came down on business for Rocky," I said. "He told me to come so I came."

"You work for Rocky?" asked Palermo.

"Yes. For now."

The boy brought me a rum collins and I sipped it. Palermo said, "You ain't been in the organization long, I hear."

"No," I said.

"We don't want you here," said Bottolino. "You take the next plane out, you understand?"

I shook my head at him. "I don't take orders from you. If you have a beef, settle it with Rocky, not with me."

"We'll do that," said Palermo. "Meanwhile you get out."

I lit a cigarette and looked over the Cuban next to me. He was dressed in tan tropical silk and there was a bulge under his coat over his left breast that could only have been a gun.

I said, "How long do you think I'll stay healthy if I go back to New York tonight?"

"You won't stay healthy here," said Bottolino. He turned to Palermo. "You want to keep arguing with this guy?"

Palermo said, "You know the orders. What you want me to do?"

"We put him on the six o'clock," said Bottolino.

I sipped my drink and considered jumping the Cuban and taking his gun away from him. But that wouldn't have solved my problem. Then I'd have angry Cubans as well as angry Sicilians after me. I said, "There was a workman and a red-headed girl on the plane coming down. Were they your people, Mr. Palermo?"

He shook his head. "No." He turned to the uniformed man who had brought me to this house. "You make those two, Manny?"

"Sure," Manny replied. "They was with this dame—Masters."

Palermo wrinkled his brow in thought. "You go and check on her at the Palace. I don't want anything to happen to that dame until I talk to her!"

The uniformed man left. Joey Palermo tapped his elegant two-toned shoes on the rug as though he were doing a dance. "Why don't you want to be nice and go back?" he asked me.

"Two reasons," I said. "I've got business to do. I've got a date with a girl tomorrow morning."

"What business?"

"I thought you knew."

"No, we don't know," said Bottolino angrily. "You know damned well we don't know."

"I'm supposed to make a deal for the El Capitan casino," I said.

"I'm damned!" exclaimed Palermo. "That double-crossing Batista! That lousy greaseball!"

"How far has the deal gone?" demanded Bottolino.

"The price is set. I've got to arrange the conditions."

"I bet Rocky got those other two places already, then," said Palermo. "He say anything to you about the Mirador and Greasy Joe's?"

"No."

Bottolino got up. "Come on, Andradi. I'll take you to the airport personal. We ain't got too much time."

I said, "Why are you doing it this way? You're not going to stop Rocky by chasing me out of Cuba. I can phone from Miami and get Batista's boys to come over and make the deal. You know that."

Bottolino's face flushed angrily. "We know how to stop Rocky," he said. "We know how to stop you, too."

Palermo said, "Cuba belongs to us and we don't want you here, Andradi. You go make your deal in Miami and see what good it does you."

I got up. I said, "O.K., let's go to the airport."

I got to Miami in time for dinner and made the first course a hot dog at the air terminal. The redheaded workman's girl had been on the same plane, coming back alone. I wondered about her while I ate my frank. As I left the counter I saw her move in beside an airline pilot and give him a speculative look. It seemed she was a girl on the prowl.

I phoned a FANG number and got a woman with a brisk, no-fooling voice. I gave her my identification and said, "I've just been chased out of Cuba and I've got a date there tomorrow morning at eleven. I want to get back, but not through customs and not with any police notice. What can you do?"

"We can arrange a private plane tomorrow morning," she said. "We can land you at Havana and take you through the North American Oil hangar. Call me back in an hour and I'll give you the details. . . . Wait a minute—didn't you fly down this morning with two-eleven?"

"Two-eleven when?"

"Nine A.M."

"Yes."

"We've lost touch with her. When did you see her last?"

"At the airport after we'd landed. She was waiting to go through customs."

"She's missed three contacts. It looks serious."

I thought of the workman and Palermo's concern for Connie. I said, "There's a lead right here at the airport. If you can get me a plane right away, I'll go back to Havana and hunt for her."

"Just a moment, please."

I looked out the phone booth across the waiting room and saw the redhead at the hot-dog counter talking to the pilot. Then the FANG operator came back on. "I'll have a plane for you at the Atlantic Air Service hangar in fifteen minutes. The pilot will be Ray Wright. Ask for him there. He'll know where to take you."

"There'll be two of us," I said.

I went back to the hot-dog counter, now well crowded, and stood near the redhead. I got another hot dog after a few minutes, then moved behind the redhead and reached over her shoulder. "Pardon me, I need the mustard," I said.

61

She drew aside slightly, frowning in annoyance. The pilot beside her said, "I'll call you tomorrow night in New York. Good-bye, honey."

He squeezed her hand and backed away from the counter. I pushed into his place and squeezed the mustard on my frank. Then I looked at her and smiled. She was regarding me with displeasure.

I said, "Didn't I see you on the flight down to Havana this morning?"

She didn't know whether to be friendly or to run. After a moment she nodded assent. "Yes."

I leaned close to her and spoke confidentially. "I've got something that will interest you. Let's go where we can talk."

She shook her head. "Leave me alone."

"It's business," I said. "You could make a lot of money."

Her face relaxed. "Well all right. Why didn't you say so?"

I took her arm and walked her out, eating my hot dog. I got her over to the Atlantic Air Service hangar on the far side of the field by taxi without any argument. There was a big Beechcraft on the apron with its two engines idling and a young guy in shorts and a loud sports shirt was standing by the wing talking to a mechanic in white coveralls.

He came over to us as the taxi pulled away.

"Mr. Andradi?" he asked.

I nodded. "You Ray Wright?"

"Yeah. You ready to go?"

The redhead said, "Wait a minute! Where are we going?"

I smiled at her. "What's your name, honey?"

"Jeannie."

I said, "Jeannie, this is Ray Wright, our pilot."

She shook hands with him. She turned back to me. "Well?"

I took out my wallet and picked out a new $100 bill. "I want you to go back to Havana with me," I said. I offered her the bill. "For this."

She didn't take it. She pouted, "You said business."

I said, "Don't you trust me, Jeannie?"

She snorted. "No."

I picked another C-note. I said, "Would this much interest you?"

She said, "I've got to be back in New York tomorrow night. All my baggage is back at the terminal. I don't want to go to Havana. Going back there isn't business."

"All I want you to do, Jeannie, is to take me to your boy friend you went to Cuba with and introduce me. Then Mr. Wright will fly you back here and you can catch a plane to New York. Isn't that worth two hundred dollars?"

"Are you queer or something? You'd give me two hundred dollars just for that?"

"Sure. No strings attached."

She took the two bills. "All right then."

We followed Wright to the small ladder that led into the cabin. The wash from the propellors caught her silk skirt and she held it down and giggled. "You're going to get your money's worth," she said. "I haven't got anything on underneath!"

I helped her up the ladder and into a seat in the cabin. Wright followed, slammed the door, and went up forward.

We were airborne within minutes and heading south down the coast. Jeannie was looking out the window. She seemed preoccupied. After about a half-hour she turned to me and said, "You know, I thought you just wanted to go to a hotel with me. . . . I meet the craziest people. Over in London we used to call them weirdies."

We landed at Havana airport in a little over an hour and taxied to the North American Oil hangar north of the terminal. There was a car waiting for us and there were no customs officers or police in sight.

Ray Wright told Jeannie, "I'll be waiting right here when you want to go back."

We got in the car, driven by a smartly dressed young Cuban, and she told me we would wait for her friend Louie at El Chico. She was sure he wouldn't be there this early, but it was the best place to wait, she said.

I said, "You suppose he's with Connie Masters?"

She had big blue eyes and she opened them wide at me as though I'd said something obscene. "Why would he be with her."

I shrugged. "I thought he came down here to take care of her."

She said angrily, "You take me back to the airport. I don't like you!"

I said, "Well, let's go to El Chico first and have a drink, now that we're on the way."

She thought that over, then shrugged a shoulder and said doubtfully, "O.K. Just one."

The club was packed and we went to the circular bar in the front. Jeannie had forgotten her anger and asked the head waiter whether he had seen Louie, and he said no. We found two places at the bar near the cash register. The show was on and we could see a corner of the stage through the arch. A quartet of Negroes was singing. I ordered rum collinses and we sat side by side and silent until they came.

She said, "Cheers," and we sipped. Then she said, "Louie won't be in for a long time. Not for hours."

"Can't we go and meet him?" I asked.

"He wouldn't like that."

"He knows who I am, doesn't he?"

"Yeah. I guess he does."

"Well let's go then. I'll take the responsibility. I'll tell him I insisted—that you had nothing to do with it."

She didn't want to. It took two more rum collinses and a third $100 bill to persuade her.

Apparently she was a girl who couldn't handle her rum. Her speech became thick and she needed my help to walk out to the car.

We drove west out of Havana at her direction and turned down a dirt road towards the sea just beyond Marianao, some ten miles out of the city. A jetty and fishing boats were etched in the bright moonlight, and a half-dozen small fishermen's huts huddled around a cove less than a mile across. We stopped at the end of the road, at the edge of the beach.

I said, "Now what? Where's Louie?"

"Kiss me first. . . . you know, I like you."

"Louie'd cut my throat if he caught me kissing you." She laughed. "He would at that!"

"Well, where is he?"

She pointed out to the middle of the cove. "Out there. On the *Estrellita*. We've got to wait here until he comes in."

I couldn't see anything through the car windows. I got out and walked down to the edge of the water. Then I saw it, a forty-foot sports fishing boat riding without lights about a mile off-shore. When it rocked to the gentle swell the moonlight was reflected from the windshield. I went back to the car. Jeannie was just getting out.

"You see it," she asked.

"Yeah. Let's go out there."

"How?"

"We'll steal a boat and go for a row. It's a wonderful night for it."

She giggled. "All right. You row."

I went around the car and told the driver to go back to the main road and wait for us for two hours. If we didn't come back by then, he was to return to the airport and notify the pilot of the Beechcraft that we wouldn't need him.

I went back to Jeannie and took her arm and helped her towards the jetty. After a couple of steps she kicked off her shoes, then sat down and took off her stockings. "I won't need these," she said.

64

I couldn't persuade her to take her shoes along. She was at the giggling stage and everything I said was hilarious.

I found a small boat at the corner of the beach and the jetty. It was hauled up on the sand, but there were no oars. I went along the jetty hunting for some and found a pair in a boat about halfway out. When I got back Jeannie was curled up in the sand in the lee of the boat, sleeping.

I shoved the boat into the water, then picked her up and put her in the stern. As I reached the seaward end of the jetty I saw a rowboat coming across the water towards us. It could have been coming from the *Estrellita*. I swung in close on the opposite side of the jetty and shipped the oars.

Jeannie was wide awake by then and asked me what was the matter. I shushed her and she talked louder. I reached for her and clamped a hand over her mouth. She struggled valiantly and hit me several times in the face with a free fist, but I was able to keep her from attracting the attention of the other boat. As it came closer, I could see two men in it. They went up on the beach and got out, walking away quickly up the dirt road.

When I released Jeannie she swore at me and demanded that I put her ashore at once. I resumed my rowing out to the *Estrellita* and tried to soothe her but she would not forgive me. Every few minutes she would utter a new obscenity. Then suddenly, as we were closing on the *Estrellita*, she started to giggle again. It was at that instant that the *Estrellita's* engines came to life with a roar and the riding lights were turned on.

I pulled mightily on the oars the last few yards and caught the stern rail of the boat just as she got under way. I got the painter around the rail, then climbed aboard. Up amidships at the controls inside the pilot cabin was Louie, his back to me. The light from the binnacle lit up his face and I recognized his profile as he looked out the starboard window.

I was halfway to him when he turned and saw me. He flipped the throttles shut, then reached under his coat. When he turned back he had a gun in his hand.

"Who the hell are you?" he demanded.

He switched on the overhead cabin light and stared at me with disbelief. "How the hell did you get on board?"

"I rowed out," I said. "You're Louie Pizzari, eh? Where's Connie Masters?"

Suddenly his eyes squinted as though he were in pain. He seemed to be looking not at me but slightly to my left. Then the gun roared twice. I felt nothing—no slam of

65

bullet and no numbing shock. He had missed me both times.

There was a whimper behind me—a sound that a kitten might have made. Then the thud of a falling body. I turned and saw Jeannie lying on the deck, blood oozing from her smashed face through her flaming hair which covered it.

I turned back to look at Louie. He was shaking his head.

"Now I got two damned dames to get rid of," he said.

NINE

WHILE HE WAS TYING ME UP IN A FORECASTLE BUNK, Louie Pizzari said, "You shouldn't have come here, Mr. Andradi. You make me look bad."

There was a serious, worried expression on his face and his eyes were wet and sad. He reminded me of a cocker dog I had as a kid who would get that same look when I'd try to induce him to get off my bed on hot summer nights.

"Where's Connie Masters?" I demanded once more.

He shook his head. *"Bell' arti parrari picca.* You shouldn't ask me that. You know better. . . . Look, Mr. Andradi, I got a reputation. I'm Louie the Disposer. I work for all the *capo mafiosi.* I'm a good workman. So they give me this job and now you come and try to spoil it."

As he worked with the half-inch manila line, I tensed the muscles of my arms, legs, and shoulders to get all of the slack possible. He didn't want to hurt me, and he put little of his strength into tightening the lines.

I said, *"Si moru mi drivocu si campu t'allampu."* This is one of the ancient and dire Mafia threats: "If I die I shall be buried; if I live I shall tramp you out."

He leaped against the bunk opposite mine, holding the rope that bound my ankles. "Please, Mr. Andradi, don't say that. I am just a workman who takes orders. Why should you hate me personal? If you try to tramp me out, I will have to kill you. No one is stronger than Louie Pizzari."

He took the half-inch line and twisted it around his arm and hand. Then suddenly he strained, his eyes bulging with the effort. The line parted. It was a trick and I knew the trick—to cut one lien with another by pulling against it. But with half-inch manila it took tremendous strength—more than I had. "You see?" he said.

"Nevertheless, if you harm that girl, *t'allampu.*"

He finished tying me and stood looking down at me. "Now we go out to deep water. When we get back to Havana, there will be just you and me. . . . I will call Don Nicosa and ask him what I should do with you because you have tried to spoil my work. Maybe, Mr. Andradi, he will tell me that you are my next job."

"You work for Don Nicosa?" I asked.

"Sure," he said, "don't we all?"

He left me and the engines were revved up. We were under way again. I started working on my bindings and after a half-hour of painful struggling I decided that I had been wrong—that Louie had tied the ropes tight enough for his purposes. After ten minutes of resting, which became more painful than my struggling because of my cramped position, I went back to work on the ropes.

I have no idea how much time passed then—perhaps as much as two hours—and I had finally succeeded in working some slack in the binding around my wrists when the engines were slowed. I could hear Louie moving around, down the ladder from the bridgehouse and to the cabin aft. Then there was a thumping at the stern and the faint scream of a woman—it seemed thin and far away and the terror that was in it could have been more my own imagination. There were three quick pistol shots and those could not be mistaken. After a few minutes the engines were speeded up again.

I redoubled my efforts on the ropes, disregarding the pain and the torn flesh, and finally I got my hands free. I rested for a time, then untied my legs and rubbed the circulation back into my ankles. My feet and hands were numb and my back felt as though Louie had been tromping on me, but after a few minutes of rubbing and exercising in the pitch-black cabin, I felt all right again.

The forecastle door led into the galley. There was no light there and I moved carefully. There was a small vestibule with a ladder going up to the bridgehouse. Faint light from the binnacle seeped down there. I looked up and saw Louie's legs through the hatch. They were huge columns sheathed in blue slacks. He was wearing white canvas boat shoes and they were planted on the deck as though attached. Astern was the engine room and I opened the door silently and went through a passage to the after-cabin. A dim bulb was lit on the overhead and I saw bunks on each side against the bulkheads. The bunk on my right was mussed and there was a long length of half-inch manila on top of the white spread.

Under the pillow was a red suede bag I had seen before, on my way from New York to Havana. I opened it and it was empty. But there was the familiar Arpege scent that came from it. I snapped it shut and put it back under the pillow. I started back astern and kicked something with my foot. I leaned down and picked it up—a red shoe with openwork toe and a high, slim heel. I'd seen that before, too.

I dropped it on the bed and went through small double-doors onto the rear deck. I crouched on the deck and looked forward. I saw Louie as I had first seen him when I climbed aboard, standing at the wheel.

I straightened up and I yelled, "Louie!"

He jerked his head around and looked at me. The dawn was coming up fast and there was no question that he could see me plainly. He performed the same motions he had the first time. He closed the throttles, then turned back to me with the gun in his hand.

I stood waiting for him. I looked around at the deck, getting its topography well fixed in my mind. Up ahead of me was a large wet place that had been recently washed down. This was the place where I'd seen Jeannie laying dead.

Louie stopped two feet from me, pointing the gun at me, and said, "All right. Now I will tie you up again."

I said, "Was that Connie Masters you shot and threw over the side?"

"You talk too much," he said scornfully.

He moved suddenly towards me, the gun held in the flat of his hand. He moved remarkably fast for a man of his size and he almost caught me unawares. He swung his huge right arm with the gun to smash me on the side of the head. He had lost patience.

I ducked under his swinging gun-hand and came around with the side of my palm as hard as I could against his throat, in the judo manner. Then I grabbed his gun-arm and applied the leverage and pressure that could have broken it if he continued to struggle.

He gave forth an enraged roar and grabbed my hair with his left hand and jerked my head back. He almost broke my neck. Then his knee hit me in the back and I was forced to release his arm. He knew a trick or two and his great strength was overpowering. He continued to roar, and there was a gurgling from his throat in between the bursts of sound, so I must have hurt him with the blow. I hurt him but I didn't slow him down.

I twisted away from his knee and hit his gun-hand just as he shot. Then the gun was against my head and the hammer clicked. It clicked three times. He had not reloaded after killing Connie and Jeannie.

I was punching, kicking, kneeing, and staying in as close as possible to avoid a clubbing with the gun. It didn't seem that I was being effective and I was wondering how long I could keep it up. Then he got in a blow on my left shoulder near my neck with the gun and I felt intense pain. A fist smashed me in the face and I started to sink

69

to my knees. I made an instinctive grab for his huge legs as I went down and I hugged them to me as I had learned to do on the football field. The gun hit me again on the top of the head, but there was no force in the blow. I had him off balance and he was falling backwards. He got one leg loose and kicked, grazing my hip, but he was still falling.

Then there was a roar louder than the rest and his other leg twisted out of my grasp. I saw Louie hit the water with a splash. His roar was suddenly cut off as his head went under. Then he came up thrashing his arms and gurgling. The boat was moving slowly and was five yards from him.

I got up to my feet and hurried forward to open the throttles. Louie was going to have to join Connie Masters and his Jeannie. To keep him quiet.

The sky was cloudless and the sun was just rising above the horizon in the East. The tradewind blew a steady ten knots and the sea swell was gentle. Cuba had to be to the south and Florida to the north. I set the automatic pilot on a northerly course, steering a few degrees east, and set the throttles halfway. Gas guages showed one tank three-quarters empty and the other full, but since I didn't know how much they held I couldn't guess at the cruising range. That was a chance I'd have to take.

I couldn't go back to Cuba. If the boat was traced and I was connected with it, then I was finished. If I could get rid of the boat, I might be reasonably safe.

I went below to the after-cabin and examined my cuts and bruises. I found iodine and adhesive and patched my head and shoulder. There was a wardrobe in the cabin and I rummaged through it and found a T-shirt big enough. There was a plastic shirt-bag and I wrapped the two bundles of money and my wallet in that and tied it around my waist. Then I shaved with the boat-owner's razor, threw my discarded clothes over the side, and settled in a fishing-chair to wait for the Florida Keys to appear on the horizon.

I must have dozed for several hours. When I opened my eyes the sun was high and beating down on me. I checked the gas and the time. I found the one tank now empty. The *Estrellita* had run about three hours on a quarter-tank, which should give me twelve hours on the remaining full tank. I was cruising at about ten knots, so twelve hours would equal 120 miles. That was ample for where I had to go and what I had to do.

At 4:10 P.M. I sighted land ahead. I switched off the pilot and steered to the right, approaching gradually. There were binoculars in the pilot house and within an hour I was able to

70

see cars on the causeway that connects the Florida Keys.

There were scores of boats in this area, from outboards to big sports fishermen. I kept as far away from them as possible. I passed several towns and small harbors, then came to a long stretch of empty land where the road went inland. At the northern end of this key was a larger town, which I later learned was Key Largo. I picked this for my debut ashore.

It was then 7:50 P.M. and still light, so I turned southwest and sailed for an hour into the dark. Then I turned back on the opposite course and sailed for another hour, which should have put me back where I had been. There was a lighthouse off to my left that blinked white and red and a string of lights on the shore that came from street lights and the houses of the town. I went to within a mile and a half of the shore, then stopped the engines and let the *Estrellita* drift.

I turned out all lights, including the riding lights. I took off my shoes and threw them over the side. I took a flashlight from a clip at the side of the control panel and went down the ladder to the engine room. It was hot and smelled strongly of oil. I found tools in a box on the bulkhead and picked out a small crescent wrench. At the back of the engines I located the gas line from the port tank and I unscrewed the connection just below a valve. The gas streamed out to the floor boards and ran into the bilge. I bent the copper tubing back and forth until there was a rupture in it, then tightened the connection. The gas continued to stream out the hole I had made.

I went into the after cabin and got the rope with which Connie had been tied. I coiled it and took it to the engine room and soaked it in the escaping gasoline. I laid an end of the rope on the floor under the gas stream, then carefully uncoiled it to the vestibule and threw the rest of it out a porthole which I opened. I went out to the deck quickly, lit the gasoline-soaked rope with my lighter, and dived overboard.

It was a shallow dive and took me away from the boat. I swam strongly about ten strokes, then dived again, this time as deep as I could go. I stayed under until the bursting point, then came up. I was too soon by a full second. The *Estrellita* exploded in my face.

I was under again before the debris began falling. By a miracle, or because I had been far enough away, I was unhurt. When I surfaced again, the superstructure of the *Estrellita* was burning fiercely and she appeared to be down

71

by the stern and sinking slowly. I swam towards her and got to her side. The heat was scorching but I was able to avoid being burned by keeping under water. I found the dangling rope from the vestibule porthole—the one damning piece of evidence I needed to destroy. I tied the rope around my waist and swam away. Halfway shore I untied it and let it drift.

I came ashore on the beach north of Key Largo. The *Estrellita* had disappeared. Several boats, including a Coast Guard lifeboat, were churning around in the area sweeping the water with searchlights, hunting for bodies. I lay on the beach among sand dunes for a half-hour and rested, then got up and started for town. It was a warm, humid night and my wet clothes actually felt comfortable. But I had to do something about them. That came first.

With money it is not difficult to get anything. I followed a man of my own height and weight from a bar and accosted him at the door of his house. I bought his seersucker suit, which fitted perfectly, and his shoes, which were a half-size too large, for forty dollars, twice what they were worth.

Then I walked back to the center of town, found a garage open, and hired a car to take me to the nearest airport, at Florida City some twenty-five miles north. At 11:30 P.M. I was back at the hot-dog counter at the Miami air terminal.

My FANG contact in Miami was a middle-aged, hard-faced native named Pete Howell who would have looked more at home at sea than behind the wheel of his new Lincoln. He picked me up at the airport, then drove fast out Highway 41 across the Everglades. I told him the full story of my trip to Cuba, since he didn't tell me how much of it he knew, and gave him the details of the *Estrellita*, Connie Masters, Jeannie, and Louie Pizzari.

He made no sign that he was hearing me and asked no questions. When I was finished he said, "You going back to New York?"

"I should get back as soon as possible."

"I'll arrange a plane for you tonight."

"That's all?"

He nodded. "We're busy here in Miami just now. Willie Lombardi has moved down here with his fight racket."

I said, "This caper of mine ought to bring FANG all of the action it needs."

He gave me a thin smile. "It will, but that's all in the past.

That's been set up and it's working out. Louie Pizzari was a good touch, Andradi."

His attitude annoyed me. He was too off-hand. He'd said nothing about the most important point of all. I said, "I suppose Connie Masters was a good touch, too? You certainly got her knocked off fast, didn't you?"

He took his foot off the throttle and let the car slow down. It was the only sign that anything was bothering him. "I was Connie's teacher and she was my friend," he said. There was a long pause. "We can't win 'em all. . . . I'm going to suggest we use Louie Pizzari for our first announcement of Anti-Mafia. You be prepared for it, Andradi. It's going to be a shock to the Dons and they won't be in a good humor."

I said, "I'll take care of myself. I won't forget how careless you were with Connie."

He nodded. "You do that."

He had a radiophone in the car and he called an operator and ordered a plane to take me to New York. Then he turned the car around at a road junction and drove me back to the airport, to the Atlantic Air Service hangar where I'd been the night before. There was no further conversation on the way back. At the hangar he shook my hand, said good-bye, and left in a hurry.

I stood on the apron waiting for someone and presently the same Ray Wright came out of the hangar. He told me we would take off as soon as the plane was gassed up.

We landed in New York at La Guardia shortly before 8:00 A.M. and I was back in my apartment at 9:00, putting in a call to Rocky at the Waldorf Towers.

A girl answered, a tinge of Boston in her voice. She told me she didn't know where Rocky was. "Who are you?" she demanded.

"I'm his brother Danny."

"Oh—I've heard of you. I'm Patsy."

"Yes. . . ?"

"He's told you about me?"

"No."

"He hasn't! I wonder why not?"

"Look, Patsy, you don't know where he is, do you?"

"No I don't. I haven't seen him for two days, if you want to know."

I got rid of her and tried Rocky's office in Brooklyn. He was not there and I could get no information. A man told me in Sicilian that it wasn't wise to talk over the telephone.

I tried two more numbers, then the St. Charles Hotel on Central Park West, which was Mafia-owned and operated for the convenience of the Dons and their Ivy-league Brothers.

73

Rocky had been there the night before but had left at 3:00
A.M.

That was as close as I could get to him. It looked ominous,
in a way. It looked as though Brother Rocky was on the run.

TEN

I SLEPT MOST OF SUNDAY, GETTING CAUGHT UP FROM MY two sleepless nights. At 4:30 P.M. I was awakened by the telephone. I picked it up on the second ring.

"Andradi?"

"Yes."

"This is Vincent Carmi. You got back from Cuba, eh?"

"I'm back."

"We want to see you."

"O.K. Where?"

"A couple of the boys will pick you up in half an hour, in front of your place."

"Fine. I'll be waiting."

"You do that, Andradi."

He hung up. I got up and showered and dressed, putting on a tropical suit and a new white shirt. I tried to keep my mind off the two boys who were going to pick me up. "Two boys" meant two workmen, and two workmen could mean bad news. I found myself perspiring and my collar was wilting before I got my jacket on. I thought of taking a gun or a knife—FANG had given me a .380 automatic and a couple of German trench knives with retractable blades—but I discarded that idea as foolish. If they were going to get me, they'd do it from the car as they drove up. Guns and knives wouldn't help me. . . . I found some assurance in the fact that Louie Pizzari had tied me up rather than kill me. I found some more in Palermo and Bottolino, who had me put aboard a Miami plane rather than dump my body into Havana harbor. So maybe the Professor did want to talk to me. . . . Maybe.

I was on the sidewalk in front of my building at five o'clock. There was little traffic at that end of Fiftieth Street. Two cabs came by, then a delivery truck from a florist. Then the street was empty. A black Buick turned in from First Avenue and moved down the block. It moved slowly and, it seemed, too deliberately, as a car would on some murderous errand. I was perspiring again. I stood by the curb. The Buick stopped opposite me. I recognized the driver as Jake Lamassa, Rocky's workman with the scar. Beside him was another *bassa mafioso*, about as ugly as jake, and he looked

75

me over in a speculative way. Jake motioned for me to get in the back and the other one opened the door. I got in.

There was no conversation. We drove to Fifty-first Street and across town to the West Side. We turned up Eighth Avenue and stopped before a brownstone next to the St. Charles Hotel. Jake said, "You go in there, Mr. Andradi. Ring the bell. Someone will meet you."

I got out of the car and climbed the steps of the brownstone. There was a bell in a brass plate to the right of the inside door and I pushed it. The door was opened immediately by a young Sicilian in a white coat.

"You Mr. Andradi?" he asked.

"Yes."

He swung the door wide. "Come in. You are expected."

I followed him down the hallway to the rear of the building. We went through the last doorway on the left, to a small room furnished as a den. One wall was covered by heavy drapes hanging from the ceiling. My escort pushed these aside and revealed a steel door. He unlocked this with a key and bade me follow him. We entered a dimly lighted passage, well carpeted, which could have led nowhere but into the St. Charles Hotel. We went down a flight of steps, around a couple of corners, and stopped in front of an elevator door. My escort held the door open for me to enter.

"Press the top button," he said. "Someone will meet you."

I closed the door, pressed the indicated button, and went up. I have no idea how far, but it seemed at least to the top of the hotel. When the elevator stopped the door was opened and I looked into a huge room with an oaken table across the length of it, like the board room of a corporation. Facing me in the doorway was the Professor.

"Come in, Andradi," he said, holding out a hand. "We've been waiting for you."

I stepped out of the elevator and took his proffered hand. He steered me to an end of the table where seven Dons sat smoking cigars. The chairman was Vito Nicosa and I went to him and shook his hand. The others were Frank Magardi, Lou Caruso, Joe DiMassi and Leo Gamma, all of whom I'd met, and Dons Sammy Giorgiano and Marko Gambetta—two new names to add to my roster of Mafia elders. Both were impressive in an *alta mafioso* way and rated high in the hierarchy, judging by the respect accorded them.

I had to assume this was a council of elders, a top-level business meeting of the Brotherhood, for only on such occasions would you find a group of Dons together in daytime in a secret place, without women and food and wine. Such councils decided all matters of importance to the organization —matters of policy and of life and death.

It did not escape me, novice that I was, that three Dons whose names were important in the East were absent—Dons Rocky Montana, Charlie Giosa, and Steve the Waiter Fischetti.

I was told to take a seat at the far side of the table next to the Professor. I was given an excellent cigar and I was asked if I'd like a drink. I shook my head. "I seldom drink," I said.

Don Nicosa did the talking and questioning. He spoke in English and in Sicilian, switching to the *gergo mafioso* when he wanted to make a particular point that was a matter of traditional policy. The Mafia commandments are all set down in this slang and are taken seriously by the Brotherhood. The single penalty for violation of these rules of conduct is death.

"You know *omertà*?" Don Nicosa asked me.

I nodded. "Yes sir."

"Do you live by *omertà*, Andradi?"

"Yes sir."

"What is your first loyalty?"

"To God and to the Brotherhood, Don Nicosa."

"We will find out about that. *Sangu lava sangu.* ("Blood washes blood.") Why did you go to Cuba?"

"I was sent there by my brother, Don Montana, to arrange for the purchase of the El Capitan Hotel and casino."

"You have arranged this?"

"No sir. Don Palermo and Don Bottolino requested that I leave Havana, so I went back to Miami. I have not been in touch with Batista's men."

"Who was to purchase this hotel?"

"My brother and Don Giosa and Don Fischetti had formed a syndicate for this."

There was murmuring and nodding around the table. Don DiMassi sneered at me, *"L'omu chi parra assai,* eh Andradi?"

I nodded at him. "Would you have me be silent before the elders, Don DiMassi?"

"Enough of that!" exclaimed Nicosa. "You knew of this syndicate, Don DiMassi. You and Don Gamma were both invited to join it and you have not given me as much information as Danny Andradi." He turned to me. "How much money was involved?"

"The total price was to be fifteen million, paid in New York. I have $200,000 I was to give as a down payment."

"You have it with you?"

"Yes, sir." I took the two packages of thousand-dollar

bills out of my pocket and put them on the table. There were exclamations from several of the Dons.

The Professor reached for the packages. "I'll take charge of these," he said.

There was further questioning about the Cuban business. The Mirador and Greasy Joe's were mentioned as having been purchased by Rocky's syndicate. Then Don Nicosa said, "This confirms our decision. Please indicate now if there is any disagreement."

No one spoke. Several nodded and the Professor tapped me on the arm. "We have a job for you, Andradi. We hope you will not disappoint us."

He was smiling at me in a cynical way, as though he anticipated that my next question would enable him to drop the bomb.

I said in Sicilian, "I am at the disposal of the Elders. I will do what I am told to do."

The bomb didn't drop. Nicosa nodded at me, his face serious. He said, "You do not disappoint me, Danny Andradi. . . . On the plane down to Havana did you talk to the girl Masters?"

"Yes, sir. We sat together."

"There was one of our workmen on that plane, with a red-haired girl. You saw him?"

"Yes, sir. He sat just behind us."

"Have you seen him since?"

"No, sir. I saw him for the last time at the Havana air terminal. He was with Miss Masters."

"Have you ever heard of the Anti-Mafia, Mr. Andradi?"

It was a question I had been prepared for since Miami, but now that it was before me I found it difficult to dissemble. I was like a runner waiting for the starting gun, who falters at the first step because he is over-anxious.

"The Anti-Mafia? No, sir, I have heard of no such organization. Is there such a thing?"

I felt I was giving a lousy performance. I felt as though all of them there were seeing through me. I was afraid to look around at their faces.

Frank Magardi took a 4 x 5 filing card from his pocket and passed to me. On it was typewritten:

SANGU LAVA SANGU

THE MAFIA WILL BE EXTERMINATED. THE FIRST TO DIE IS LOUIE PIZZARI, WHOSE BODY TODAY FLOATS IN FLORIDA STRAIT. NO DON

AND NO WORKMAN WILL ESCAPE OUR VENGE-
ANCE.

THE ANTI-MAFIA

I put the card on the table and shook my head. "This is probably from a crank. It sounds crazy to me."

"Not if Louie Pizzari's body is in Florida Strait," said Don Nicosa.

The Professor introduced the workman as Johnny. He was like all *bassa mafiosi*, a Sicilian peasant with a broad, serious face and a stocky body. I met him in the lobby of the St. Charles. I had been told only that I was to meet this Johnny and help him.

The Professor said, "Johnny knows what to do. He will tell you what he needs from you. Good-bye, Andradi. Don't let us down."

Johnny and I left the hotel and got into a new Ford double-parked on Central Park West. He got behind the wheel, made a U-turn and started uptown. He said, "Your brother Rocky goes to the Linden House barber shop every Sunday at seven. This I am told."

I said, "It's possible. I don't know his habits."

"We'll find him there," he said. "But I don't know Don Montana. I've never seen him and he's never seen me. You understand?"

I nodded. "That's clear enough."

"We will go to Central Park South and I will let you out. You will walk into the Linden House and wait in the lobby until you see me. Then you will go down to the barber shop in the arcade under the lobby and you will speak to your brother. Not to anyone else. Just your brother."

I nodded agreement. I was afraid to talk. I knew my voice would have given away my astonishment. I fought to keep my thoughts objective—that I was merely to identify a hoodlum for Mafia execution.

It was a monstrous and unbelievable charade the Mafia had dealt me in. It was not that I cared for Rocky. Everything I had been doing had helped to bring about his condemnation, and I was aware of it. But now, I was the one who would lead his killer to him. It was a burden that very nearly overwhelmed me.

"What's the matter?" said Johnny. "You don't like the idea?"

I shrugged. "Naturally not. But I'll do what I have to do. You want to head downtown now?"

He made another U-turn and drove fast and expertly to

Central Park South and Seventh Avenue, where I got out. I walked leisurely to Sixth Avenue and went into the lobby of the Linden House. It was crowded at this hour. Arriving guests formed a line before the desk. I stood at the entrance to the flower shop to the right of the doors and waited for Johnny to show up.

Then I saw him coming. I walked to the rear of the lobby and down a flight of marble steps to the arcade on the floor below. Fifty feet along to the left was a round red-and-white barber pole under a canopy held up with spears. I went into the shop. Rocky was in shirtsleeves with his tie off, just getting into the second chair. The barber, a small bald-headed man with gold-rimmed glasses, was standing beside the chair holding the barber cloth in his hands.

Rocky looked big and tough and arrogant and there was nothing agreeable about him. Nothing that I liked. But he was my brother. He said, "Hi, kid. Hunting for me?"

I said, "I wanted to tell you I was back."

He laughed too loud. "I hear they chased you!"

"Yeah, I got chased."

"Why didn't you stay down and call 'em over to Miami?"

"I thought of that. I thought you'd better handle it."

"I'll handle it," he said as the barber put the cloth around his neck. "I'll handle all them bums. . . . I'll call you tonight late, Danny-boy. Now I'm busy."

"O.K.," I said.

I turned and walked out of the shop. There were about a dozen people in the arcade and on the steps, all hurrying to somewhere. I didn't look at any of them. I started up the steps and got to the first landing, where the stairway starts curving back, and paused a moment to light a cigarette. Then I continued up.

I was in the middle of the lobby when the shots came. There were three muffled blasts, not very loud. They had a mushy sound; it wasn't the sharp bark of a pistol fired in the open.

I kept walking. The people checking in and out and waiting for dates to show up and just wandering around gave no sign of having heard anything unusual. I didn't see anybody running or any excitement.

I got a cab outside and went for a ride around the park. I had never felt so heart-sick, so completely desolate.

I phoned Tony at the parish house from a drugstore on 110th Street and told him I wanted to see him.

"Can you come up, Dando?" he asked.

"I'll be up."

I took a cab to the Bronx and was ringing the parish

house bell in a half-hour. Tony opened the door and came out. He took me by the arm.

"Let's go next door where we can have some privacy."

We went into St. Mary's, an old red-brick structure with a huge rose window above the portal. Tony took me through a side door to the altar and we went up the aisle to a pew in the rear. There was a dim light over the altar; the high-vaulted ceiling was lost in blackness. Over to our right was a statue of the Virgin and a score of candles flickered there.

Tony said, "You're in trouble, Dando?"

"Rocco is dead," I said.

"Killed?"

"Yes. I helped to kill him. An hour ago."

He put his hand on my arm. "That is a bitter thing to know."

"He trusted me. I think that I am the only one he trusted. ... So now he's dead."

Tony bowed his head. He might have been praying. I sat in the gloom of the old church and tried to think it through, to find some reason in it, some justification. I couldn't. The only thing I could think about was that I had betrayed Rocky, and all of the reasons were insufficient.

Tony raised his head. "You are working with Commissioner Orsini?" he asked.

"Not exactly, but we'll call it that."

"And your indictment and conviction—they were a part of it?"

"Yes."

"Now Rocco—he's a part of it, too?"

"Yes."

"Don't give up, Dando. It's got to be done and you must do it."

"No," I said. "I don't think I can now. Not any more."

Tony grasped my arm. "What are you saying? You must!"

"Is that the advice of a priest?" I said bitterly.

"It is the advice of a priest, of your own brother, and of a man who is proud of his Italian heritage," he said quietly.

"I've killed Rocco!" I cried. "Can't you understand that?"

He put his arm around my shoulder. I put my head on my hands on the forward pew. I couldn't stop the tears and I felt ashamed of them.

"He was my brother, too," Tony said, "and I cry for him in my heart as you do. I think of him as we were together as children—how Rocco was always the strongest and how he protected us. ... Do you remember the time we three went to Sheepshead Bay to go swimming and the gang of boys attacked

81

us, and how Rocky drove them off? He was the strong one, Dando, and he should have brought honor to us. He should have made us proud that we were Andradis and Sicilians from Castellammare. Instead he made us ashamed and he broke our mother's heart. You know that, don't you, Dando? You know that she died because of the evil that was in our brother Rocco?"

"Yes, I have always known that," I said.

"Rocco was her favorite," he continued. "When he went to prison she ceased to live. He took her with him into that place. . . . Men like Rocco must always die at the hands of their brothers. You have been the instrument. That's all, Dando, an instrument. It cannot be a personal thing, for if it were not you it would have been another man—another brother."

"And my own feelings—are they nothing?"

"No," he said emphatically. "You must have courage. You must have the courage to carry through this work."

We sat there together for a long time—it may have been an hour. The storm within me subsided and the doubts and remorse ebbed away. There was a great, indescribable comfort in having Tony near me—closer to me than he had ever been in our adult life.

"Why don't you come up tomorrow morning and attend communion? Confession would help you. You've been away from the Church too long, Dando."

I shook my head as I got to my feet. "I have confessed tonight," I said. "I can't come back to the Church until my job is done. I will not be a hypocrite."

We walked back down the aisle together. "You will be forgiven if you do the job," he said. "The Church will wait for you."

ELEVEN

THE FUROR AND INDIGNATION OVER THE EXECUTION IN the Linden House barber shop of Rocco Montana spurred the Congressional committees on racketeering and criminal organization into renewed activity. There followed a blizzard of subpoenas with, as was expected, a small percentage of *alta mafiosi* caught in their snowfall. But as usual the overlords were left in peace, for their names were not newsworthy and too little was known or suspected about them. Vito Nicosa, Frankie Magardi, Vincent Carmi, Sammy Giorgiano, Marko Gambetta, and Lou Caruso, to name the six Mafia Dons who I had discovered to be the most powerful, were secure in their obscurity.

Deportation proceedings against Frankie Costello and Joe Adonis were pressed, to be sure, and in these two the government had corralled a couple of important second-string hoodlums, but the working organization of Mafia was left alone. It may seem unreasonable that FANG, knowing what it knew, did not seize this opportunity to reveal the upper Mafia hierarchy and assist in its prosecution, but experience had taught us that Congressional inquiry and legal prosecution for such omissions as non-co-operation and perjury was like trying to kill flies with pingpong balls.

Any revelations FANG could have made would have been premature and might very well have canceled out all of the work I had done. No possible good could have come out of subpoenas for Magardi and Nicosa and the rest of those *alta mafiosi* I was smoking out. We didn't know enough yet. We were just beginning to get a picture of Mafia in America, but we were still too far away from the real source of its power, from the traditional fountainhead of the Brotherhood. That is what I had to find.

The press, radio, and television took up the story of the barber-shop execution with a zest beyond expectations, and cries went up from all media to supress the underworld figures who had so affronted the peace and dignity of a New York Sunday evening.

Hundreds of thousands of words were written and spoken. Fact and fancy were about evenly balanced. Some few who had studied the Mafia and understood the methods of the criminal conspiracy made astute guesses as to the facts of the killing, but their accounts lacked the sensationalism the public demanded. Those who captured the national interest wrote and spoke of a gang war, of the fanciful invasion of Rocky's territory by rival hoodlums, of a great underworld upheaval.

Unnoticed by all of these commentators and by the Congressional experts on crime who were quick to get aboard this bandwagon of publicity were the simultaneous exectuions of Charlie Giosa and Steve the Waiter Fischetti, whose bodies were found early Monday morning in an abandoned automobile at the edge of a garbage dump outside of Secaucus, New Jersey.

There was no hint that Giosa and Fischetti had been associates of Rocky, nor was it guessed that they had been on a par with him as Dons of the Brotherhood. They both had criminal records and these records were summarized in the brief stories of their demise, but they were adjudged by the various news agencies to be minor hoodlums who had run afoul of other minor hoodlums. It was Rocky alone who got the send-off, and it was not unjust that his obituaries should have matched the noise and color of his living.

The New York police were not so naive, but what they knew and what they suspected they didn't give to the press. They, of course, had Commissioner Orsini to keep them up to date. A detective by the name of Kelley took me to police headquarters on Centre Street the next morning. The questioning lasted for about a half-hour and was civilized, with no tempers. There was a second detective, a police inspector, and an assistant district attorney.

Kelley asked most of the questions. "You talked to your brother just before he was killed?"

"Yes. In the barber shop."

"Just how long before was it?"

"I don't know exactly. From what I read in the newspapers, I would judge he was shot just after I left the hotel."

"Is that so? You heard the shots, of course?"

"No, I didn't hear the shots."

"You must have run out of that place very fast. You didn't have more than a minute to get up the steps and through the lobby."

"So you say."

"So I say. So does everybody else. Why don't you tell the truth, Andradi?"

I shrugged in the Italian manner.

"What did you talk to your brother about?"

"I'd just got back from Cuba and I wanted to tell him I was back. That's all."

"Did you talk to Charlie Giosa and Steve Fischetti before they were killed, too?"

"No. I know them only slightly. I haven't seen either of them for months."

"But you know they were killed at the same hour your brother was gunned in the barber shop, don't you?"

"I read the newspapers. I didn't realize it was the same hour, but you say it was."

"It was. You were working for your brother, weren't you?"

"No. I'm not working at all right now."

"You were working for your brother and you were working for Giosa and Fischetti. You went to Cuba for them. We know all about that, Andradi."

"That is not correct."

"How many times was your brother shot?"

"The newspaper said three times. That's all I know about it."

"How about Giosa? Was he shot three times, too?"

"I don't recall."

"You don't recall! And Fischetti. He was stabbed with a knife, wasn't he?"

I shrugged. "If you say so. The newspapers said he was shot, too."

"You know we can get you for violation of parole, don't you?"

"You can? Because I talked to my brother last night?"

"You answer the questions!" said the assistant D.A. in a nasty voice. He was a little bird-dog man named Tully who had once been one of my drinking companions. "We can make it tough for you, Andradi."

"I don't know any answers, Mr. Tully," I said. "I don't know who killed by brother. I don't know who killed Giosa or Fischetti. I have nothing to do with their business and I don't know any of their associates. Why don't you go out and arrest the guys who did these murders?"

It went on that way for a half-hour, as I say, when suddenly it was ended by a phone call and I was taken to an office on the second floor, given a couple of newspapers and magazines to read, and told to make myself comfortable.

It was a small office, furnished with a desk and three chairs and a couple of filing cabinets, and there was a grimy window overlooking Centre Market Place. I sat at the desk and smoked and read the *Herald Tribune* and the *Journal-American* accounts of the murders of the three *mafiosi*. I didn't feel anything at all reading about Rocky. I was reading about a stranger, a hoodlum with a name I knew, but nothing about him touched me.

An hour later Deputy Commissioner Orsini came into the office. He closed and locked the door after him and came to a chair beside the desk and sat.

"We'll keep you down here for another couple of hours," he said. "Make it look better."

"O.K."

"How are you?"

"Fine."

He said, "Who killed them?"

"You go to hell," I replied.

He smiled at me. "You're all right, Danny. We picked the right man. You're doing a fine job."

"So you say."

"You need anything?"

"From your two-bit police department?" I said. "What could you guys give me?"

We both laughed then and he got up. He said, "Somebody will come for you in a little while. Good-bye, Danny."

"So long."

He unlocked the door and left. I went back to my reading. I was free in time for a late lunch.

The next day there was the funeral for Rocky. Some thirty black Cadillacs and Buicks followed the hearse and the three open cars filled with flowers. It started from Vizatelli's Funeral Home in Flatbush after a lengthy service that I didn't listen to and wound across Brooklyn to Calvary Cemetery in Queens. Tony and I rode alone in the first car which followed the cars of flowers. In the next two were the eight Dons who had condemned Rocky to death. There were twenty carloads of Rocky's lieutenants and executives and back down the line were three of Rocky's girls. The rest of the mourners were Andradis and Turrinis from Brooklyn, New Jersey, Pennsylvania, and upstate New York.

Tony said, "We're quite a family, Dando."

"Yeah," I said, "but the *mafiosi* still outnumber us."

The pastor of our former Brooklyn church read the graveside service. Tony and I stood side by side in front of the others. There were no tears. I'd already cried my cry for Rocco. When the first clods of earth fell on the coffin, Tony turned away and went along through the crowd. I joined the eight Dons and we walked back to the cars.

Don Nicosa fell into step beside me and spoke in Sicilian. "The police didn't bother you?" he asked. He called the police by the Mafia appellation "Uncle Angelo."

"Just stupid questions," I replied.

"They kept you for a long time."

"Four hours. They're sadistic bastards." I said this latter in English. I didn't know the word for sadistic in Sicilian.

"You have done very well," he said. "Better than I expected, Danny."

"Thank you, Don Nicosa," I said.

I rode back to Manhattan with Nicosa, Frank Magardi and Sammy Giorgiano. We went first to the St. Charles Hotel and dropped off Nicosa and Giorgiano. I shook hands with both, said *"Baccio le mani,"* then Magardi and I were driven back to the East Side.

As we approached the new Chambers Building on 56th and Madison, a huge monument to Mafia wealth, where Magardi had his offices, he said, "You'll be working for me now, Danny."

"Fine," I replied. "You tell me what you want me to do."

"We have problems," he said, sighing and waving his cigar. "I've been hunting for a bright boy who can handle people, someone with imagination. You come to my office when you're ready to help me. It's Connor, Wythe and Company, twenty-fourth floor. How would next Monday suit you?"

"Monday's O.K., Don Magardi."

"You need anything—money?"

"I've got enough for now," I said.

He took out his wallet and selected a $1,000 bill. "Take this. You've got to have money in your pocket."

He waved away my thanks. The car had drawn up to the curb in front of the building and he waited for the driver to open the door. He got out and said, "Monday morning, Danny. Around eleven."

The car took me to my apartment. I was at a low ebb. I lay on the bed and thought about Connie and dumb Jeannie and the workman, Louis Pizzari, then Rocky. . . . I needed the kind of faith and confidence Tony had found in the Church, but I didn't have it and I didn't know where to get it.

Perhaps a girl like Trina Templer could give it to me, if I could know her and trust her, and if she would believe in me. It was a ridiculous sort of hope, as I looked back upon it, but typical of us romantics, who put everything together sooner or later on the basis of a Great Love. We are always sure that life's problems will be solved when we find The Woman—no matter how often the realities have demonstrated the contrary. We never learn.

When I woke up I felt pretty good. Sleep is even better than a Great Love, sometimes. I showered and made some coffee. There wasn't so much to this FANG business, and faith be damned. My job was simple—to work against the Mafia from the inside. And I was on the inside, solid. Right over Rocky's dead body.

On Thursday, a couple of days later, I was honored by a visit by two *mafiosi* of impressive aspect—the Professor, crisp and immaculate, and a youngish, compact, hard-stepping *paisan* with a face of truly distinctive evil. Actually he was rather handsome, his features regular and nicely tanned by the Florida or Las Vegas sun. I found that all of his evil was in his eyes and that you hardly noticed the rest of him once you had looked into them.

There had been a phone call and then they came up, climbing my four flights and arriving in a critical mood. The Professor introduced his companion as Johnny Castle (formerly Castigli), and I learned in due course that he had gone to Harvard, was a C.P.A. and actuary, and was top executive of Connor, Wythe & Co.

I had never been briefed on Castle. He was a new one to FANG and to me, so I listened to him carefully. Unlike most *mafiosi*, he liked to talk about himself and he couldn't resist references to Harvard and his career.

They came into my living room and looked around disdainfully. They sat side by side on my divan and they lit up cigars. I lit a cigarette and sat across the coffee table from them in my one good chair.

After several minutes of chit-chat, the Professor said, "You live like a true *mafioso*, Andradi. Very modest. No show. Not even a very good piano."

I had to assume he was being sarcastic. I said, "I don't have to impress anyone, Don Carmi."

"Is that a fact?" he replied.

Castle gave me a small sneer and looked at the worn spot on my rug near the door. He said, "I saw you play a couple of times for Columbia. We beat you bad."

"We?" I said. "You and who else?"

"Harvard," he said. "I didn't play football. The boxing coach wouldn't permit it."

"Boxing, eh? That's a sort of esoteric sport, isn't it? They tell me all the fights are arranged."

The Professor cut in quickly, "We'll gossip later, Andradi. We received another *billet-doux* from the Anti-Mafia. Don Nicosa asked me particularly to show it to you. That's why we are here."

He pushed a filing card across the table. I picked it up and read the typewritten message:

NOW YOU HAVE LOST THREE DONS—MON-
TANA, GIOSA, AND FISCHETTI. THE CUBA
DOUBLE-CROSS WAS SET UP BY ANTI-MAFIA SO
THAT THEY WOULD BE KILLED. WHO WILL BE
NEXT?

THE ANTI-MAFIA

"What crackpots!" I said.

"Oh?" said the Professor. "You are implying that they didn't set up this affair in Cuba?"

"I don't *know* whether anybody set it up," I replied. "It doesn't sound reasonable that it was a plant. That would mean Batista himself was in on it and I don't buy that."

"Not necessarily," said the Professor. "Batista could have been victimized by smart operators who knew all the facts. . . . Let's say somebody in our organization was in touch with Anti-Mafia, feeding them information. Then it would have been easy to arrange this Cuban affair, wouldn't it Andradi?"

Johnny Castle chimed in, "It would take only one yellow-belly to do it."

I met his inimical stare. I nodded at him. "Just one." Then I said to the Professor, "That's always a possibility of course, but from what Rocky told me I would judge he didn't need anyone to prompt him to buy into Cuba."

"What did he say, exactly?" he demanded.

"He told me first that he had a new operation lined up that would far overshadow his Brooklyn enterprises. He indicated he had been working on it for some time and that it was his own idea. Later he told me it was Cuban gambling he was moving into and he described Don Palermo and Don Bottolino as bunglers who had mismanaged their casinos and needed to be replaced. He gave me the strong impression that he was acting with higher authority when he asked me to go to Havana and arrange for the purchase of El Capitan. . . . He said nothing that would indicate he was working with people outside the Brotherhood or against our best interests."

I hoped I had not laid it on too thick and that Rocky had not talked too much to Joe DiMassi and Leo Gamma. But that was a chance I had to take. If I revealed knowledge that would support the Anti-Mafia claim, then the next step would be to tie me up with them.

"You didn't tell us this before," said the Professor.

"I wasn't asked. The question of Anti-Mafia was not raised."

Castle said, "You rode down to Cuba with this Connie Masters, didn't you?"

I nodded at him. "That's been established."

"She tell you why she was going to Cuba?"

"Just in a general way. She said she was going to swim and lie around and rest. A vacation."

"She mention Don Palermo?"

"Not that I recall."

"Try to recall," he said nastily.

"I've tried. No soap."

"She told you, didn't she, that she had a date with Palermo that night and was going to tell him all about you and your brother and your double-cross of the organization."

I said, "You'd make a lousy lawyer, Castle. Such loaded questions are for children."

He half-rose out of his seat. "Watch your tongue, Andradi."

"Watch yours, Castle. One more crack about me double-crossing anyone and I'll throw you out of here."

Then he did get up. The Professor grabbed his arm. "Sit down, Johnny!" he ordered.

Castle sat down reluctantly. He was still the boy-boxer from Harvard feeling his muscle.

The Professor said sharply to me, "Keep it friendly, Andradi. We're here under specific orders from Don Nicosa."

"Did he order Castle to accuse me?" I demanded. "No Andradi takes insults from the *contadini*."

Castle reacted properly at that. He became enraged. A *contadino* is an illiterate peasant and the word is used by *mafiosi* only with contempt.

But he didn't get up again. He said with all the menace he could pack into it, "I'll catch up with you one day, Andradi."

I smiled at him. "You do that, Castle. And *scupetta a mugghieri nun si 'm orestano*." (Never lend your gun to your wife.)

The Professor said with pedagogic asperity, "What's the trouble with you, Andradi? Are you being deliberately provocative?"

I shrugged at him. "I wouldn't be any good to you, Don Carmi, if I let people walk over me. . . . I've got no beef with your friend Castle so long as he remains civil."

"We have to find out about this Cuban business, now that the Anti-Mafia has entered into it," he replied. "Certainly you appreciate our concern?"

"I share it," I said. "Such an organization is a menace to all of us. I'll help you any way I can."

He regarded me as though he were back in the classroom

listening to a not very bright pupil. "I've been puzzled why a boy with your background and education should suddenly turn anti-social and throw it all away."

"Probably for the same reason you did—and Mr. Castle. I'm no different from any other Sicilian whose family background impels him to follow the Mafia tradition."

He shook his head at me. "The traditions of the Andradis and the Turrinis are not specifically Mafia, I've found. They were rebels, as are all Sicilians, but they were not noted *mafiosi*. There is a difference, my boy."

"You have been warned against me and my family?" I asked. "I don't know where you could have picked up information like that."

"You don't? I'll tell you, Andradi. From a most revered Patriarch in the hills behind Palermo."

"Your revered Patriarch could be wrong, Don Carmi. I am a *mafioso* now."

He gave me a skeptical smile and got up. Johnny rose with him and the two moved towards the door. I held it open for them.

In the doorway the Professor turned and said, "Don Nicosa and Don Magardi like you, so the rest of us will put up with you. If I were the boss, you'd be in Florida Strait with Louie Pizzari."

I bowed to him. *"Baccio le mani,"* I said.

The Anti-Mafia was like its antonym organization in that we had our elders and our councils. The next Anti-Mafia council I attended was on the Saturday evening after Carmi's and Castle's visit to my apartment. It was set up by FANG because it was considered that the facts I had gathered were sufficient for a further discussion of Anti-Mafia policy.

Our council was every bit as imposing as the Mafia meeting at the St. Charles, although we lacked the board room and the secret access. But we did have something even the Mafia could not have achieved. We had a private railroad car.

There were seven beside myself. There were Smith and Jones, Commissioner Orsini, a Federal judge from the South who was sitting in Philadelphia, an assistant to a member of the Presidential Cabinet, a noted atomic physicist who had come East from Arizona for the meeting, and an official of the New York Central Railroad, who had arranged our meeting place.

We arrived separately at Grand Central and went through a gate on the upper level with the passengers boarding the Empire State for Albany and the West. At the front end of this train, ahead of the baggage and mail cars and behind the engine, was a stainless-steel lounge car. Curtains were drawn on all windows and there was a guard standing just inside the car door. He nodded to me as I got to the door and opened it for me, saying my name. He knew me all right.

The interior of the car was lighted and seven chairs had been moved around a long table covered with a white cloth, supporting platters of sandwiches and pots of coffee. I was the fifth to arrive and I shook hands with Smith and Jones and Orsini and was introduced to the atomic scientist. Then the Cabinet assistant, the judge, and the railroad man arrived, our guard bade us adieu, and the car door was locked.

The surprise to me was that the judge took over the meeting and conducted most of the inquiry rather than Smith, whom I had considered the No. 1 man. I will call the judge Williams. He was a large man, second in size only to the huge Jones, and he had a merry manner and friendly words for me prior to our business session. Then he became the stern jurist and admonisher of the wicked, and I had a fleeting recall of standing shamefully in Special Sessions and being sentenced for a crime I had never committed.

The judge said, "The cogs of our machine are beginning to mesh, thanks to the excellent work of our group, and we are met here to formulate our next moves. . . . However, I came to listen, not to orate. Let's discuss the Mafia hierarchy, first. You Danny—if you don't mind my becoming familiar so quickly—you review the reports you've been making to our directors."

I said, "I've been working on the Mafia system of territorial divisions principally and I am reasonably certain now about the overlords in America. Vito Nicosa is overlord of the Northeast, Marko Gambetta the Southeast, Sammy Giorgiano the Middle West, and Lou Caruso the Far West. All the background data I have on these four comes from FANG, so I will let someone else present those details.

"The Cuban gambling and narcotics operations appear to come under control of the Northeast rather than the Southeast. At the Mafia council to pass upon the execution of my brother, Vito Nicosa had the authority. In Havana, Joey Palermo and Vince Bottolino confirmed this with their references to Nicosa rather than to Gambetta.

"The Mafia today is under the tight control of Nicosa and two Dons closest to him, along with the three other territorial overlords, rather than under general councils of the Dons of the various territories.

"A probable reason for this is the Apalachin debacle. It does not now appear to be practicable to hold large conclaves of the Dons. I believe all future Mafia councils will be smaller and that the rule of the Brotherhood will be more concentrated. Actually, six men rule the Mafia in America—the four overlords and two others.

"These others are Frankie Magardi and Vincent Carmi. Magardi, with his truckers' union and jukebox monopoly, operates in all four territories. I believe his narcotics activities also are nationwide. Carmi is Nicosa's chief lieutenant and the brains of the Mafia organization in the East, if not in the whole country. He is personally concerned with gambling and narcotics and, unlike the others of these *capo mafiosi*, does not maintain any legitimate business fronts.

"Vito Nicosa rules the Northeast as well as the Mafia council. The number two man in the council is Frankie Magardi and the number three man is Vincent Carmi. Then Caruso, Giorgiano, and Gambetta, in that order. But Nicosa's rule is confined to America. On matters of general policy, and particularly on the executions of Dons, he awaits the decisions of the Patriarch of the Mafia, in the hills behind Palermo. That is still the traditional fountainhead of the Brotherhood, as it was from the beginning."

The Cabinet man spoke next. He took several pages of notes from his pocket and referred to them as he recounted the backgrounds of the territorial overlords.

"Marko Gambetta," he said, "operates principally from Maryland to Florida. He is mainly concerned with gambling and, as an outgrowth of this, the fight racket, which he controls nationally. His lieutenant in boxing is Willie Lombardi, who recently moved into Florida and has bought popularity in the police departments throughout Dade County. He gets what co-operation he needs. All fights held under his auspices are fixed, of course. The winners and losers are known, which makes gambling coups possible.

"Gambetta lives quietly in a house on the Severn, outside of Annapolis, with his wife and four children. He is well thought of in his community; he contributes to charities and is a member of various Anne Arundel County service clubs. He is the owner of two large roadhouses, both of which feature legal slot machines. His police record in Baltimore is one arrest for assault, no conviction, and, going away back, an arrest for disorderly conduct in a house of prostitution, fined fifty-dollars and costs.

"Lou Caruso lives in Beverly Hills, in a fine house on Serra, and has no police record under that name. He owns much California real estate and a brokerage house, Caruso & Sons, with offices in Los Angeles, San Francisco, San Diego, and Palm Springs. He owns a large percentage of the Peacock Hotel in Las Vegas and the nationwide C.M.P. Trucking

Lines. He maintains a house at Malibu and has a secret hideaway in Palm Springs, known to us. He has a wife and two children, who stay pretty close to Beverly Hills and go to Malibu in the summer for a couple of months.

"Sammy Giorgiano lives in Chicago, in a hotel apartment on the near North Side. He has an imposing police record dating back to Prohibition, but with only two convictions. One was an attempted murder, later reduced to simple assault and a twenty-dollar fine when the victim recovered. The other was a narcotics charge, a first offense, with a sentence of three months. Today Sammy is a respectable citizen, as such things go in Chicago. He owns a group of cleaning and dying establishments, a chain of laundries, a hotel, a couple of bars, and he has a large interest in Fulmer-Robinson & Company, wholesale drug house. He's considered to be a solid business man and his past sins are forgotten.

"Vito Nicosa is another with an imposing police record, under three different names, and Commissioner Orsini tells me a recent analysis of charges brought against Nicosa and their disposal indicates he owned district attorneys in Brooklyn and Manhattan. Nicosa is an important contributor to Tammany and at one time controlled the Kings County Democratic organization through his financial support. He thus owned one mayor as well as the county prosecutors.

"My report on Frankie Magardi is incomplete as yet. We have only recently learned about him from Mr. Andradi and we are still digging. He appears to have used the names of Magardino, which may be his real name, and Maggio. When we definitely tie these up with him, we will know more about him."

There followed a further discussion of the six *capo mafiosi* by Orsini, who added detail about them from the New York and other police department files. Orsini dwelt particularly upon narcotics operations and gave a full picture of this traffic, from Lucky Luciano in Naples and Rome to the various Dons and their organizations in America.

By this time our train had arrived in Harrison, where the electric engines of all Grand Central trains are detached, and our car was switched to a siding. An hour later we were attached to a train returning to Grand Central. As this train slowed down for the stop at 125th Street, Judge Williams said:

"We are still lacking our key Mafia figure—the Patriarch who dwells in the hills behind Palermo. We should know who this man is and how and where to reach him before we proceed with our executions. I am well acquainted with *omertà* and so I doubt that we are going to get this information in America. We must get someone to Sicily. We must have a man who will be sent to Palermo on Mafia business. What do you think, Mr. Andradi?"

"I agree," I said. "I'll have to determine how this can be achieved. It will take time. I've got to win greater trust, to prove myself further. I'm certain I can create the opportunity but it won't be quickly."

"Any idea what means you will use?" Smith asked.

"Narcotics are still the Mafia's prime source of income. Perhaps I should concentrate on that."

Judge Williams said, "Then it is agreed, I take it? Barring some unforseen crisis, we will delay our extermination program until we know about the hills behind Palermo."

Jones said, "I should want to feel free to execute any of these Dons if a situation should arise that would warrant it."

"You are free to do that," said Judge Williams. "I am merely stating a general policy. . . . I will not be disturbed if you do away with any of them, Mr. Jones."

TWELVE

THE MAGARDI ENTERPRISES COMPRISED THE JUKEBOX monopoly, the truckers' union (with a younger brother as president), ownership of Diamond Records, one of the largest of the recording companies; control over all heroin that entered New York and several other ports, a chain of funeral parlors in Brooklyn and Manhattan, the Homestead Finance Company, a usurious small-loan outfit; and control over the East Harlem gang, also known as the 107th Street gang.

Like all Mafia Dons, Magardi's first inclinations were towards crime and vice. He regarded his legitimate businesses merely as a means to legitimize money collected from the underworld. He cared little whether these honest enterprises prospered. He assumed that those working for him were thieves and he assumed they were stealing every possible dollar. But if he could use his funeral parlors as narcotic drops, then the bookkeeping was of minor concern. If he could send a chunk of underworld cash through the loan company and thus get most of it back as legitimate earnings, then he was satisfied. It was an upsetting way to conduct a competitive business and it kept the several relatively honest executives who worked for him in a constant turmoil, but they didn't know what Frankie knew. They didn't have Frankie's view of the financial horizon.

It is traditional that Mafia Dons don't work. Work is for suckers. Work is for the ignorant, the *contadini*. There are several Mafia apothegms covering this. One could say that a primary commandment of the Brotherhood is that a *capo mafioso* must live off the labor of others. So the honest Magardi enterprises were run by non-*mafiosi*, who knew nothing of the Brotherhood that controlled their destinies. Many were of the underworld, but they were not the Sicilian elite who controlled it.

The one exception to these precepts of work and profits was Diamond Records. The truth is that Frankie Magardi was stage-struck, that he was fascinated by these people of the music world. He had discovered that with a company like Diamond, he could make it pay off in a lot of unusual and satisfactory ways.

96

Frankie owned almost fifty per cent of the good pop singers in the business, signed to recording and agency contracts, which gave him ten per cent of their earnings no matter where they worked. He kept them all working constantly in various Mafia night clubs all over America and in Havana.

As a sideline, he had set up a nationwide association of disc jockeys so that he could be certain Diamond Records would be given preference on at least one radio station in every city and town across the country. He kept his disc jockeys in line with regular weekly payments and with shares of stock in Diamond Records—a neatly tied-up bundle of persuasion. When something stronger than peaceful inducement was needed, he had that readily at hand.

But the aspect of recording that interested Frankie most was the artists themselves, female gender. This is a business beseiged by singers from all of the states and territories and not a few from Europe. A recording company is the clearinghouse and the goal for all the ambitious girls of the world who have ever sung in a choir or at a party or in a high-school show. And most of them who finally reached such an objective as Diamond are pretty, for they have been well-screened along the way by the requirements of show business. Frankie, as the boss of Diamond, had his pick. He could have any of them, except an occasional Trina Templer who didn't need patronage, and he kept the largest and most luscious harem of the whole Mafia in various hotels and apartments around Manhattan.

Frankie wanted me for Diamond Records. He wanted me as a buffer and for ideas and for growth. This was the one legitimate business in his portfolio that he insisted should prosper on its own and for itself. He demanded the stature that such success would bring him personally, for it was a stature among the only people he admired, the people of show business. In this show world he was Frankie Magardi the entrepreneur, and there was no one who would assail his position on the grounds of birth or social background or criminal record. A successful impressario was sacrosanct.

I called on Frankie Magardi on Monday at 11:00 A.M. at the Chambers Building on Madison. He had a suite off the huge layout of Connor, Wythe & Co. on the twenty-fourth floor, using their general reception room but no other of their facilities. Connor, Wythe are actuaries handling all of the odds-making and banking for betting commissioners and horse rooms throughout the country, and are operated by the so-called Syndicate, which is a loose term for the gambling organization of the underworld. The Syndicate comprises hoodlums of all races, various non-Mafia gangs, and a sprinkling of *mafiosi* who control it. Connor, Wythe was under closer Mafia control, for the one who ran this company was Johnny Castle.

Magardi had a spacious office and a tough young male secretary named Mike Lotto, who looked me over with much interest and little deference. I accepted a cigar and sat in a deep leather chair facing Frankie's modern oval desk with its battery of eight telephones.

"We've got to do something with Diamond Records," Magardi said after a time. "It's got to be bigger. You get what I mean?"

"You want to expand?" I asked.

"Sure. That's it. We got to control more of the field. We got the best artists, we got the two top A. and R. men in the business, but we got too much competition. Them other bums out-sell us four for one—five for one."

"You mean all together or separately?"

"No, all together. All we been getting this year is a fifth of the total business. That ain't enough, Danny-boy."

"How about their singers and their bands? Can we get any more of them for Diamond?"

"Some, maybe, but not enough. These guys have got smart and they're using the same kind of contracts that I got, so it's tough to break 'em loose. . . . I want you to come up with some ideas. I want you to tell me how I can put 'em out of business."

I said, "That's the Mafia method—to wreck them."

"What's wrong with the Mafia method?" He was immediately belligerent.

"It's out of date—obsolete," I replied.

"You tell me a better way!"

"Sure. Buy 'em up. Consolidate. All that takes is money and it's legal."

He thought about that for a couple of minutes. Then he shook his head. "I like my way better. It don't cost so much."

"It won't cost you anything if you do it right," I said. "You use tax money. You use the money you would pay the government if you declared all of your income, and you get some of the other boys to come in with you on the same basis—make it a syndicate. Then you use the profits from Diamond. It becomes a legitimate investment and you don't have to juggle your tax books and pay big fees to lawyers to keep you clean."

"What if they won't sell?" he asked.

"They'll sell. They're all for sale if you have enough cash and persuasion. . . . Let me ask some questions around the business and find out what's available right now and how much it'll cost. Then I'll draw up a plan and estimates and we can go over it and pull it apart. . . . I'm not trying to sell you anything, Don Magardi. You ask me a question and I'm giving you an answer."

He nodded and puffed on his cigar. "Who's going to do all this business?" he asked. "I ain't got time for nothing like that."

"I'll run it for you," I said. "I'll set it up and I'll run it. All I need from you is money."

He scowled at me. "Yeah, you'll run it and you'll steal all the loot."

"Not all," I said. "There'll be plenty to go around."

Then he laughed. "You young guys got too much vinegar. O.K., Danny-boy, you draw up this plan and we'll have a look at it. . . . I got an office for you down the hall and a secretary by the name of Marie—a niece of mine. Don't you go making no passes at her."

He winked at me and got up and I followed him out through his ante-room and along the hall to the second door. This opened into a small reception office and behind the desk was a pert brunette with harlequin glasses and a very red mouth. Frankie introduced her as his favorite niece and she followed us into the office beyond. It was a large room tastefully furnished in bleached mahogany and chocolate leather and it looked out on a terrace formed by a set-back in the building.

"What do you think, Danny?" Magardi asked.

"It's fine," I said. "Just fine."

"My last boss was Steve Fischetti," volunteered Marie. "He's deceased."

"I hope I stay healthier," I said.

Magardi squinted his eyes at me. "See that you do, Danny," he said. "You keep out of the way of the Professor and this Johnny Castle. They don't like you much."

My FANG contact was Jones. My problem needed the top echelon of the Anti-Mafia. We met in an 180th Street Bronx Park express of the East Side subway going uptown at noon on Tuesday. We rode to the end of the line in the same car, but at opposite ends, and I followed him out of the station and into the Bronx Zoo. I joined him at the lion enclosure and we stood side by side and watched the jungle beasts dozing in the shade.

"Good to see you again, Danny," he said. "How goes the fight?"

"Passably. I've talked myself into a corner. Can we consolidate one or two big recording companies under Diamond, along with some of the smaller companies?"

He shook his head. "That's a tough one. You'd need millions and a lot of luck. . . . I don't know much about the record business, but I understand it's cut-throat competition, with some very hard-headed boys at the top. I don't know how you'd induce any of them to sell out. The take is too big when they hit it right."

"Well, that's my problem. We have unusual means of inducement on occasion. I need a complete survey of the businesses first—capitalization, ownership, grosses, earnings, and particularly any soft spots. Can you get me that?"

"Yes. We'll go to work on it right away. But we won't like this consolidation idea, Danny. It will put too much power in Mafia hands. You make it a legal set-up and there's nothing in the world we can ever do to bust it."

"I've thought of that," I said. "There'll be a built-in self-destroyer."

"So you say. I'll need details."

We started walking, pausing now and then before cages and animal runs. I bought some peanuts and I gave them, bag and all, to a camel who leaned his head over the fence and smacked his lips at me.

I said, "The consolidation I am planning could constitute a monopoly in restraint of trade, in violation of the anti-trust laws. In due course this would become known and· suits would be filed by the government. That is, after I've done my Anti-Mafia job, dead or alive."

"I see," said Jones. "A good point—but the Mafia has lawyers, too. Will they stand still for it?"

"By the time the lawyers get around to it, it'll be all done. I want to go about it slowly, one company at a time. I'd start with the smaller outfits and get them into line first. Then I'd knock off the big ones. It wouldn't become a monopoly until we had the last of our purchases. . . . I'm counting on the avarice of these people to ignore the dangers of monopoly, just as it worked out with the International Boxing Club. Those boys wouldn't stop until they owned it all, and when they finally got it the government swatted them. They had lawyers, too—some of the best."

"A good example, Danny. I'll get you the survey you need. Let me know what other help we can give you. . . . How about this Magardi? He as bad as they say?"

I shook my head. "Not to me. He's my papa. But I've got a boy I wish you'd look into. This Johnny Castle I told you about, who's running Connor, Wythe and Company. He's

100

suspicious of me and the Anti-Mafia, and it's just possible he may find out something. Magardi tells me he's after me."

"We'll check on Johnny Castle."

"But not like you handled Connie Masters," I said.

Be-Kay Records had one singer who amounted to anything—a juvenile delinquent by the name of Tommy Lopata, who was about No. 3 on the teen-age idol scale and was coming up fast. My survey of the recording business, a twenty-page presentation assembled by FANG, was in the hands of Magardi and was being debated by several of the Dons, including Nicosa and the Professor, but I didn't want to wait for their decision. The way I could impress the Dons was to start moving, to show results, to give them a concrete illustration. I wanted this Tommy Lopata and Be-Kay Records for that purpose. The survey showed they were in trouble. It was a soft spot. With all of the promotion Diamond could give him, Lopata could sell a million of his next recording. Of this I had been assured by Max Murtha, Diamond's Artists' and Repertoire man for pop and rock 'n' roll.

I had met Murtha in Magardi's office and now I was making my first visit to Diamond's headquarters in West Fifty-fourth Street just off Eighth Avenue. They had their own twelve-story building with offices on the lower floors and recording studios up above. Their manufacturing plant was in New Jersey, on the outskirts of Newark, but some distribution was made from Fifty-fourth Street.

Murtha's office was on the tenth floor, across a hallway from Studio A where the big bands worked. It was my introduction to a recording studio but I knew what to expect. I had been spending my nights for a week being briefed by experts dug up for me by FANG, learning about the music business and their patter.

"Come in, come in," greeted Murtha, jumping up from his paper-littered desk and extending a hand. He was a dynamic, roly-poly little man with a perpetual half-smoked cigar in his mouth, seldom lit, and a gruff, clipped manner of speech that had been peeled of most expressions and intonations of politeness. "What do you want, boy?"

"I've been hearing about this Tommy Lopata. I think we should get him."

"A bum. A real jerk. But we could use him."

"Be-Kay owns him?"

"Yeah. Them crumbs."

"Who owns Be-Kay?"

101

"Manny Friend is the front man. I don't know who put up his dough but it's a cinch he didn't."

"Get him over here. I want to talk to him."

"Uh-uh. We don't let that thief in the building. He'd walk out with the generators. . . . You really want to talk to him?"

"I'm going to get us Tommy Lopata."

"You *think* you are. That's been tried by experts."

"Everyone's for sale," I said. "You ever try to buy him with a lot of dough?"

"No—but I bet you've got an idea!" He picked up a phone and dialed a number. "I'll set it up for you. Maybe if you showed Manny Friend a ten-dollar bill he'd jump off the Empire State."

Then he got Friend on the phone. "Manny? This is Max. . . . No, don't talk, just listen. I got a guy here, Danny Andradi, who will be over to see you. Danny's got a bankroll and he wants to talk. . . . No, I ain't doing you any favors. You'll find out. . . . Yeah, you can shove it." He hung up and pointed his cigar at me.

"You go over there, Danny. Twelve-fifteen Brill Building. Keep one hand on your dough and the other on your gun. . . . Now where was I?"

He looked at his watch and whistled. "Jeeze!" He moved to a huge speaker in a corner of the room and flipped a switch. The room was filled with sound, a beautiful contralto singing over a full-band backing, "—*my careless love. Days are cold and nights are colder; love is old but tears are older . . .*"

The music soared and this voice seemed to edge itself into the corners of my being. There was an earthy, caressing quality that called out to me in a very personal way. It was almost disconcerting. I'd never cared for girl pop singers and I didn't know Lee from Day. Music yes —the operas, the masters, and a lot of good jazz—but now I was hearing for the first time this personal appeal that I suppose accounts for the popularity of most singers.

Suddenly the song was cut off and a trumpet blew a glissando down to the bottom. A man's voice said, "That's what I mean! That's what I want in there! The phrasing is good that way, so keep it. All right now, from the top. We'll cut this. Turn 'em on, Eddie."

The song began again, after a short band intro, and I sat on the edge of Max's desk and listened. I felt chills up and down my spine, as I had before at the Met, when Lily Pons or someone close to her soared in an aria.

As the last note died away Max said, "That's the way I like 'em. Solid."

I came out of my trance. "Who is that?"

He looked at me with disbelief. "You mean you don't know?"

I shook my head. "I'm kind of new in this business."

"Brother, I'll say! That, son, is just the greatest—Trinia Templer."

I said, "She's here—recording?"

"Sure. Where else would she record?"

"Can I see her?"

He shook his head. "You, too, eh? . . . We'll go in. You know her?"

"I've met her."

"O.K., but it's not going to do you any good. That gal's not for you, Danny."

As we crossed the hall to Studio A I said, "The opinions about that seem to be unanimous. But I'm still going to hear it from the lady herself."

Trina was talking to the bandleader, Sammy Harrow. She had her back to us. She was wearing slacks and she was a girl who could. She had on a white silk shirt, cut in the style of a man's, and she waved her left hand as she talked to emphasize her points. There were a lot of people in the studio and Max introduced me to some of them and I shook hands, but I wasn't paying attention and I don't remember them. I was paying attention to Trina.

Then she turned around and she saw us and she smiled and waved at Max and switched it to a scowl for me. We walked up to her and Max said, "You know Danny Andradi? He's running Diamond now—he's your boss."

She didn't offer me her hand. She said, "You kept me waiting."

"I got kicked out of Havana," I said. "I couldn't get back. Will you please accept my apology?"

"No. You could have phoned."

"I couldn't. I wasn't within miles of a phone."

"A likely story."

"It's true. . . . I've never regretted anything so much. The next day I was back in New York. I didn't want to make a fool of myself, so I didn't call you."

"Let's forget it, then. I was just stood-up. Good-bye, Mr. Andradi."

Max poked me in the side. "Didn't I tell you, Danny? She's not for you!"

Trina had started to turn away. She swung around on Max. "You keep out of this," she said.

"Me!" Max exclaimed. "Why, I was just telling . . ."

"I heard you. I'll decide that, and it's none of your business."

I said, "You heard her, Max. Keep out of it."

He looked at us as though we were crazy and he backed away. "Screwballs," he said.

I said to her, "Let's go and talk."

She looked unfriendly. I took her arm and steered her to the last row of seats at the back of the studio. She almost resisted but not quite. By the time we got to the seats she was neutral. I gave her a cigarette and lit it for her, then lit my own.

I said, "I'm not running Diamond Records and I'm not your boss. Max was trying to give me a buildup. I work for Frankie Magardi."

She nodded. She said, "You were a lawyer, weren't you?"

"Yes. I was. I was disbarred."

"I know. I asked about you. Columbia, football hero and all that. Now you're a what—gangster?"

"In a way. Hoodlum is the term I use."

"Magardi's a hoodlum, too, isn't he?"

"Yes, we're a pair."

"My brother was trying to explain it to me in Havana— he's the one who looked you up. He said you and Magardi are probably Mafia, and he told me what the Mafia is. It's fascinating in a way, with all that tradition of evil. Sicily is a lot like Ireland and their constant revolting against England and authority, only the Irish never developed the criminal angle of the Sicilian Brotherhood. . . . I'm mostly Irish, so I understand revolt."

"The Mafia hasn't been revolting for two hundred years," I said.

"I know—now it's the underworld. But it doesn't fit you, somehow. Magardi yes, but not you. I've been wondering a lot about you and there's something very fishy. Odoriferous."

I smoked for a little while in silence. Then I said, "There's an explanation for everything. Sometimes it isn't what you expect, sometimes it is. If we ever become good enough friends, I'll tell you some of it."

"You'd have to be able to trust me?" she asked.

"That's it."

"Well . . . all right."

"All right what?"

"Nothing. . . . So now you're in the record business. I suppose I could go out with someone in the record business. Talk shop and all that. . . . It's done every day."

"Sure."

"Well, don't sit there and say sure. Ask me, you dope."

"Dinner tonight, Trina?"

"O.K. Ambassador at seven-thirty. Pick me up."

"Right."

THIRTEEN

M ANNY FRIEND WAS ANOTHER ONE LIKE MAX MURTHA, outwardly—a washed and pressed and manicured Max Murtha. Otherwise there was the cigar usually unlit, the abruptness and lack of politeness, the dynamic pushing and moving and doing.

He said, "So you got a bankroll, eh? What you want to buy?"

"You," I said.

He moved around in his chair and tapped his feet on the floor. "You're a fresh bastard. Who you with?"

"Magardi."

"Magardi! You trying to scare me?"

"You can be scared," I said.

"What's Magardi want?"

"I've told you."

He laughed, a hard, humorless bark. "You couldn't buy me for a million! Be-Kay's swinging like Goodman."

I said, "You're swinging like Monday night in Hoboken. You're as high as a coal mine. Let's turn off the hot water and run some cold. What's the clinker in your kasha, Manny?"

He moved around some more. He threw his cigar into a tarnished brass cuspidor. "Let's go down stairs and get some coffee."

We rode the elevator in silence and went into Dempsey's off the lobby. We took a table in the back, where Tin Pan Alley foregathered day and night to dream about their profits and the big one coming up.

"You buying?" asked Manny.

I nodded. He ordered coffee and cheesecake. I took the same. I said, "All you need is money. We got money. Stop acting like Gromyko."

He sighed. "It's this goddamn punk, this Lopata. He's got hisself a statutory with a little sixteen-year-old bum. I spend forty grand to date keeping them blood-suckers off his back. That's all the dough in the world, but they're still hungry. Them lousy sonsofbitches. A disgusting dame and her no-good daughter. A fat pig who sits and tells me about her

106

clean young virgin and every other girl in New York's a whore but not her Cathy. . . . You know what this little tramp does? She goes up to Tommy's hotel while he's out on a singing date and she strips and climbs into bed and waits for him. So they call it rape. You mind if I put a cigar on the check?"

He went to the cigar counter and picked out a Corona-Corona, and came back stripping off the covering.

I said, "Everybody's got troubles. How much do you need?"

"How much do I need! Christ, you name it! You get a pig like that, there's no end to it."

"I'll end it. I'll take over Tommy and the rape, both. Fifty grand for Be-Kay."

Then the screaming began in earnest. I was a robber. I would steal from my own mother. I was a snake and a hyena and a leech. I would snatch pennies from a blind man and rob the poorbox of my own church. I was a hoodlum and Magardi was a hoodlum and we belonged in prison.

I said, "When you're all through crying, wipe your eyes and we'll go back to your office and draw up the papers. You're lucky I'm giving you fifty and not twenty-five, with what you owe the manufacturer and the truckers and a couple of bands and your landlord. . . . You want to take fifty now or twenty-five later?"

He got up. He said, "When do I get the cash?"

I said, "I'll give you a couple of grand down when we sign and the rest after we've gone over your books and find out what we're buying."

"You know what you're buying," he said. "You're buying Tommy Lopata. . . . Make it three grand, Danny."

Twenty-one was crowded but a lot of people around New York knew Danny Andradi, hoodlum with a future, so we got a choice table in the bar. We got a lot of attention, too, from the stag line. Trina in a green dinner dress a shade darker than her eyes made all the rest of them look like frumps.

When we sat down and ordered our drinks, she said seriously, "Is this your idea of a night out, Danny?"

I looked at her for a moment and all I could think of was what it would be like to take her in my arms. I said, "No."

"Why, then?"

"I thought you'd—no, that isn't honest. I thought of myself. I thought of you with me in Twenty-one, where people are seen."

"You wanted us to be seen?"

"I wanted to stake a claim on you. I wanted the boys to know that you were with me—that you were my girl."

"Or you'd mow 'em down?"

"Well—no. Not that drastic."

I lit a cigarette for her and she leaned back against the banquette, blowing out smoke and looking at me through it. Then she said, "On the plane to Havana that day you said something to me that no one has said since I was a little girl. You said, 'You are a very nice person, Miss Templer, just as I thought you would be'. I'm not a nice person, Danny. I'm the most un-nice person you've ever met—selfish, self-centered, ambitious, heartless, cold—all of the things that make a woman a real bitch. I've broken my father's heart and my mother's heart and I've used people and mistreated them to get what I've wanted. I'm sensitive to people who are as calculating and bitchy as I am, so I read you. One way or another you're going to become Danny the Big Shot, and I'll do as a starter. Maybe it'll hit the columns—Trina Templer holding hands with Danny Andradi at Twenty-one . . ."

Our drinks came and we lifted our glasses in a silent toast. I said, "That was a fair opening argument. I said something else to you on the plane, too. I don't remember the exact words, but it had to do with impact—the way you impressed me. The implication was plain, I think, that I had fallen in love with you from afar, or would at the slightest provocation. . . . I don't care much whether you think you're self-centered and calculating. Most people are who amount to a damn. As for being cold, that we'll find out about. I don't think so. Maybe you just haven't found your man yet."

She nodded. She said, "A fair rebuttal, but off on a tangent. Love's got nothing to do with it, or with us. And you're not my man."

"I suppose it wouldn't seem so, as we sit here in Twenty-one. All right, so I goofed. Let's drink our drinks and get the hell out."

She shrugged. "The food's good here."

"I know where it's better."

"Suit yourself, Danny."

We got a cab and went to the West Side, to a small restaurant on Forty-sixth owned by one of the great and unknown Italian chefs. He had been a chef for forty years on the big Italian liners and this was his way of retiring—a slight, bent old man by the name of Crespi who had wanted all his life to own his own restaurant.

Trina had said little on the way over. Apparently she'd become bored with introspection and my intentions. When the cab stopped she said, "Is this it?"

"It is."

"I'd rather not, if you don't mind."

"I do mind. This is where we dine. This is one of the fine restaurants of the world, regardless of its looks. Stop being a snob; it's unbecoming."

She got out and she stood on the sidewalk while I paid the cab. When I turned around she was standing with her legs apart and her hands on her hips, ready for battle.

"I don't like to be pushed," she said.

"O.K. I don't like to push."

"I'm not a snob."

I moved close to her and looked into her belligerent eyes. "No, you're the girl I love."

"How can you say that!"

"It's the easiest thing I've ever said."

She put her arm in mine. "All right, lead on. Let's eat."

I held the door open for her and I said into her ear, "You see? You're not so different."

Signor Crespi shook my hand and kissed Trina's when I introduced her. He took us to his own private booth, which was beyond the restaurant proper and next to the kitchen. He said, "For you, Signor Andradi, there is always my own table."

The booth had curtains across the front and he closed them. Trina picked up a spoon and tapped it on the table. Then she threw it down. Then she poked my hand with a finger.

"The next song I sing I'm going to sing for you."

I said, "I'm going to thank you for that in the only way I know how."

She was sitting across from me at the round table. I got up and went to her side. I leaned down and kissed her on the lips.

She drew away as though I had burned her. I put my arm around her then and I held on and finished what I had started. She fought me furiously for a moment, then suddenly she had stopped fighting and she was kissing. There had never been anything like it in my world.

Signor Crespi rapped on the sill outside. I went back to my seat. He brought us wine and glasses. He said, "I will give you lasagna and scampi and a roast. Do you wish to eat now?"

Trina was repairing her lips. She moved one shoulder

109

slightly. I said, "Any time at your convenience, Signor Crespi."

He bowed. He sighed. He said, "I get the message."

Then he was gone and I reached across the table and took Trina's hand. I said, "That sums up all of my arguments. The defense rests."

She bowed her head. She said in a very quiet voice, "I don't know what's happened—yet. It's something . . . I've never felt this way. Don't be light and gay, Danny. Just . . . just kiss me once more."

So I did. Believe me, that first one was nothing. Nothing at all.

Tommy Lopata was a good-looking boy of twenty-three, well set-up, with black, wavy hair and light blue eyes. The dream-boat type. He had a full, sensual mouth but now his lips were pressed in a stubborn line and he regarded me with animosity.

He said, "You got a hell of a nerve, busting into my suite like this! I didn't get to bed until after five and now it's only nine-thirty! What do you want?"

The coffee table was stacked with dirty liquor glasses and filled ashtrays. Through the open bedroom door I could see the edge of a bed and a mass of blonde hair on a pillow.

"How old's the girl?" I asked, motioning with my hand.

His face got red and there was fear in his eyes. "She's old enough. She's over twenty. You the police?"

"No." I took the Be-Kay contract from my pocket and handed it to him. "Read that. I'm your new boss. You work for Diamond Records and you work for me."

He glanced at the contract briefly, a grin spreading over his face, then folded it and handed it back. He was relaxed now and he turned on the charm. "Diamond Records! Brother, that's great! That puts me right up there in the big time!"

I said, "Not yet. First you've got to get honest."

"What do you mean honest?"

"Get rid of the girl in there and we'll talk."

"Get rid of her? Suzie's staying! Man, I just found her last night!"

"Get her out anyway. I'll wait."

"You go to hell! Who do you think you're pushing around?"

"You," I said. I moved to him and slapped his face, not hard but hard enough.

He let out a cry and doubled up his fists. "You sonofabitch! I'll kill you!"

I slapped him around with careful effectiveness, not hurting him but letting him know that I could. He flayed wildly with his arms and kicked, but his feet were bare so he did no damage. I gave him a quick judo fall that really jarred him and he lay on the carpet groaning. Then the girl was coming at me with a shoe in her hand and a wild look in her eyes.

I said, "Drop it, Suzie. Go back and get dressed. You're leaving."

She stopped in front of me with the shoe raised. "You leave Tommy alone, you filthy ape! You leave him alone!"

She had on a thin, nylon nightgown not woven for casual callers. She saw me looking at her and she suddenly folded her arms over her breasts and backed towards the bedroom.

"Get dressed," I told her. "You're going home."

I picked Tommy up and tossed him into a chair. Then I sat in another facing him and I said, "I'm big enough and Diamond Records is big enough to make you behave. Don't make any mistakes about us. We've got a large investment in you and we're going to protect it. You either go along or you're through. Completely washed up. You have no other choice."

I lit a cigarette and waited. He felt his chin and his arm, then sat back in the chair and looked at me with hate.

"I've got friends," he said. "You won't stay healthy long."

I said, "Oh, for God's sake, now I've got to do it all over again!" I got up. He cringed down in his chair.

"Don't hit me," he pleaded. "Please . . . I didn't mean that."

I said, "You mean it but you're yellow. All right, send your friends around. Tell them to come in a group and bring guns. . . . What a punk you are!"

I turned away in disgust and went back to my chair. Suzie came out of the bedroom, dressed in a dark blue suit and wearing a small hat. She was a pretty little girl, but no class. Just a body that would get her by for another few years. She was carrying an overnight case and a big pocketbook and she was angry. She strode to the door and flung it open.

"Good-bye," she said. Then she hesitated and looked at me. "You're right about one thing. He *is* yellow."

The door closed with a bang.

Tommy was almost crying. "Now you've lost me Suzie!"

I said, "Cheer up, Tommy. We're going to go out right now and get you a girl. A wife by the name of Cathy."

Manny was right about this Caroline Bryan; she was a pig. She talked incessantly in a high, whining voice and her tactic was to daze you with words, then pick your pocket. So I yelled at her and she shut up for a moment, her loose, wet mouth hanging open.

"They're going to get married today!" I said. "I told you that! You sign this permission for your daughter so we can get on with it. Either that or I bring charges of blackmail. I've got you cold on blackmail, sister. You want me to call the police?"

"You wouldn't dare!" she said. "They'll arrest him first for rape! You think I don't know anything?"

"They'll get him sure, but they'll get you, too. We'll fight this rape frame-up and we'll make his name the biggest in the country. A frame-up by a lousy mother who uses her daughter for a decoy! You think we won't sell records then?"

"You just try it! I dare you!"

The phone was across the room beside the door. Tommy was sitting next to it in a chair facing me and he was sweating, his eyes on the floor. Over on the divan, beside her fat mother, sat little blonde Cathy, a real cute dish if you didn't look too closely. Her skirt was too short and too tight and she showed too much leg, but they were pretty legs. Her blouse was too skimpy and cut too low so she showed too much breast, too, but that was pleasantly full. She had an avid look on her face and she wet her lips constantly with a pink tongue. She was the only one enjoying it.

I crossed the room and picked up the phone. I dialed a number and a man answered. I said, "This the police? My name's Danny Andradi and I'm at 398 East 71st Street, Apartment 7B. There's a woman here I want to charge with blackmail. You got the address? . . . All right, I'll swear out a warrant for her arrest, but I want her arrested now. I've got—"

Suddenly the phone was yanked out of my hand and fat Caroline gave me a push that sent me halfway across the room.

"Are you the police?" she said into the phone. "Well you come right over and arrest this boy who raped my daughter —she's only sixteen and he got her up in a hotel and kept her prisoner all night. . . . Yes, that's it. He's right here. My name's Caroline Bryan. You hurry. I'll keep him here."

She had backed up to the door and she stood holding the phone against her stomach and there was a look of triumph on her face.

"Now you're in the soup!" she exclaimed. "I've called your bluff!"

"How about the money we paid you?" I demanded. "You think you can double-cross us?"

"You and your blackmail!" she said scornfully. "I can prove I got every cent of that money from my ex-husband. Do you think I was born yesterday?"

I went back and sat down to wait. Little Cathy was jumping with excitement. Tommy wiped his forehead with a hand that shook. Fat Caroline leaned against the door and grinned. Then the doorbell rang.

The two men showed their badges and said they were detectives. One took out a new notebook with a black cover and a ball-point pen. He was the smaller of the two, but both were large men, with weather-beaten, tough faces. The one with the notebook was Al Jordan and the other was George Albee.

"You Mrs. Bryan?" Al asked Caroline.

"Yes. I'm the one talked to you on the phone. This is the man right here who raped my daughter—his name's Tommy Lopata. He's a singer. He got her in this hotel room and—"

"Wait a minute," said Al. "I'll ask the questions and you answer them. Just answer what I ask you. Right?"

She looked at him resentfully. "I was just trying to tell you—"

"Yeah," he interrupted, "I heard you. Just answer the questions. How old are you?"

"I'm—well, I'm forty."

"What's your full name?"

"Mrs. Caroline Brown Bryan. I'm divorced. My husband was—"

"Yeah. What's your daughter's name?"

"Catherine. You spell it with a C. She's a—"

"Yeah. How old?"

"Sixteen."

"When?"

"What do you mean when? She's sixteen, like I said. She's a sweet, innocent—"

"Yeah. When's her birthday?"

"Oh. February fourteenth."

He turned abruptly from her and faced Tommy. "You're Tommy Lopata?"

Tommy looked up startled. He nodded. "Yes, sir."

"How old are you?"

"Twenty-three."

"You know this girl, Catherine?"

"Yes."

"For how long?"

"Since a couple of months ago. July twenty-eighth."

"Where did you meet her?"

"In my bed. I came home from the island where I'd been

113

singing—at the Pines—and she was in bed in my hotel room."

"That's a lie!" screamed Caroline. "He's just trying to—"

"Quiet!" roared George. It was the first word he had spoken and it was loud.

"You have relations with her?" Al continued.

"Sure. That's what she was there for. What was I going to do, kick her—"

"Yeah. You know how old she was?"

Tommy shook his head. "I had no idea. When I saw her the next morning I figured she was pretty young, but she claimed she was nineteen."

"Is that a fact? Well—she tell you anything about herself? Was she a virgin?"

"God, no! I mean, she's been around plenty. She told me she's done the same thing with a couple other guys in the business, this Harold—"

"Never mind. Then what happened?"

"I got rid of her about ten o'clock. That afternoon her mother called me up and said she was going to have me arrested for statutory rape. I got hold of Manny Friend—he owned Be-Kay Records—and I told him. Me and Manny went up to see her and Manny gave her five grand."

"That's a lie!" screamed Caroline.

"You'll have your chance in court," George told her. "Right now, shut up."

"You gave her five thousand dollars," prompted Al. "Then what?"

"Well—she kept calling. Every week it was another five grand."

"There any records of these payments?"

"Oh sure. We kept records—Manny and me."

"Anything else?"

"Well, Manny told me he was going to take a tape recorder up one time. One of those little portable jobs. Later he told me he had a tape of the whole transaction and that it was enough to hang her—"

"You crooks!" screamed Caroline. "You filthy crooks!"

George shushed her. Al turned to her and said, "Leave me see your bankbooks, Mrs. Bryan."

"I will not!" she yelled. "You've got no right—"

"Quiet!" said George.

Then I spoke up. I said, "I'm representing Mr. Lopata, as an official of Diamond Records. I want you to arrest Mrs. Bryan on a charge of extortion, as I told you over the telephone. I think you've heard enough to know we can make the charge stand up."

114

Al nodded at me. "O.K., mister. She's under arrest."

George took handcuffs out of his pocket and reached for Caroline's wrist.

"No!" she exclaimed, backing away. "No, please! I'll get you the bankbooks! I'll give them to you! Don't arrest me!"

George dropped his hands. "Get 'em," he said.

She hurried out and down the hallway. I looked over at Cathy. She giggled at me. "What do you know!" she said.

Caroline was back within a minute, holding three savings bankbooks in her hand. She gave them to George. "Take them. Just leave me alone. Leave me alone!" She sank into a chair and started to sob.

George looked at each of the books, whistled low, then put them in his pocket.

"What you want us to do, Mr. Andradi?" he asked me.

"As long as we get the money back, I'll drop the charges," I said. "But she's still got to sign permission for her daughter to get married."

"I'll sign it!" said Caroline. "Where is it?"

I produced the paper and she read it, the tears still streaming. Then she wiped her eyes with a handkerchief and went to the coffee table and signed the permission with my pen.

I nodded to Cathy and said, "Let's go, Cathy. It's your wedding day."

She jumped up and got a coat from a closet in the hall and we five left—Cathy, Tommy, the two detectives, and I.

On the way down in the self-service elevator George gave me the three bankbooks.

"O.K.?" he asked.

"O.K.," I replied. "A real professional job."

"We get half?" asked Al.

"That's the agreement."

"It's sure as hell better than driving a truck," said George.

Cathy let out a whoop. "It's a frame-up!" she exclaimed happily. "You're not cops at all! I knew it all the time!"

FOURTEEN

THINGS WERE TOO SLOW.

Personal success as a hoodlum I had. I was in solid as the white-haired boy of the great Don Magadri, No. 2 *capo mafioso* of the country. Since my coup on Be-Kay Records and Tommy Lopata, I could write my own ticket on Magardi's enterprises. My merger plan for the recording business had been approved and was waiting only for the formation of the syndicate and the accumulation of the cash needed to put it into effect.

Bassa mafiosi had begun to call me Don Andradi. I had arrived, despite the animosity of the Professor and the suspicions of Johnny Castle. I was invited to dinner at the home of Vito Nicosa at Sands Point and I was invited to go to Florida or Las Vegas for the sun whenever the spirit moved. There were never less than a dozen $1,000 bills in my pocket, and most of the time I carried fifty or more of them. I was asked to join combines for the purchase of narcotics to be imported, and for each $1,000 I put up I received some $14,000 back.

I drove a black Cadillac Eldorado and I had a regular table at the Pavillon and another at the Colony. I still had my small apartment on East Fiftieth, but that was for a reason. That was to adhere to the Mafia commandment against ostentation. It was acceptable to be ostentatious in most of your living so long as you retained one humble association.

I was a *capo mafioso*. Not a Don yet, formally, but soon to be.

But in my Anti-Mafia world, no action. The FANG program was marking time, waiting for me to get the critical information needed. I had obtained confirmation that the Mafia hierarchy were in constant touch with the "hills behind Palermo" and that no important decisions were made which would affect the Brotherhood without the approval of the Patriarch—but who he was and where exactly to find him remained their secret.

The stepped-up Congressional inquiries into crime were beginning to show an effect within the Brotherhood, and

116

the atmosphere throughout the ruling echelons of the underworld was one of nervous apprehension. Much of the activity against them was attributed to the Anti-Mafia. The fine beginnings of alarm we had achieved with the Cuba debacle and the deaths of the three Dons and Louie Pizzari were slowly snowballing into solid, icy fear.

The Committee on Rackets had moved its hearings to San Francisco. Word had spread throughout the Brotherhood that one of the oldest and most revered of the Dons in that area had "blown his top" and was talking too much. At least one council of Mafia elders was held, in Chicago, to consider the case of this talkative Don Fred Vitali. I got one hint from Frankie Magardi that Vitali wouldn't live long if he didn't clam up.

All of these items were on the positive side, but for me personally there was nothing but frustration. It was not my idea to work indefinitely for the advantage of the Mafia, building up their enterprises and buying their heroin and driving their competitors out of business. Just so much of that and I found myself filled with disgust.

Palermo was still 6,000 miles away. The opportunity I was seeking to get there had not materialized. I needed a crisis within the Mafia to put my plan into effect. Something had to be done, I felt.

Late in November I called a FANG contact and I said, "I want a meeting with Smith. Fix it up. I'll call back."

"That's impossible. He's not available."

"Well, damn it, make it Judge Williams, then."

"Don't ask that, Mr. A. It's highly irregular. Where are you calling from?"

"Phone booth, Grand Central."

"That's where you called last Monday. Don't talk in the clear. Just answer yes or no. Otherwise use code."

"Yes," I said.

"After your Monday call we received another, using the identification you had just given. The voice didn't match so we cut it off. An effort was made through the telephone company to trace our address. You've had competition in a booth next to yours. Maybe you've got it right now. We'll have somebody there in three minutes and nab him for you."

I said, "Look, damn it, I want to see Margie tonight. I don't care who she's got a date with. You tell the boss that this is Danny Andradi."

"O.K., if you say so. I think you're wrong. Call back in an hour. I don't think I can arrange the contact."

"All right, then. Tomorrow night. Keep her available, you hear?"

I banged up the phone and was outside the booth immediately. I didn't look at the booths on each side. I took out an address book and studied several pages. Then, still looking at the book and not where I was going, I pushed open the door of the booth to the right of the one I had been in. A woman's high and indignant voice protested. I looked up into a pair of angry gray eyes behind spectacles. There was a little black Skipperkee on the floor and he began yapping at me.

I retired in confusion and went back into the booth I had just vacated. I put in a call to Trina, still out in Las Vegas at the Peacock, and told the operator to charge it to my phone on Fiftieth. I kept a watch to see who would pass outside.

Trina. There was another problem in the world beyond the Mafia. And the FANG frustration was as nothing compared to the Trina impasse.

After our night at Crespi's and those first kisses—after the most memorable night I had ever spent—she suddenly froze up like a Vermont winter. She was in New York for the next two days and refused to see me—said she couldn't possibly because of all her commitments. She was polite, distant, and maddening. Then suddenly she took off for Las Vegas, a full week before she had to be there for her show rehearsals.

She was running. . . . I phoned her every day and most nights and she never refused to talk to me, but she talked as though I were a brush salesman and all my brushes were the wrong size. . . . I've never claimed to know anything about women. I'm not that stupid. But I did think I knew what a kiss meant and I did think I knew what was in a girl's mind when she told me, as we said good-night, "I'm very happy, Danny." That's why I'd bought the ring, which I was still carrying around in my pocket. I thought I knew.

She came on the phone. She said, "I've been trying to get you. You haven't been home."

"I'm not now. I'm in a booth."

"Listen, Danny. I've got to see you."

There was a note of panic in her voice. This was still another Trina, and I'd never met this one at all.

I said, "O.K."

"O.K.? O.K. what?"

"I'll do it."

"I don't follow you. . . . Danny, I'm in trouble! Don't you understand? I must see you! Immediately!"

"I said O.K."

"Oh. . . . You'll be out?"

"Yes."

"What's the matter? Can't you talk?"

"No."

"Oh. . . . Listen, Danny—are you listening?"

"Yes."

Then her wonderful voice dropped very low. She said: "I love you."

"What!"

She'd hung up. I listened to the buzz on the line for a moment, then dropped the receiver on the hook and leaned against the wall. I felt as though someone had hit me—right in the heart. I caught a fleeting glimpse of Johnny Castle hurrying by the window of my booth and I went out and tailed him. I wasn't thinking of what I was doing or why. I was thinking of those three words of Trina's.

He went across the rotunda and up the steps leading to Vanderbilt Avenue. He stopped halfway up and looked around—probably for me. I was out of sight by then, behind an abutment below. As I started up a moment later I noticed another character following along, a guy about my own size but some older, not a typical *bassa mafioso* but not of the upper class, either. He looked like a competent hard-guy, from the brief glance I caught of him. . . . So this Johnny Castle was no dummy. And Danny Andradi *was* a dummy.

I wandered out to Vanderbilt Avenue and saw Johnny a half-block away on Forty-third, walking fast. I followed along. It was just getting dark and an excellent time for him to give me the slip. I let him do that. I stopped at the corner of Madison and looked up and down, feigning confusion and annoyance. I walked back to Vanderbilt and into Grand Central.

I'd been thinking about the subway system and the hour and decided I'd take the I.R.T. East Side to Spring Street. I crossed the station and went down into the subway and waited for a local. I took a seat in the deserted first car and waited for Spring Street. I was at the front end of the platform and I started to walk back. There were only three men and one woman on the platform, all of whom had gotten off the local. One of the men was my tail. He had been in the car just behind mine and he walked slowly towards the exit. He was carrying a newspaper and he dropped it. He leaned down to pick it up, taking his time, and I passed him.

I didn't turn off the platform at the exit. I kept walking to the rear and when I got to the end I stopped and lit a cigarette, holding it so it couldn't be seen, for it is unlawful in New York to smoke in the subway.

The *mafioso* was some twenty feet up the platform, leaning against the wall under a light and reading his newspaper. He was paying no attention to me at all. So I paid no atten-

119

tion to him. We were the only two on the platform. The change booth was out of sight and nobody was coming through the turnstiles. I smoked. He read. Time passed. Then I heard the rumble of a train. I looked up the tracks but saw no lights. It was an express on the other track. It came closer fast and rushed by with that rattling, banging rhythm peculiar to the I.R.T. It was a rhythm I'd known all my life. It was New York. After a while more rumbles and more rhythms as an express roared uptown and a local squealed to a stop on the opposite track, then ground back into motion. Locals don't run often at that time of the evening. It was a long wait.

Then it was coming. First I heard it, then I saw the upper two lights, then the lower pair. It was coming fast. I threw my cigarette, which had gone out, to the tracks and walked fast to the *mafioso*. I stopped in front of him and swept the paper out of his hands. I said in the Mafia slang, *La furcæ pri lu poviru!* ("The gallows for the poor!")

There was a startled expression on his face. Then there was no expression as I whacked my palm with full strength against the side of his neck. I caught him as he fell and heaved him to the tracks, with the train fifty yards away.

I ran to the exit. I slowed down to go through the turnstile, putting my hand up so my face would not be seen by the station agent. As I reached the stairs, I heard the train's whistle wailing an alarm. I kept running and then slowed to a normal pace as I reached the top. I walked over to Broadway and got a cab back uptown.

That ought to flush out Johnny Castle. If FANG wasn't ready to start something, I was.

There were odds and ends to clean up. There was a phone call to Frankie Magardi to tell him I was going to Las Vegas for a week or so.

"That's O.K., Danny-boy, you do that. You got a rest coming to you. You going to the Peacock?"

"Yes."

"You say hello to Lou Traffacino for me. I'll phone him you're coming. I think I might have a job for you out there, Danny-boy. I think you're the one who can do it."

"Glad to, Don Magardi."

There were two phone calls to FANG contacts. They were a nuisance because I had to assume my phone was now tapped. I packed a bag and went out, driving my car to the parking lot across from Radio City Music Hall. Then I bought a ticket and went into the theatre and wandered around until I was certain there was no tail. I phoned from the lower lobby.

The first conversation was brief and pointless. It added up to no meeting with FANG brass that night.

I said, "While you guys are snoozing, there's a stiff at the Spring Street I.R.T. station. But don't make it Anti-Mafia, for God's sake. It was my tail."

"What's the story?"

"Some other time. I'm in a hurry. I'm going West."

I hung up and called a second FANG number, which was used only for a particular purpose.

I identified myself, then said, "I've got to be in Las Vegas tonight. Tell me how."

"Just a minute." I waited about four. Then the man's voice came back, "Floyd Bennett. Within an hour. Commander Perkins at Operations. You got that?"

"Yes. I'll drive to the field. Black Eldorado license N-67824. It's got to be picked up and driven to Las Vegas, for my cover. The keys will be under the floor mat. I'll check into the Peacock in five days—that'll be Sunday night. The car's got to be there. I'll meet the driver somewhere. You name it."

"Just a minute." Two more passed. He said, "Sunday at seven o'clock P.M. at the Sal Sagev Hotel. That's downtown, near the railroad. You got that?"

"O.K."

I left the theatre, retrieved my car, and drove to the West Side Highway. I made doubly certain there was no tail and I wasted a lot of time going down deserted streets. Then I went downtown and through the tunnel and around the rim of Brooklyn to Floyd Bennett field, which is the U.S. Navy airfield. The rest of it was routine. Commander Perkins and a civilian pilot by the name of Allison and a big Navy experimental jet with a Delta-wing and four huge engines. We screamed off the runway at 9:10 P.M. and landed at the Las Vegas airport at 10:10 P.M. Las Vegas time, picking up two hours in time zones and making it in three hours and twenty minutes flying time, which Allison apologized for as being very slow for that plane.

He taxied to the far end of the field and told me I'd have to get out there. The terminal building was about a mile away.

"I asked the tower for transportation for you but it looks like you won't get it," he said. "It's a nice night for a walk."

"What's this caper?" I asked.

"We're top secret," he said. "We don't want people looking at our airplane yet."

"I'm people."

"No you're not. You don't exist. And I never made this flight."

I walked. It was a nice night but I didn't enjoy it. My bag was heavy and I wanted to be on a phone to Trina.

I called her from a booth outside the terminal. I got her after a short wait. I said, "Don't use my name. Come out to the airport and pick me up. I'll be out on the highway."

"My God! You here already!"

"Just come out here. Don't say anything."

"Right."

She was there in fifteen minutes. She was driving a white Ford convertible. I flagged her down as she started to turn into the airport. I threw my bag into the back and opened the door on her side.

"Move over," I said. "I'll drive."

She moved over. She was wearing black Bermuda shorts and a black silk shirt and there was a white scarf around her head. Her beautiful legs were bare and well tanned and she had on white beach sandals. She curled one leg under her and watched me critically as I got under way. She was frowning.

I drove away from town, on Highway 91. I said, "I'm not supposed to be here until Sunday night around seven o'clock. I'm supposed to be driving across. I've got to trust you that far. If I'm identified by anyone in Las Vegas before then, I'm dead. I don't mean that as a figure of speech. I mean killed. You follow me?"

"Yes. I follow you." She was still frowning.

"O.K. Now if you didn't mean what you said over the telephone, you know how to get rid of me."

"That's not funny."

"I didn't mean it to be."

"Will you kindly pull over to the side of the road?"

"Sure." I pulled over. I parked amid the tumbleweed and cactus.

"Turn off the lights," she said.

I turned them off.

"Now let's start all over again. I'm your girl. I've told you for the first time that I love you—just a few hours ago over the phone. You haven't seen me for more than a month. You're supposed to love me. You haven't said so, really, but the way you moon around it could be. . . . So now you see me. I'm right here, just this far from you. You don't say, 'Move over, I'll drive.' You say something else, or you do something else. . . . Well?"

122

I put my hand out and touched her on the shoulder. "I do love you, Trina."

Then she came into my arms and we kissed. A long time passed. Then she pulled away and she sighed. "I've been waiting too long for that."

"So have I. . . . More?"

She nodded and we resumed. Then after a time she moved away from me because you can do only so much kissing. I got back behind the wheel, turned on the lights, and continued driving.

"Your car?" I asked.

"No. Rented. Where are we going?"

"I've got to phone. I'll stop at a gas station. . . . Have you forgotten the big crisis? You told me you were in trouble. That's why I'm here."

She moved close to me and I put my arm around her.

"When I'm with you there's no more trouble," she said. "Magardi's been after me."

"After you! Why?"

"I had it out with him once, just before I signed my contract with Diamond. Just business. No personal relations. I thought it was all settled. Now he says if I'm not nice to that horrible Johnny Castle, he'll ruin me. He insists I come back to New York immediately. He was on the phone this morning and he told me if I didn't take a plane today he'd make a bum out of me. The way he said it, Danny! It was like a death sentence!"

I felt a shiver go through her body and I tightened my arm around her. I said, "This'll take some figuring."

We drove on in silence for a couple of miles, going slow. There was no doubt in the world Magardi could ruin her professionally, and there was no doubt he would not hesitate to do it if he had sufficient reason. But why Johnny Castle? What suddenly had stirred up this mess of trouble?

"You ever been out with Castle?" I asked.

She shook her head. "I met him just once, when I was singing at the Algiers. He's so evil, Danny! He frightens me! And I don't think he cares about girls at all. I think he's a fairy. I just can't figure it."

I thought some more. Then suddenly all of the pieces fell into place without my even trying. It was so obvious I was abashed at my dullness. Castle had been tailing me and listening in on my phone calls. I had been making daily calls to Trina, so he knew how I felt about her. This was his way to get me where it would hurt most. So he had gone to Nicosa and had induced him to give the order to Magardi—a most reasonable request for one *mafioso* to make to another.

I said, "My coming out here makes it worse. However, we're in this together now. You and me against them all."

She snuggled against me. "You make me believe that," she said.

"The problem is how to get Castle away from the Mafia so I can handle him." I was thinking aloud and talking too much in front of her. I felt too comfortable with her.

"I could lure him for you," she said. "You know, the *femme fatale* like in the spy movies."

"You drop that idea fast," I said with emphasis. "You want to get your head bashed in?"

"Well I could. It's not an impractical plan at all."

I patted her head. "Stick to your singing, darling. Keep out of my world. One of us in it is enough."

"What are you, Danny?"

"Me? I'm a hoodlum. A hoodlum with prospects."

"No, seriously. Tell me."

"One of these days, Trina. . . . Well, it's a question of my life-expectancy. In my business you don't die of old age. If I live, I'll tell you. I promise you that."

"Aren't you being a little too, too?"

"Perhaps. Let's forget about me. I'm away out on a limb with you, Trina. I thought there was no one I'd trust as far as I've trusted you. The only outsider who knows as much as you do is my brother Tony."

"He is a priest, isn't he?"

"You really have looked me up—yes, up in the Bronx. What I want to impress on you, darling, is that one unguarded word from you—maybe something you might say in anger or some reference entirely unintentional—and that would be my finish. These people are not playing games. They are deadly serious. They are the most vicious fanatics the world has ever known."

"Magardi, Castle, people like that?"

"Those are the ones. Frank Costello, Joe Adonis, Lucky Luciano. Big names. The Mafia."

"All right. You be the hero. But if anything happens to you, then I'm going to die, too. Just remember that."

I stopped at a gas station at a crossroads, told the boy to fill it up, then phoned from a booth outside. I called a FANG number in Las Vegas and a man answered. When I'd given him my identification he said, "Been expecting you. What's boiling?"

"Me. I need a hideout until Sunday. I've got a girl and she goes, too."

"That'll compromise you if it's a hideout," he said. "You off your rocker?"

124

"I'm already compromised. This is Trina Templer. She knows enough to fry me."

"We'll take her off your hands. Where are you?"

"Wait a minute, buster. You do this my way. She stays with me."

There was a long silence. Then he said, "You've got me in a bind, chum. I'm supposed to make such decisions."

"Not with me you don't. You ever heard of Connie Masters? I don't trust you guys with women."

"Touché. O.K., where are you?"

"Highway 91 about twenty-five miles south of Vegas."

"What are you driving?"

"White Ford convertible. The top's down. Nevada plates. A rental car. Girl and me."

"Start driving north, slow. I'll make like a cop and pick you up with a red light."

"Done."

I went out and paid for the gas, then started back the way we had come. Trina had a worried look. "What now?" she asked.

"I fixed up a hideout for us."

"For us? You mean, you and me?"

"Yep."

"Look, darling, aren't you kind of taking things for granted?"

"What things? We've gone over this. We've covered all the angles."

"We have? I'm not going to spend the night with you. I'm going back to the Peacock."

I pulled over to the side of the road again and turned off the lights.

I said, "You're my girl. I don't know what those words mean to you but to me they have a literal connotation. They mean you belong to me. Things that belong to me I take care of. I wouldn't do anything in the world to hurt you, any more than I'd hurt myself. So, you're not going back to the Peacock while I'm not there, and I can't be there until Sunday. The minute Johnny Castle hears I've left New York he'll come barrelling out here. If he finds you alone at the Peacock, he'll make it miserable for you. Also, there is the small item of your knowing too much about me. He's a bright boy, Trina, and he'd get you to talk. I came out here to protect you, and I'm going to do it, and protect myself to boot, in spite of your moral scruples."

"You're quite a speechmaker," she said. "If you think you can scare me into setting up housekeeping with you until Sunday, you're daft."

"Is that what you think, Trina?"

She moved away from me. "Whether it's what I think or not, I'm going back to the Peacock. Lou Traffacino is my friend. He'll knock this Castle silly."

I started up the car again and drove slowly. Maybe I hadn't handled it right, but I'd lost her completely. I could feel the ice between us. Everything I had had and had held in my arms was gone.

I said, "I'm going to have to kidnap you then, if you won't come willingly. You know too much about me and I don't trust you any more."

"You just try it!" she exclaimed.

"I will," I said.

FIFTEEN

I HAD NO MISCONCEPTIONS ABOUT JOHNNY CASTLE. I DIDN'T doubt that I could take him, but before I could do that I would need opportunity, and it would have to be an opportunity with no possible kick-back to the Mafia.

By killing his man in the subway, I had told him, "Come and get me." He would know who had done it, as though I'd sent him a wire. But ours was a personal feud and I had to keep it that way, without involving the Brotherhood, or I wouldn't be able to touch him. Now Trina had entered the picture and had messed it up good. Any appearance with her and a fight over her with Castle, and the whole Mafia would know about it. He'd been smart enough to stake his claim with Nicosa and Magardi. All I had was a yen and the memory that she had said she loved me.

We were halfway back to Las Vegas, Trina sitting on the far side of the seat and hostile, when the car came along side and a red light flashed at us.

"The police!" she exclaimed. She couldn't resist a smile.

I pulled up. I told her, "Wait here until I talk to them."

She grinned at me. I walked back to the car which had stopped just behind us with the red light still flashing. I leaned my arms on the door and bent over and looked into a tough, confident face. He was about my own age and he was holding a gun in his lap.

I said, "You nervous?"

"I don't know you."

I identified myself. I said, "I'm having trouble with the girl. She doesn't want to come along. I'll need help."

"O.K. Follow me. We turn off to the left up aways. It's our stand-by communications center and it's yours until Sunday. The icebox and deep-freeze are stuffed. There's a phone behind the right bookcase, which swings out—direct line to H.Q. The radio stuff is locked away and—"

He broke off suddenly. Trina was running towards us.

I moved away from the door. "Officer," she said, "will you take me back to the Peacock? I don't want to be with this man any more."

127

He said in a tough voice, "You want to make any charges against him, lady?"

"I—no, I just want to get back to the Peacock."

"O.K. You ride with me. He's going to follow. I'll see he doesn't trouble you."

"Thanks, officer," she said. She backed away and looked at me, and the flashing red light lit up her triumph. Then she walked around the car and got in beside the FANG agent.

I returned to Trina's car and followed his car, which had pulled out ahead. We went about sixty for several miles, then turned off to the left at a crossroad. We went along this road for some five miles, still going fast, then drew up beside a driveway flanked by a high wire fence. There was a sliver of moon and a skyful of stars and in their light I could see the silhouette of a low house and rising behind it the lattice of a slim radio tower.

He got out and came back to me. He said, "Go in the driveway. There's a garage around in back. Put the car away. The front door's open. Light on the left. Need anything else?"

"You'll have to cover for the girl," I said. "Send a wire from Los Angeles over her name—Trina Templer—to Lou Traffacino at the Peacock. Tell him she's gone to L.A. for a few days."

"O.K. Put the car away and come and get her."

I ran the Ford into the garage and came back. I didn't forget to take the keys out of the car.

Trina was steaming and the FANG agent was holding her by the arm. "What is this?" she demanded as I opened the door. "This man is not a police officer!"

I picked her up in my arms and lifted her out. She started banging at my face with a free arm before I could tie it down. She yelled, "You put me down! You let me go, you—you gangster!"

I held her firmly against me and started up the driveway. The FANG agent tooted his horn in farewell and drove away. Trina continued to struggle and to call me names. She had a wiry strength that was surprising and I had my hands full carrying her. I put her down on the porch, holding one wrist firmly, opened the door, and turned on the light with a switch to the left.

I said, "You can fight as long as you want, but it's not going to do you any good. There's just you and me out here in the middle of the desert and you won't get any help. . . . I wish you wouldn't, Trina. I don't want you to hurt yourself."

Then suddenly she was crying, her head bowed. She had

128

stopped fighting and she let me lead her inside. A couple of table lamps lit up a comfortably furnished room, with deep chairs and a huge coffee table with a thick glass top in front of a big divan. She walked wearily to the divan and sat in a corner, curling her feet up under her. She dried her eyes with a handkerchief from her bag. I lit a cigarette for her and handed it to her. She took it without looking at me.

I said, "A half-hour ago, holding you in my arms and kissing you, I thought I had found everything I'd ever wanted. Now that's all gone, apparently. Maybe it couldn't have rested on a very solid foundation. But I don't blame you. There's nothing very savory about me and my job. Everybody told me, from Connie Masters to Frankie Magardi to Max Murtha, that you were not for me—that I was way over my head. Now I can see they were right. You're not for me because you don't believe the things I tell you and you don't trust me. You believe I would take some mean advantage of you just to get a quick roll in the hay. . . . If there's no trust, there's no love, so let's forget it. I won't keep you here any longer than I have to for your own safety and for mine."

She crushed out her cigarette. She still didn't look at me. She said, "You still making speeches?"

I said, "I'm going to make one more, just for my own satisfaction. You can listen to it or not. Back in New York, after that first night we had been together those few hours, I did a foolish and extravagant thing. I thought that you meant it when you kissed me, and I thought I knew what a kiss meant. I bought you this."

I reached into my pocket and took out the small box I had carried for so long. The gold paper with the Cartier imprint had become frayed and the white ribbon was soiled. I leaned over and tossed it in her lap.

"It's yours, Miss Templer. Call it a memento, or loot, or whatever."

I turned and walked away, to explore the house. I went to the kitchen first and found the refrigerator and deep freeze well stocked. I suddenly realized I was hungry and I made a peanut butter sandwich and drank a couple of glasses of milk. Then I went into a bedroom, passing through the living room. Trina was motionless on the divan. I didn't look at her. The bedroom had a large double bed with a candlewick spread and starched white curtains and hooked rugs. Adjoining it was a bathroom and a shower. As I came out of the bathroom, Trina was standing in the doorway. Her face was smudged from her struggling and her tears and her hair was mussed and she looked like a gamin in her black shorts and

129

shirt. . . . No, I hadn't got her out of my heart yet. If I ever could.

She came over to me and her right hand was clenched. She stopped in front of me and extended her hand. The ring was in it. She said, "Put this on my finger."

I did as she bade. Then suddenly she threw her arms around my neck and kissed me. It was—well, I would say it was at least a $52,000 kiss and that we were now all even. Then she backed away from me and sat on the edge of the bed, looking at the ring.

"It's the most beautiful thing I've ever seen," she said. "You must love me to have done this. Some day I'll stop making mistakes about you. . . . I've always wanted an emerald, Danny. You have read what was in my heart."

I said, "Isn't this a kind of sudden switch of mood, Trina?"

She shook her head. "No, you've got to understand women better. . . . I'll make a speech now. Back in New York that night, when we first found each other, it scared the lipstick off me, Danny. I was really frightened. So I ran away to Las Vegas. Then tonight. You kissed me again and I got frightened all over again. That's all."

"What are you frightened of? Me?"

She shook her head. "No. Of myself."

"It doesn't make sense to me, but if you say so. . . ."

She looked at the ring, twisting it so the light caught it. "Now we're engaged," she said, "so—well—it's different."

"What's different?"

"Oh, you know—me being kidnaped." She laughed. "I mean, spending the night with you. . . . Turn off the light, Danny."

I turned it off by the switch at the door. There was light from the living room and through the window were the stars and the sliver of moon. She was lying back on the bed, her hands under her head, kicking her feet.

"I've got no nightclothes, no creams, no curlers—none of the absolute necessities. That's one reason I insisted on going back to the Peacock. But no mere man would understand that! I'm going to be a real mess in the morning and it's all your fault."

"Are you still scared?"

She rolled her head from side to side to indicate a negative. "Not any more." She looked up at the ceiling. "Danny . . ."

"Yes?"

"You're—you're scared now, aren't you?"

I was near the door and I leaned against the jamb. "I guess so—you could call it that."

"Don't be."

I looked at her for a time and I wouldn't let myself think how much I wanted her. She kicked off a sandal in my direction and it fell to the floor at my feet. She kicked off the other one and it landed on top of the dresser. Then she suddenly rolled over on her stomach and put her arms around her head.

"Danny," she said. She spoke into the bedspread and her voice was muffled. I could barely hear her.

"Yes?"

"Don't just stand there."

I took off my jacket and hung it on the back of a chair. I took off my tie and dropped it over the jacket. I sat down on the edge of the bed beside her. She didn't move and I didn't move. . . . How had she known I was scared?

"You remember what I told you over the telephone?" she asked. She was still speaking into the bedspread.

"Sure."

I leaned back on an elbow and looked at the back of her head. Then suddenly she was in my arms and we were holding each other as close as two bodies can be, kissing with a hunger we had not dared to show each other before. Here suddenly was an aroused, passionate Trina demanding love —a basic, earthy woman with no restraints upon her desires. The contrast to her previous façade of guarded suspicion was unbelievable. There never has been a woman like Trina. . . .

As we lay with the starlight coming through the window and the soft night breeze off the desert cooling our bodies, she whispered, "Now I know why I've waited."

I couldn't match that so I kept quiet.

She leaned over me, grasped my hair with her two hands in the wild, tender way of her lovemaking, and kissed me. Then she asked, "You like me, Danny?"

"For me, you're perfection."

"I've given it some thought."

"I'll tell you what you were wrong about, though. You're not cold and heartless and calculating."

She laughed in her throaty way. "Maybe I'm not so cold— that was a surprise to me, too. But I'm calculating. I'll show you."

So she showed me . . . .

This was Wednesday night—a Wednesday in December I won't forget. Late Thursday afternoon while Trina was in

131

the kitchen fixing coffee, I heard the bell of a telephone. It was ringing from a box up near the ceiling in the bedroom closet. I looked in the closet and saw nothing but a row of clothes hanging and a couple of suitcases up on a shelf. Then I remembered about the bookcase and I went into the living room. I tugged at the corner of the right-hand bookcase and it came away from the wall. Behind it was a recess and in it was a telephone.

I picked up the receiver. "Yeah?"

I got an identification number and gave one. Then he said, "All hell's broken loose. Fred Vitali up in San Francisco has been assassinated. We've got to go into action. No more delay on our program."

I said, "Give me details."

"Vitali had been talking to the Rackets Committee—you know about that. His wife and daughter were killed in an automobile accident a month ago. They were crowded off the road by a truck. The truck belonged to Lou Caruso's C.M.P. Trucking Lines and Vitali had been a wild man since. With what we know about Caruso, we can guess the reason, but the Committee doesn't know that. They've been keeping him under wraps, but this afternoon they produced him publicly for the first time, in their hearing room in the Federal Courthouse.

"He was shot through the window with a high-powered rifle from the roof of the building across the street. Shot in the head just above the left ear. A Don has got to die for Vitali. We're all agreed on that. FANG has decided it must be Caruso. You're in the clear until Sunday night and you know him and can get to him. It would take us a week to set it up and by that time he'll be running. Vitali has given his name to the Committee and Caruso knows a subpoena will be out for him. We've got to act immediately. We want to make this a public announcement of Anti-Mafia. Our debut in America."

"Where is Caruso right now?" I asked.

"Palm Springs with a dame, but he won't be there tomorrow."

"O.K.," I said.

"We'll send a car and a helper. It'll take two. He's got a bodyguard."

"Send a baby-sitter, too. I'm not leaving Miss Templer alone."

"Will do."

I hung up the phone and closed the bookcase. Trina was standing in the kitchen doorway looking at me. She was

132

wearing a large bath towel draped in the Hawaiian manner. It was unfair competition for Anti-Mafia.

She said, "Listening to you on a telephone is maddening. You say nothing! What was the other side of that conversation? Some siren after your virtue?"

"I've got a job. I'll be gone until tomorrow."

"What am I going to do?" she wailed.

"There'll be somebody here to talk to you."

"I don't want to talk to anybody! I won't do it!"

"You'll do it. You're kidnaped, remember? You've got no say at all."

She shook her head at me and came over close. "Maybe you could keep me kidnaped but not anybody else. I'm going back to the Peacock and I'm going to kick Johnny Castle right in the shins."

"You're going to stay—what's the matter with you, Trina? Haven't you found out enough to realize the dangers of this business?"

"I'm not afraid any more. I'm not afraid of you and your goons and I'm not afraid of Johnny Castle. Don't you worry about me, Danny. I can take care of myself."

"No," I said. "You stay here. We sent a wire for you to Lou Traffacino saying you were in Los Angeles, so you're covered. Wait until I get back and we'll decide what to do."

She grinned at me. "We're wasting an awful lot of time talking when we should be saying good-bye."

So we said good-bye.

My assistant was Carter Hills, my gunnery instructor at Higganum Farm so long ago, and we greeted each other as old friends. He had a souped-up Oldsmobile with California State license plates—the same as the police use—and once we got over the Nevada line he opened it up to over a hundred and kept it there as long as traffic permitted. We picked up police cars coming down the Baker grade and again south of Barstow, but in both cases they abandoned the chase when they got close enough to identify our State plates.

Hills had never been talkative and we rode the first couple of hours in silence. I was still back with Trina and I had a lot to recollect. Then I got my mind up to the present and I asked him, "Does FANG know any details about this Vitali assassination?"

He nodded. "We know who did it."

"Who?"

"Couple of guys from New York. We don't know who set it up, but we'd been following one of them, a character named

Johnny Castle, and he led us right to the San Francisco plant."

"Who did the shooting?"

"Castle, we think. We didn't get close until it was too late."

"They got away?"

"Sure. We had one man and they had an army."

"Where'd Castle go?"

"He was headed south, driving a car loaned to him by Lou Caruso's lieutenant, Nino Catania. We'll pick him up in Los Angeles."

"No you won't," I said. "He won't go to Los Angeles. He'll go to Las Vegas."

That ended the conversation for a time. Some fifty miles later Hills asked, "Weren't you the one involved in this Johnny Castle business back East?"

"That's right."

"He's good, but you're better," he said. "We made you better."

I said, "I'll find out."

As we reached the bottom of El Cajon Pass I brought up the subject that had been on my mind from the first. "You've told me why we get Caruso. Does that mean the rest of the FANG program we laid out is canceled?"

"Nothing's canceled," he said. "We're just making a slight adjustment to altered circumstances."

"I can't get even close to this Palermo business," I said. "Nobody uses a name. It's like a bad nightmare—a vague, shadowy sort of menace that has no identity."

"People are saying Luciano is the number one man; that he's the brains of the organization."

"That's not correct," I said. "Luciano was not consulted about me and my family background, nor did anyone ask him about my record merger or the general strike. Those are things I know about. He didn't order Vitali's execution either; you can be certain of that. It comes from those hills up behind Palermo and nowhere else—not Rome or Naples. Luciano is the brains of the heroin traffic and that lets him out."

"You going to Palermo yourself?" Hills asked.

"That's what I'm planning," I said. "But first, Johnny Castle."

"First Lou Caruso," he said. "This night isn't over yet."

SIXTEEN

There is a sign out in the mesquite that says, "Palm Springs—Speed Limit Strictly Enforced." Carter Hills took his foot off the throttle and let the big car coast to a halt, stopping well off the highway. There was still no city in sight as he opened his door and got out. The dashboard clock read twelve forty-eight. He said, "Let's pick some weapons."

I got out and met him at the rear trunk. He opened it and selected a wood case from among several stacked in the back. In it were a half-dozen objects wrapped in white cloths. He selected one, unwrapped it, and handed me a .38 Colt. "I suggest this for your belt," he said. He took six shells from a box and handed them to me. I loaded the gun and put it in my belt. He picked a gun for himself and loaded it. Then he picked out another wood case, a long one. It contained two shotguns of twelve gauge with very short barrels. He picked one up and handed it to me, then got a couple of shells for it.

He said, "The sawed-off shotgun is a weapon of terror, so we use it. Also, it leaves no bullet with identifiable chamber markings. . . . Have you a stomach for this, Danny?"

I looked down at the gun and shook my head. "No, but I'll do it. That's what I signed up for."

I put the two shells in the breach, snapped it shut, then double-checked the safety. He slammed the trunk and we got back into the car. I held the shotgun in my lap, the muzzle pointing at the door. We were under way again, to the desert hideaway of Lou Caruso.

We went through the business district, past modernistic stores and motels and restaurants, then made a right turn towards the mountains for a couple of blocks, then a left turn and another right. We were on a wide street lined with expensive bungalows and redwood fences and plantings of coconut and banana palms. Several of the houses were ablaze with lights and gave forth the sounds of partying. It was not the sort of street to which you would expect violent death to come a-calling in the night.

We came to a halt in the middle of a block and Hills turned

off the lights. He said, "It's that corner house up on the left. Caruso's still there or I would have got a call."

"A call?"

He pointed under the dash. "I've got a short-wave. If he'd moved out it would have been on the air."

He checked the gun in his belt, then took a long, slim-bladed knife from a leather sheath under his armpit and put it up his sleeve, hilt down. He said, "I'll go get the bodyguard. He's sitting in that car parked over near the garage. Give me five minutes. Then you go in. When I hear the shotgun I'll drive right up to the front door. If you don't come out, I'll go in and get you. O.K.?"

"O.K.," I said.

I waited. I saw Carter Hills stroll to the corner, then move quickly towards the garage and disappear behind the parked car. There was a house across the street with a radio or hi-fi going pretty loud and I listened with a part of my mind to a Rodgers and Hart ballad. The voice couldn't match Trina's. . . . No sound came from the car at Caruso's and I saw no movement. I checked five minutes on the dashboard clock, then got out. I put the shotgun under my coat with the muzzle down and held the stock tight against my side with my right arm. I walked to the corner and looked at Lou Caruso's house. A cinder-block wall and a redwood fence cut off most of my view of it. Apparently the living room faced the rear, where there would be the inevitable swimming pool and barbecue grill. The main entrance was just beyond an asphalt car-park to the right of the garage. The fan-light over the door showed dim illumination and there was a crack of light through an Italian blind on a window to my left. I saw no sign of Hills.

I started walking across the asphalt to the front door. I didn't know what I was going to say or what I was going to do. My mind was not that far ahead. I was not thinking beyond each present instant of time. I was aware that my heart seemed to be pounding with an unusual fuss and the soft night breeze seemed cold. I felt chilled and uncomfortable. Music was coming from the house but I didn't hear it until the instant I lifted up my left hand to press the door-bell. Then it flooded over me—the March from Aida, and it seemed somehow appropriate. I pushed the button. There were answering chimes and there was a momentary discord with Verdi.

The door opened and a pair of black, dull eyes looked out at me. They were in a woman's face, a puffy, dark-skinned Indian woman's face. One of the Digger Indians, who are the maids and houseworkers of Palm Springs.

I said, "I want to see Mr. Caruso."

"Who's calling?"

"I'm from Mr. Nicosa. You got that, Nicosa?"

She nodded, then closed the door.

I stood and waited. The record came to an end and then there was complete, heavy silence. But it wasn't silence, either, because there were crickets all around calling through the night. . . . There were no windows looking out on the stoop so I was not under surveillance. My position was pretty good, if Caruso came to the door. I moved the shotgun around a few inches so I could grab it quickly.

Then the door opened again. I was looking into the same black eyes in the same puffy face.

"Come back later," she said. "Mr. Caruso is busy."

"Later?" I repeated stupidly.

She nodded. She started to close the door. I put my shoulder against it and pushed hard. She fell back with a cry of dismay, glowered at me for an instant, then fled through a door off the entry hall.

I stood in the hall and looked ahead into a huge living room with a beamed wood ceiling that sloped down to glass doors and windows across the entire side. Beyond was a lighted swimming pool and awnings and a dining area. To my left there was a hallway that led to the bedrooms. Nobody was in sight.

I stood there and listened. Not a sound. Then I moved forward slowly—and right into the gun-range of Lou Caruso, hidden against the near wall of the living room beside a huge potted palm with a .45 held steady in his right hand.

"What do you want?" he demanded. "How did you get by Aldo?"

His eyes were blank and hooded, as I remembered Rocky's would get. He barely moved his lips when he spoke.

I said, "I've got something for you, Don Caruso."

"Damn, lying punk!" he said, his voice still low. "What do you mean using the boss's name? You crazy? You don't know *omertà* yet?"

He switched to Sicilian and called me all the filthy names with which that dialect abounds, moving closer to me with the gun pointed at my head. "You think I don't know what's going on? I talked to the boss an hour ago. He didn't say nothing about you. Why did you come here?"

I kept my voice low to match his and I kept it steady— God knows how. I was looking down that gun barrel at extermination.

"He told me to bring you this."

I took the shotgun from under my coat, my movements

137

slow and careful. I didn't take my eyes from him or his gun and I expected I would see the muzzle blast at any instant, and that would be the last thing I'd see.

Suddenly he moved. He crashed his gun against the side of my head. My hands were holding the shotgun and I didn't have a chance. I fell to the floor and dropped the shotgun. He started kicking me and I folded my arms over my head and lay there for a moment, gathering my senses. The blow from the gun had jarred me to my heels, but the dizziness passed quickly.

He was kicking my arms, trying to reach my face with his shoe. I grabbed his foot and twisted as hard as I could. There was the snap of a bone and he screamed. He fell with a thud, still screaming. Then he began calling Aldo at the top of his voice.

I got to my knees and hunted for the shotgun. I don't know why I didn't think of the pistol in my belt. I guess the beating had driven all thoughts from my mind but the job I was to do with that gun. I found it behind me and picked it up. I looked over at Caruso and saw his hand lifting up his .45 from the floor. Apparently he had dropped it when he fell. He was moaning, cursing in Sicilian, promising to kill me.

The question was which of us was going to shoot first. I felt my reflexes had failed me, that I was moving with fatal slowness. It seemed an eternity before I got the shotgun swung around to him and my finger on the trigger. Nothing would move fast enough. Then he was aiming his gun. I couldn't understand why he hadn't shot minutes ago. I pulled the shotgun trigger and the kick of the gun almost broke my shoulder.

Then I got to my feet and walked out the front door, which was still open, not looking at the horrible mess the shotgun had left of Lou Caruso.

An hour after dark we were bouncing along the country road to the communications center. Hills had said nothing since San Bernardino, where we had stopped briefly at a gas station to phone. As we neared the house he slowed down and asked me, "You need any help with this Castle?"

I said, "I want to handle him myself. I'll figure some way to flush him out. I'll go to work on it after Sunday."

"You'd better keep that thirty-eight. You think he's found out anything about you that would compromise you with the Mafia?"

"I doubt it. I don't see how he could. I've been careful and lucky."

"You haven't been careful with that girl, from what I hear. She could hang you."

"Not Trina," I said, perhaps a trifle smugly. "She wouldn't do anything to hurt me."

"So you say. Women don't fit into an assignment like yours. There was never a woman you could trust with a secret."

"Not Trina," I repeated. "And while you're on women, don't forget that Indian of Caruso's. She can identify me. Have FANG take care of her."

He shook his head at me as he turned into the driveway. He stopped beside the front porch and we got out. Then the woman we had left with Trina—a stolid dame of forty named Elsie Downes whose regular job was telephone operator at the Peacock—came running out the door waving her arms.

"She's gone!" she yelled. "She got away!"

I got out and stood facing her. "When?"

"Right after you left, Mr. Andradi. She hit me on the head with something—right here—while I was lying down." She lifted up the hair over her right temple and there was a strip of adhesive tape there. "She tied me up with a clothes line—not tight but it took me some time to get free. I heard the car start and then she went speeding out the driveway."

I reached into my pocket. The Ford keys were gone. Hills was standing beside me and he put a hand on my shoulder.

"We'd better go after her right away," he said.

I vetoed that. "It's too late. Any harm she was going to do is already done. Now FANG is going to have to trust her, too, whether they like it or not. I'll get hold of her Sunday night when I make my debut at the Peacock and find out what's happened. Until then, the only practical thing for me is prayer."

"We'll check at the Peacock," he said. "If we find out anything we'll call you. We've got a phone operator on the board now and Elsie goes back on at four o'clock."

"O.K.," I said.

Elsie went back in the house and got her handbag and an overnight case. She drove away with Hills and I went into the house and tried to sleep. I couldn't for a long while. I couldn't stop thinking about Trina—wondering what she had said to Johnny Castle by now and whether it was too much. If it was, I'd never have any more problems with women.

139

On Saturday morning Carter Hills returned to my hideout with two days of newspapers from Los Angeles, San Francisco, and New York, with their blazing headlines on Mafia and Anti-Mafia, and an urgent request from FANG for me to abandon Johnny Castle and re-establish contact immediately with Frankie Magardi.

The FANG high command wanted to know what was happening among the *capo mafiosi* since the assassination of Lou Caruso and the public advent of Anti-Mafia.

Hills also brought me word of Trina. She had gone directly to the Peacock. She had met and talked to Johnny Castle, then had put through a telephone call to Magardi. She had not been able to reach him and she left word that she would accept his ultimatum. She asked him to let her return to New York and fulfill her singing engagement at the Algiers.

"We couldn't get any line on what she told Castle," Hills said, "but it appears certain you're still in the clear. He put through no calls to the East, which he would have done immediately if he'd found out anything. . . . You'd better forget that woman, Danny. Just hope she'll keep her mouth shut until we get hold of her."

"Leave her alone," I said. "FANG is going to have to put up with her. I've told you that. You pass the word on up."

"The order has gone out to pick her up as soon as she leaves the Peacock," he said.

"It's got to be canceled. If I'm willing to trust my life to her, that's got to be good enough for FANG."

Hills reluctantly phoned, quoting my attitude and demands accurately to several persons. While he talked I looked at the newspapers. The front pages were almost exclusively devoted to the assassination of Fred Vitali, the subsequent gunning of Lou Caruso, and the advent of the mysterious Anti-Mafia.

The Thursday papers were jammed with Vitali and the San Francisco hearing-room assassination. It was called a Mafia killing and all the papers stated he had been murdered because he had violated the conspiracy of silence —*omertà*. There were photographs, diagrams, editorials, and enough facts and speculation about Mafia to convince the most skeptical. Also, for the first time, some of the actual rulers of the Mafia were named—Frankie Magardi, Lou Caruso, and Vincent Carmi, although their full importance was not guessed.

Nicosa wasn't mentioned, nor were Marko Gambetta and Sammy Giorgiano. There was no hint of a Mafia Patriarch in the "hills behind Palermo." But it was a good beginning.

The Thursday papers said subpoenas had been issued for Magardi, Caruso, and Carmi, and that all three had vanished from their usual haunts and were in hiding.

Where the murder of Vitali had shocked and horrified the public because of its implications of underworld supremacy, the gunning of Caruso in his swank Palm Springs hideaway was the first act of violence that gave people hope the fight was not all one-sided.

The Anti-Mafia was welcomed to the battlefield of the crime war with rejoicing. On every front page appeared the facsimile of the filing card which had been sent to all newspapers and press associations:

SANGU LAVA SANGU

DON LOU CARUSO, MAFIA OVERLORD OF THE FAR WEST, IS DEAD. HIS ASSASSINATION AVENGES THE MAFIA MURDER OF FRED VI-TALI. NO MAFIA DON WILL ESCAPE THE PURGE OF

THE ANTI-MAFIA

Speculation about the Anti-Mafia was endless and the guesses ranged from an organization of rebel gangsters to a secret society pledged to exterminate Italian mobsters. Only in *The New York Times* was there a paragraph that hinted at the truth, and this was so worded that it meant little enough. The *Times* reported:

"It was learned on good authority that the so-called Anti-Mafia is a nationwide organization dedicated to removing the stigma against Americans of Italian descent left by the nefarious Mafia. The organization operates without official sanction of any kind, although it is not expected that the F.B.I. and local police agencies will oppose it and seek to curtail it, our informant stated."

I combed through the newspapers for anything that might indicate Mafia reactions. The only significant facts were that Frankie Magardi and Vincent Carmi were hiding out (with Caruso dead) and that several other known Dons had disappeared from their neighborhoods.

Hills put in more calls after settling the Trina Templer problem, then told me my car was in Flagstaff, Arizona, and would be held there for me.

141

"I've arranged a plane for you and you can be in Flagstaff in an hour or so," he said. "Let's get going."

Hills drove me to Las Vegas airport and we went around the rim of the field to the far side where a jet was parked. It was an Air Force trainer, built for two. I climbed into the right-hand seat and shook hands with the pilot. He closed the canopy, lit the burners, and we taxied to the end of the runway. In a little over an hour we set own at a field on the outskirts of Flagstaff, and I was on the telephone at an Air Force hangar.

I got Magardi's tough young secretary, Mike Lotto, after a half-hour and three numbers. I told him, "I want the boss to know where he can reach me right now. I'm going to wait at this number for one hour. It's a phone booth and safe. You tell him."

"I can't do it," he replied. "You ought to know better. That's not—"

"You do it," I cut him off. "You do it or *t'allampu.*"

There was a moment's silence. "O.K.," he said.

Twenty minutes later Frankie Magardi was on the phone. He spoke in Sicilian and so rapidly it was difficult to understand him.

"Come back and take over the business," he said. "Call me as soon as you get in. Mike Lotto will give you the number. Thanks, Danny. Good luck."

I put in a call to the Peacock and asked for Trina Templer. I had to wait while she was paged. I gave the operator Max Murtha's name.

Then I heard her voice, "Hello, Max darling!"

"Trina!"

"Oh!—ah, how's the record business?"

"You can't talk, eh?"

"No, not at all, Max. Just having lunch."

"Yeah, with that Johnny Castle, I bet!"

She laughed, in the unforgettable way she had when she was teasing me. "I've been waiting to hear from you, monkey. It took you long enough to call. How about that new song you were telling me about? You want me to cut it?"

"I'm on my way back to New York right now," I said. "Can you catch a plane today?"

"Oh Max! Do I have to?"

"Yes. There's a flight that leaves Los Angeles at four o'clock and gets into New York at one A.M."

"But this is Saturday, Max! You're not going to cut any records Sunday!"

"Make that plane, darling. I've got to see you. I'll meet you at the airport."

"All right then, if you say so. I'll see if I can get a plane this afternoon. Good-bye, Max."

I stood looking at the buzzing receiver, feeling all right again. No more doubts.

SEVENTEEN

THE PRESSURE ON THE MAFIA WAS MOUNTING. NOT ONLY had FANG thrown a real scare into the Dons with Lou Caruso, but various Federal agencies were bedeviling them with increasing effectiveness. No longer did any of the *capo mafiosi* appear at the fine restaurants and night clubs; no longer did they stroll through the streets of their cities collecting homage from their inferiors; no longer did they seek to keep up publicly their masquerade of honest citizens.

In that disastrous December the ownership of hundreds of legitimate enterprises were transferred to non-Mafia hands —to wives and relatives and others who could be trusted and who could not be linked directly to the Brotherhood. There was a general flight from the limelight. Records of ownership of everything from automobiles to gambling casinos, from funeral parlors to beer halls, were quickly shifted away from the underworld.

It was in this atmosphere of unrest and fear that I returned to New York the Saturday before Christmas. I got into Idlewild on a flight from Phoenix at 8:30 P.M. and went directly to the Chambers Building. I found Mike Lotto alone in our offices, drinking black coffee and eating a bologna sandwich. His attitude of superiority and the marked lack of deference he had been so careful to maintain had suddenly vanished. This switch by Lotto was a significant weathervane. If I had had any doubts about my position in the Mafia, they were gone now.

"The boss told me to wait for you," he said. "Anything I can get you?" He was on his feet and bowing to me in the approved manner for underlings.

"Get the boss on the phone," I replied.

"You are to use his office," he said. "He will not be back for a long time. I work for you now."

I sat behind Magardi's oval desk and put my feet up on the polished surface. Then one of his eight phones buzzed and Mike handed me the right one.

Magardi spoke in Sicilian again, using Mafia slang entirely.

"You take over," he said. "You're in the clear and Uncle

144

Angelo won't bother you. We got to have money. We got to liquidate. I already dumped the funeral parlors and we're selling the loan company Monday. A guy will be in with a bundle—Georgie Fanzio. Mike will get you the papers. You make the best deal you can. Get all he's got, Danny. You get the pitch? Get tough with him if you have to. He's a crumb—my kid sister's husband. . . . We got two kilos coming in on the Catalonia Tuesday. My cut is forty G's and you get it from Lupo. You know Lupo? Fine. He'll be in Jersey. Get it from him, no matter what he says. Forty G's. You remember all this? Get Mike on the other phone to take it down. . . . He's on? Good. Get hold of Johnny Castle. He went out to Las Vegas chasing that broad. The boss wants him to collect our December cut from all the casinos now. You hear, now! You tell him we got to have cash, Danny. You get that brain of yours working. I want a million cash by the end of March. You get it for me. . . . The boss says do a switch on the Carson-Akers fight down in Florida New Year's Eve. You got that? It's set up for Akers but now he wants Carson to have the title. This is between you and me. And tell Mike Lotto to keep his lip buttoned. This a private fix and to hell with the mob. I'll let you know how much we bet on Carson. Let Marko in on it but nobody else. . . . I got a lot more here. There's a guy, Ollie Hansen, wants to buy into the Harlem houses. Gentile and the Harlem mob will cry murder but the hell with them. Hansen will be in to see you. Get a hundred grand from him and give him twenty per cent. Make him go for it. And get hold of Gentile and light a fire under him. We ain't had nothing from him for a month. Squeeze him, Danny-boy. Make him sweat. That Gentile is a thief. . . . The jukebox take is away down in St. Louis. There are a couple of smart boys out there robbing me. Joey Gallio and Willie Whisper. Mike'll give you their phone numbers. Get 'em into New York right away and give 'em a dry cleaning. Scare 'em, Danny. Make 'em pray. . . . I don't know what to do with this dumb Templer broad. She's giving me the runaround. You watch her, Danny. If she don't play with Johnny Castle, dump her. That'll be your job—kill her off with sour records. . . . Take over Diamond, Danny. I told the boys already so they'll listen to you. But kind of keep my name in there. You know what I mean? . . . Now for the boss, we got a tough one. He says get hold of Rollo Roberts and light a fire under him. We set up this crumb in business and he ain't done a thing for us. The boss says a good press agent can clean us up for the public and fight all this bad mobster publicity. You ride herd on him, Danny. Get him cracking. He knows how to do it.

Christ, a press agent done it for Rockefeller, didn't he? . . . That's all I got on my list. Oh, one other thing. The boss says, what's the matter with you and Castle? He says he got a message from Castle he wants to talk to him about you. This would be Carmi's business, but Vince has gone to Europe. We don't like no bad blood, Danny. You fix it up with him."

I handed the phone to Lotto and he hung it up for me. I said, "I'm going home and get some sleep. I'll be in tomorrow around eleven and we start working."

"Tomorrow? That's Sunday."

"Sure. What's the matter with Sunday? You go to early Mass, then come here."

I went down to the street and got a cab to Fiftieth Street, left my bag, put on some warmer clothes, and started out again. It was about 11:30. Plenty of time to get to Idlewild. There was plenty of time, also, to have remembered to take my gun. But I didn't think of that until I was well into the depths of Queens.

Airliners are like Chinese. They all look alike. There were a lot of them arriving and I wandered around on the Oceanic apron hunting for the one with Trina—and, of course, Johnny Castle. I say, of course Johnny Castle. I was assuming Trina had told him I was back in New York. She'd said she was going to lure him for me, hadn't she? And she was not the type to listen to any of my warnings.

The third plane I got to was a big turbo-jet that came in screaming and parked in front of the Oceanic main gate. A red carpet had been rolled out and an airline photographer was waiting to take pictures of the inevitable Hollywood babes. Trina was the fifth to emerge on the top of the stairway and she looked right at me for an instant. I felt my heart flip and I was just about to raise my hand to her when I caught an almost imperceptible shake of her head. Then she turned and said something to the man behind her. Johnny Castle. What she said made him laugh and, laughing, he was not looking around for anybody. I ducked quickly under the wing and walked back to the tail of the plane, keeping out of sight of the line of passengers walking to the gate.

Then I hitched onto the end of the line, following an ancient, bejeweled dame carrying a birdcage with a silk hood over it. When I got into the waiting room I saw Trina and Castle talking to a workman—a carefully dressed hoodlum in a double-breasted overcoat and white scarf. He took their baggage checks and seemed to be explaining something to them as he pointed with a stubby finger. They went towards the exit. I followed along to a black Cadillac standing

146

in a no-parking zone. The car had Pennsylvania plates—a low number that looked official. I saw Johnny help Trina in, then climb in after her and put his arm around her.

That rattled me and I almost did something foolish. I got hold of myself, walked back to the cab line, and picked a cab near the end. The driver was a young guy who had the droopy, sleepy look of the thief. You get to know that look.

I got in, ignoring his command that I take a cab at the front of the line. I held a $20 bill in front of his nose and said, "You want to earn this for an hour's work?"

He snatched it from me. "Sure. I'm your boy."

We followed the Cadillac to Forest Hills. It stopped at a subway entrance and the workman got out and walked towards it. Castle and Trina got in the front seat and started away fast, heading for the Northern State Parkway and Long Island. The traffic thinned and we had to drop away back. I got as jittery as a flag in a high wind. I knew Trina expected me to stay with her. I was certain she would not be driving with Johnny Castle at this hour unless I was close. Male vanity, perhaps, but that's how I figured.

"Settle down," my driver said, "I won't lose them. I been doing this for years."

"You do lose them and I'll take you and your cab apart," I said.

He glanced back at me. He shrugged. "I guess you could at that."

It started to rain just after we got on the parkway—a cold, miserable drizzle that congealed on the road as slush and promised to turn to ice. The Cadillac didn't slow down and we were going at a dangerous speed for the cab. We barely avoided one bad skid and the Cadillac got too far ahead. Then when we came around a turn its tail lights were out of sight altogether.

"Don't lose him!" I yelled at the driver.

He nodded. There was a turnoff just beyond the curve and he plunged into this and down a hill to a road which ran under the parkway.

"They came down here," he said. "I can see their tracks. A night like this, it's easy to trail them."

We took a left turn at the bottom and sure enough there were tail lights in the distance. We speeded up and began to close in slowly. We passed through two towns and on. the far side of the second the Cadillac's stop lights went on and blinked for a left turn. I leaned forward and could see a motel sign where they had turned. "Suffolk Motel Inn—Vacancy."

"Keep going," I told the cabby. "Don't slow down."

We passed the motel and saw the Cadillac pulled up before a lighted office.

"Turn off your lights and stop," I told my driver. "Right here."

I got out and went around to his side of the car. "You scram out of here," I said. "If anybody asks you, you were never here. I've got your name and number, so if there's any talking I'll know who did it. Get me?"

He nodded. "We made a deal," he said.

I gave him another twenty, then walked back to the motel. It was a spacious layout on top of a hill. There was a lane lined with bare trees. It went down the side of the main building, which had a restaurant facing the highway. I turned down this lane, walking quietly. It took me behind the motel units, which were built in a semicircle facing a garden. At the back there was an areaway between two of the units which led to the front.

The Cadillac was parked to my right, facing a cabin with light seeping from the edges of Venetian blinds.

I took off my hat, overcoat, and jacket, folded them into a bundle and put them in the areaway out of the rain. Then I walked up to the door and knocked loudly.

"I've got more towels for you," I called.

Johnny Castle opened the door about six inches and glared at me. I was standing in the dark and he couldn't have recognized me.

"We've got enough," he growled at me.

Then I hit the door with every ounce of me and carried him off his feet into the center of the room.

The light came from table lamps, one small one beside the bed and a larger one on a desk near the door. Trina was standing in the door to the bathroom. I caught the briefest flash of her motionless attention as I jumped on Castle to put a hold on him.

Castle scrambled away from me with speed and agility that was unexpected. He was strong and fast and he knew judo or he would not have been able to slip the hold I was putting on him.

He bounced to his feet and backed against the dresser.

"You sonofabitch!" he said. "Now I'm going to kill you!"

His right hand flashed behind him to the dresser top and came up with a knife—a long, slim one such as Carter Hills had carried. He started moving towards me, the knife held wide.

"Go in the bathroom and close the door," I told Trina. "Stay there."

I didn't look at her but I heard the door close. I kept my

148

eyes on Johnny, backing away from him slowly, circling to my left, feeling the carpet under my feet and getting the arrangement of the furniture fixed in my mind. It was a large room and there was space for my maneuver. I had made this movement a thousand times at Higganum Farm. But then I had worn padded clothes and leather and a mask, and the knifepoints were dulled. Now the rehearsals were over. This was the performance—opening night.

Castle was as fast as Forest Wiley and Carter Hills and stronger than either. He was in good shape and his determination was fanatical. But he had weaknesses. His uncontrolled Sicilian temper was a weakness, and when I talked to him he became wild and almost careless. So I talked continuously.

"Lou Caruso was my pigeon," I said. "I blasted him with that shotgun while my partner took out his bodyguard. Now it's your turn, Castle."

"Sonofabitch!"

His knife whipped across my left shoulder and I got him with a palm blow across the side of the neck. His face turned purple and his eyes bulged but he kept moving. This definitely slowed him down and I saw my chance to maneuver him into position.

"I dumped Louie Pizzari into Florida Strait," I said. "I fractured his windpipe and threw him over the side of the *Estrellita*. Louie the Disposer. Tough as a petunia!"

"Sonofabitch!"

He missed with his next lunge.

"It seems to me a Harvard man should have a more expressive vocabulary than the constantly iterated reference to my antecedents. You losing your poise, sonny-boy?"

I kept him moving and striking and I feinted him off balance to the left a dozen times before I was satisfied I knew the exact rhythm of his movement in recovery. It was quick but it was another weakness.

"Trina brought you here to me," I said. "Doesn't that make you feel silly? She thinks you're a fairy."

He missed again and I kicked him in the groin as he went by. He stood still, his mouth open, sweat pouring down his face. Only the knife moved.

"No three-minute rounds, sonny-boy. No cheering crowds and seconds and a referee to keep it clean. You want a referee now, box-fighter?"

I took a deep breath and let it out slowly as he began to move in again. I feinted him once more but this time there was a variation. I moved in on him instead of away and

149

grabbed him high around the back, butting him hard in the face with my head. He let out a startled grunt.

My back and side were wide open and the knife came swinging around and jabbed into a rib with excruciating pain. But the rib stopped it and that was my luck working for me.

I had him. I butted again and I raised my knee hard. I exerted all of my strength in a tremendous, convulsive heave, with my knuckles on his spine and all of the leverage concentrated there. The butts and the knee had relaxed him just enough. The bones snapped with an audible crack and he went limp in my arms.

It was a way to kill a man.

I dropped him and backed away. I backed to the bed and sat down, feeling nauseous.

Trina took off my shirt and swabbed my cuts with towels soaked in hot water. She bandaged my arm and shoulder with strips torn from my shirt. She wrapped a couple of towels around me for the wound in my back. She cooed over me and she said a lot of intimate things. When she was through she backed off and stood looking at me critically.

"What's the matter with you?" she asked.

I couldn't stop shaking. "It's the reaction. Come here and let me hold you. That'll cure me."

She came and sat beside me and I held her. The warmth of her was even more exciting than it had been that first time. But she wiggled away from me and got up.

"You're an absolute barbarian!" she said. "You've got no —well, inhibitions. You just want to—to . . . Look. I love it. I love you and I love the way you are. But we've got to do something about him."

"I'll phone and have everything taken care of," I said. "That's no problem."

She stood shaking her head at me. "I don't want to stay in this room another minute, Danny. Can't you understand that?"

I got up. I said, "O.K., let's go then."

I drove the Cadillac to New York and abandoned it in the Bronx, just over the Triborough, taking Trina's bags out of the rear trunk. We got a cab downtown and I phoned a FANG contact from a drugstore while Trina waited. I arranged for the disposal of Johnny Castle, with a *Sangu lava sangu* card on him, then took Trina home. To my home.

It was quite a Saturday night.

The discovery of the body of Johnny Castle on Sunday morning, lying out in the Jersey Meadows with an Anti-

150

Mafia message pinned to his shirt, was a mild sensation in the press. Nobody knew who Castle was, and if a hoodlum were unknown then it was assumed he was a minor leaguer of no importance. The fact that the message named him as the actual slayer of Fred Vitali helped, but even this was not enough to win him the black headlines of a Lou Caruso.

Within the Mafia, the reaction was quite different and totally unexpected. It threw a fear into the Dons that was far beyond that which followed the assassination of Caruso. This killing was a sort of confirmation—a restatement. Caruso was a prominent figure and in his very prominence lay the constant risk that he would become known for what he was. Any *capo mafioso* had to expect that sooner or later he would be linked to the Brotherhood. But never such a specialist as Johnny Castle. The feeling seemed to be that if the Anti-Mafia knew of Castle and knew even that he had been the actual killer of Vitali, then none of their secrets was safe. There was no longer any magic in *omertà*. The conspiracy of silence was shattered.

The one bug in the *béchamel* was the workman who had met Johnny and Trina at Idlewild and who had seen them go away together. I didn't know who he was or where to find him. There was no question that he would tell the Dons Johnny and Trina were going to spend the night together. She would have been the last one to have seen him alive. If they found Trina they would make her talk. But, who were "they" now? All the Dons of the Northeast were in hiding, as were those of the other areas. The one *capo mafioso* most likely to get the assignment to find Trina was that rising young hoodlum, Danny Andradi.

I told Trina Sunday morning, "There are too many angles to this Mafia business. You were the last one with Johnny Castle. They know at the Peacock that you two took the same plane. This hoodlum who drove the car—he saw you drive away together. So you're pinned down to Johnny's last hours. You're in trouble, darling."

She grabbed my hair in her two hands and kissed me. "You worry about it."

"You'll have to let Anti-Mafia hide you away. This time I mean it."

"I'm not going to hide. I'm not afraid of anyone now— not since I've got you. I wasn't even afraid of that Johnny."

"So I noticed. He put his arm around you in the car."

"Sure. And when we got to the motel I kissed him."

"I'm damned!"

"Well—not really. He was awfully insistent. I had to give him a little one. You were so slow getting there!"

"O.K. Let's drop that subject. . . . You ran away from me out in the desert. Now I'm afraid to trust you."

"I didn't run away from you. I ran away from that dull woman—that Elsie. She slept with her mouth open. Besides, I had to go get Johnny for you, didn't I?"

"No. Look, sweetheart, I've got to go out. I want you to stay here. Don't go wandering around the streets. Will you promise me?"

"Who wants to go wandering around the streets? I'm home now."

"Well—you won't go out?"

"No."

"O.K. Don't answer the phone and don't make any calls. I think this phone is tapped. I won't call you. I'll be back this afternoon. You want me to bring you anything?"

She shook her head. "I've got everything, almost. I'll play your piano and vocalize and see if I can break your lease, so we can get a bigger apartment."

I got to the Chambers Building a little after eleven. The building was closed on Sunday and I had to identify myself and sign in on the register. I found Mike Lotto in Magardi's office waiting for me with a typewritten record of Frankie's telephone instructions. Each item was listed separately under a number. He was an efficient secretary—the business side of the Brotherhood.

I had him put in phone calls to Joey Gallio and Willie Whisper in St. Louis, to get the jukebox matter started. I told them both to get to New York by noon Monday and come up to my office. I wasn't polite about it. Then I had Mike find Rollo Roberts. He was just waking up in his hotel with a hangover and attendant remorse. I told him to come up and see me. I gave him an hour.

I had a very satisfactory half-hour talk on the phone with Gino Gentile of the East Harlem organization and told him to be around Monday morning with money. Mike got sandwiches and coffee from a drugstore at one o'clock and Roberts stayed for lunch.

Roberts didn't think much of Nicosa's idea of trying to build up the Mafia with publicity. We had an interesting talk on the Big Lie technique and how it had been used by Hitler and was still being used by the Russians. He agreed to go to work on it because I made it clear that he had no choice. At 2:30 I was ready to call it a day and get back to Trina when there was a phone call from Magardi.

He spoke in Sicilian. "Have you heard about Johnny Castle, Danny?"

"No. What about him?"

"The Anti-Mafia killed him. They dumped his body over in Jersey. Those sonsofbitches know too much! There's none of us safe now! Not a one! You hear that, Danny?"

"I'll watch out for them," I said. "They don't worry me."

"Speak in our language. These phones aren't reliable. . . . Johnny was with Trina Templer. They were going to spend the night together. One of our men met them at the airport and they took his car. This Templer bitch set him up for those bastards. We're not going to fool around with her. I've been talking to the boss. We knock her off."

"What?" I exclaimed.

"We kill her," he said. "It's your job, Danny. Find her and shoot her. Try to make it tonight. That's an order, right from the top."

"From the hills behind Palermo?"

"That's right."

EIGHTEEN

Fang put Trina on a plane to Bermuda. I couldn't go to the airport with her. I couldn't be seen with her anywhere. She was wearing a black wig with a pony tail and during the short half-hour I was with her to say good-bye, riding around Queens in a FANG car, I had the feeling I was with someone I didn't know. Only when I kissed her was I back in the familiar warmth of her.

I'd consented to Bermuda only after Smith himself had agreed to give her a twenty-four hour guard and to arrange to check all arrivals on the island by boat and plane. It was a lot of trouble for one girl in a business such as ours, where lives were held cheaper than any of our gifts, but I was adamant about that. I didn't let them forget Connie Masters. My constant references to their carelessness were sufficient goads.

Trina, of course, had objected violently at first. She had her career, she had her family and her friends. She was to open Christmas Eve at the Algiers. I told her what Magardi had said. I told her I was ordered to find her and kill her; that it was to be done immediately. That night.

She listened to me, frowning slightly. She wasn't frightened. Then she grinned at me.

"What absurd melodrama! The lover is ordered to murder his sweetheart!"

"It's a lousy script," I agreed, "but things that happen in real life are always idiotic. Only in books and plays do people act reasonably and events follow a sensible pattern. . . . You haven't got any more career, Trina. That's gone right down the drain."

She looked at me for a moment, then put her hand on my face. "Don't feel badly about it, Danny. I knew what I was doing. I've known ever since I first talked to you on that plane to Havana."

"You don't mind? You're not angry?"

She shook her head, the black pony tail switching across her shoulders. "Just come back to me."

"I'll come back."

It was an easy promise to make.

154

I returned to my apartment and found she'd moved all the furniture around, even rearranging the small bedroom. Well, women. . . . But I left it that way. It was more convenient.

I called Frankie Magardi at midnight and told him Trina Templer had vanished. I spoke in Sicilian. I said, "She's definitely not in New York. I've checked all the hotels and a couple of her friends she would call if she were in the city. She got away, boss."

"We'll get her," he said. "I'll put every man in the Brotherhood to work on it. . . . You think she's a part of this Anti-Mafia, Danny?"

"It sure looks like it."

"These damned women! I'll phone you the minute I find out anything. Then you go get her."

I took care of my Monday appointments with Georgie Fanzio, Ollie Hansen, Joey Gallio and Willie Whisper from St. Louis, and Nino Gentile. I got $250,000 in cash from Georgie Fanzio and his notes for $250,000 more. He left my office in tears, mumbling curses. I got $95,000 from Ollie Hansen and he was happy about it. I beat up Joey Gallio. He was a loud-mouth and a swell-head in his $300 suit and $300 cashmere coat, but he was tame when Willie helped him out. I didn't have to touch Willie. He was going to be good.

Nino Gentile was a surprise. He was the first *mafioso* I'd met with a smile. He had a vicious face and was ox-strong to back up his more violent whims, but he was a happy and talkative character with a good comic-book sense of humor. I liked Nino after rat-faced Gallio and I took his $27,000 offering with some regret.

"Now I'm flat as last night's beer," he said grinning. "But I got angles. I got more people working for me than ants has pants. I'll get it back. I'm having the shorts, that's why I ain't been in. This bundle I get from Jake Ribber. You read in the papers how some jelly-boys knock off Jake's can Saturday night? Say hello to the boss for me. I guess he's running like a box of epsom salts."

I said, "Ollie Hansen has bought into the houses and he gets twenty per cent. You knew we were going to do that?"

"Yeah. Ollie the Sniff. You know he's fronting for this Letty Kowalski? You know she's trying to push in on our H-racket? I'll drop him out a window. I bet he splashes like a watermelon!"

"Let him alone," I said. "He paid off and that's something you haven't been doing."

He laughed. He looked me over. He said, "I bet you

155

could give me a good go-around at that. How'd you get so big?"

Tuesday night I went over to New Jersey and hunted up Lupo Perez. I'd bought another Cadillac Eldorado out of the money I'd been collecting and I drove to Newark and went to the Carleton-Trent Hotel and up to a penthouse apartment furnished with blonde butternut and decorated with pastels and crystal—a call girl's notion of chic. There were three of them there with Lupo, but two were so high on heroin that they were elsewhere. The third was belting straight gin. When you looked at Lupo you understood why. He was the world's ugliest human with a nose flattened by fists, a crooked, wet mouth and red, watery eyes.

"You sure got here in a hell of a hurry," he said.

I pushed him into the room, not gently, and banged the door shut. The girl with the gin bottle gave me a weaving stare, then hiccuped.

"Get it up," I told him. "This isn't a social call."

"I ain't got it! I ain't collected yet! So help me, Mr. Andradi, that's the truth!"

I went to a pink chair across the room and sat. I said, "Collect, then. I'll wait."

"I can't get it tonight," he whined. "You know how them bums are! They never pay off!"

I nodded at him. "Sure. You'd let a couple of kilos get out of your hands without getting the money first. You're that stupid."

He stood looking at me for a moment, then turned and went into a bedroom. He came out with twenty $1,000 bills fanned out in his hand and shoved them at me.

"This is all I got. They wasn't two kilos. They was only one."

I grabbed the bills out of his hand. I got up and hit him hard in the stomach. He doubled over and got sick on the beige carpet.

"Get the rest of it."

He went back into the bedroom and came out with twenty more $1,000 bills. He offered them to me with his left hand, so I looked to see what his right was doing. He was holding it behind his back. I hit him again in the stomach and took the knife out of his right hand when he doubled over. Then I picked up the twenty bills from the floor and left.

It was a good knife so I kept it.

On Christmas Eve I went up to the Bronx—to St. Mary's. I sat through the midnight Mass, not thinking many of the proper thoughts, I'll confess. I was thinking of Trina, wondering how she was spending Christmas Eve. There was a second Mass right after the first, for there had been too many communicants. I waited for Tony at the side door to the altar. He came out with his two assistants and a couple of altar boys. He stopped when he saw me, then drew me aside off the path.

"Trouble?"

I shook my head. "Not this time. I had to have some place to go Christmas Eve."

He led me back into the church, now darkened, and we went to the back pew we had occupied on another occasion. The Crèche was off to the right down near the altar and there were still a few people there standing and looking, thinking their thoughts.

"Don't you always go away for a couple of weeks in March?" I asked him.

"I usually go on retreat then."

"Could you sort of skip the retreat this year and do something for me?"

"I could—yes."

"There's a girl in Bermuda. I want you to see her."

"A girl?"

"The one I'm going to marry if I live. The one I'll leave mourning for me if I don't. I want you to tell her about me. Tell her that I love her, so that she'll know when I don't come back that it's because I couldn't. . . . I guess I'm not making much sense, Tony, but her opinion of me means more than anything else. I don't expect to see her again. The more I think of what I'm going to do, the more certain I am that I won't. Along about March or April, if things break right, I'll walk into this thing. It's just too much to expect that I'll come out of it, that's all."

He said, "Why don't we wait and see?"

"No, Tony, there's no point in waiting. The chances are you'll never know what happened. Nobody will except one or two *mafiosi* who'll keep *omertà*."

"All right," he said, "I'll talk to her. But I don't like your frame of mind and I'm not going to tell her you won't be back. That's nonsense. You come back, Dando. You see that you come back."

I told him where and how to find Trina, what name she was using, how to identify himself to her guards. Then I gave him a big roll of Frankie Magardi's money, to cover the expenses of the trip and for the Church. Money I had plenty of.

The next morning—Thursday—I left for Florida, driving my new Eldorado. I should have set up a FANG meeting that day. Now everything was falling into place and I thought

I knew how I was going to get the Dons to send me to Sicily. I had to find out if FANG approved. I had to know if they would follow the plan I had conceived for the assassination of the Mafia rulers.

I was certain my plan would cause the greatest amount of consternation and do the most to reduce the Mafia to its pre-Al Capone status of a minor organization of hoodlums. The most enticing aspect of this plan was that I would be through with Mafia forever, if I survived it. On good days I was certain I would survive. On bad days I was certain I would not. Most of the days were bad.

I was impatient, yet the day-to-day work had to be done. I had to remain Magardi's white-haired boy or there would be no plan. Now FANG would have to wait until I had taken care of the Messrs. Akers and Carson. Their title fight was less than a week away and there had to be an understanding. Carson had to keep his title. Don Nicosa wanted it that way.

It was in that January, you may remember, shortly after the Carson-Akers fight and its shocking ending in the seventh round (which brought forth such cries of anguish from so many bettors) that the Department of Justice produced its own anti-Mafia thunderclap.

More than a year late but none the less effective for that, the Department had obtained secret indictments from Federal Grand Juries against all of the *capo mafiosi* who had attended the Apalachin council. On a selected day some forty of these Dons were rounded up like common criminals, served with warrants, dragged off to Federal Commissioners, and held in high bail.

The Mafia panic was on. The Dons were certain there was a connection between this dastardly legal maneuver and the dreaded Anti-Mafia.

All of the Dons produced the bail demanded in cash and were released. It is of academic interest that a part of this cash had been supplied to them by myself. It is of more than academic interest just how it came about that every Don picked up happened to have some $200,000 in bills in his pocket necessary to secure his freedom. However, that is a question others must answer.

Vito Nicosa was seized at his hideout on Lake Champlain, which was close to the Canadian border, and was hauled to a Federal Commissioner in Albany. He was just getting in his car to flee north when he was taken. He counted out $200,000 in large bills to secure his release.

Frankie Magardi was nailed on the International Bridge to Canada at Niagara Falls and was haled before a Commissioner at Buffalo. He likewise produced $200,000 bail from his wallet. Then he was served with a subpoena of the Congressional Rackets Committee and his cup ranneth over. Frankie, like Nicosa, was one of several Dons who obviously had been informed of the indictments and roundup.

Marko Gambetta, another who knew something, was arrested on the Mexican border at Juarez and taken before a Commissioner in El Paso. He produced his bail of $200,000 from a money belt which was stuffed with many times that amount, one newspaper man reported. Gambetta also was served with a Rackets Committee Subpoena.

Sammy Giorgiano, another $200,000 man, was picked up outside of Detroit on his way to Windsor. Joey DiMassi, Leo Gamma, and Nino Stalaci, to name a few of the Dons I have mentioned in this report, were taken from hideouts in various remote resorts and held in bail ranging from $100,000 to $200,000, which each produced in cash. The one name missing from this golden list, of vital interest to me, was Vincent Carmi. The Professor was in Europe.

Some forty in all were rounded up and some twenty got away, and the bail collected totaled more than $5,000,000. Now this sum is just a fraction of the annual take of the Mafia, but nevertheless it was large enough to put a critical strain on Mafia finances. It made it imperative that further income be produced immediately. It made it imperative that the liquidation of assets, already under way, be intensified —that every possible dollar be squeezed from every Mafia enterprise, legitimate and criminal.

This was my opportunity—the one I had seen building up for me. If I had thought it was ripe before, now I knew it was ready to pluck. There was no question that the whole Mafia was in trouble and needed bright, acquisitive Danny-boy Andradi to pull them out.

I was still in Florida when the honey hit the fan. I had sent well over $400,000 north to Magardi from bets on Carson. I had paid out $50,000 to Cowboy Akers and I had given Willy Lombardi $20,000 to placate him. When Willie wouldn't be placated, I had punched him in his fat stomach and had broken his nose.

NINETEEN

I GOT BACK TO NEW YORK SUNDAY, JANUARY 11, A DAY ahead of my announced arrival to Lotto and Magardi. I drove my car up the Jersey Turnpike to the bridge, then continued north on Palisades Parkway and the Throughway to Nyack and left it in a garage recommended by FANG. I got a local taxi to take me to New York and got out near a subway stop on the upper West Side. I went into a Jewish restaurant and had stuffed derma and cheese blintzes—a combination I don't advise—and at 7:30 P.M. I arrived at the portals of the Empire State Building on Fifth Avenue.

Up in the Observation Tower, closed to the public on this cold and windy Sunday, there was a quorum of Anti-Mafia elders. Smith was there, and Jones, Clark, Judge Williams, the assistant to the Cabinet Officer, Commissioner Orsini, and the railroad vice president. Missing was the atomic scientist. We sat around in a rough circle in the aluminum and plastic chairs of the sightseers.

Judge Williams said, "You tell us what you've got, Danny. The floor is yours."

I lit a cigarette and I spoke mostly to him. I said, "I can get over to Palermo now and find the Patriarch in the hills. I am certain I can flush him out and that's what I want to do. I want to finish this job and finish him. I've been on it too long.

"This isn't heroics. It's plain common sense. Today we've got everything going for us. The whole Mafia in America is on the run.

"My proposal is this: I get to Palermo. On a certain date we agree upon, at a certain time, I find this Mafia Patriarch and I kill him. On that date and time here in America, FANG assassinates the ruling Dons—Nicosa, Magardi, Gambetta, Giorgiano. Along with these you should knock off Leo Gamma, Nino Stalaci, Joey DiMassi, and Willie Lombardi. They are the next in line in the hierarchy. You do it whole-sale. You wreck the Mafia.

"I've left out one name—Vincent Carmi. The Professor is in Europe. Probably in Italy or Sicily. If he's still in Europe on our Day of Blood, then I take him. If he comes back here, then he's yours.

"That's my plan. That's what I want to do."

There was a silence that lasted for perhaps a minute but it seemed longer. Outside the wind whined dolefully around our tower. It was an appropriate obligato for the proposal of violence I had put before the company. It was as though I were receiving huzzahs for my murderous urgings. I looked around at them. Smith was leaning back in his chair, his eyes half-closed. His sharp, set features told me nothing. Jones was drawing his lips in and out, his huge body uncomfortable in the small chair, and I supposed he was thinking of his backside. He caught my eye and grimaced. The Cabinet assistant was looking at the floor, moving a foot back and forth on the linoleum. The railroad man was gazing out a window, probably assessing the weather. Clark was within himself, his arms folded tightly across his chest. Only Orsini seemed to be animated. He was smoking a new cigar and nodding his head. When he caught my eye he spoke to me.

"That's a good plan, Danny," he said. "The trouble with it is, it puts you right out of business. You'll be no more use to Anti-Mafia. *If* you live."

"It's a calculated risk," I said. "Maybe I won't live. But if we pull it off, you wouldn't need me any more anyway, alive or dead."

The judge looked around at them. "Are there any further comments?" he asked.

Smith said, "You know our thinking, Judge. You decide."

Williams looked at me, leaning forward in his chair with his arms resting on his thighs.

"No outsider has ever penetrated this Mafia fountainhead and survived. You know that, Danny?"

"Yes, sir."

"If we go in there in force, with the aid of the Italian government, which we can get, we might have a chance. What we've wanted from you, Danny, is a name and a locale. That would be sufficient for our purposes."

"You couldn't do it that way," I said. "Mussolini, with all of his dictator power, couldn't. He sent Mori down there and he failed. Ceasare Mori was probably the best policeman in Italy and he had the national police force and the whole army behind him if he needed them. He got nowhere. You know that."

The judge nodded. "We don't want you dead."

"It's not a question of my death," I said. "Let's not confuse the problem with sentiment. I don't want to die, either.

I'm telling you the only way it can be done. I can go there as a *capo mafioso*. I can come face to face with this Patriarch and I can kill him. Nobody else can."

"How can you get to him?" asked the judge.

"Right now the Mafia is desperate for money. I will show them how to make a bundle—with narcotics. I've got it all worked out. There'll be so much involved that it's unthinkable he will keep his hands off it. You've got to remember that first of all he's a thief, like all the rest of them. When the hears how much money I've got he'll have to see me. He'll see me and he'll take it from me, one way or another. That's the bait."

The judge turned to Orsini. "What do you think, Bill? Is this sound?"

Orsini nodded. "Yes. Danny knows what he's talking about."

The judge sighed and got up. He said to me, "You let us know the date you decide upon. Get your program in order first, then tell us. We'll do our part."

"O.K.," I said.

First I needed a boat. I drove out to Long Island and started visiting boatyards. In Oyster Bay I found a bright young yacht broker named Tom Riley and I told him what I wanted.

He asked me a lot of questions, then said, "You want a motor-sailer for such cruising. I know where there's a beauty."

He took me to a yard on an inlet off the bay. In a huge boat shed, high up on a cradle, was a great rounded bottom and a tremendous iron keel.

"This is the *Vega*," said Riley. "Sixty feet overall, fifteen-foot beam, and she draws eight feet one. That's too much for the Bahama Banks and a lot of other places, but if you want a deep water boat this is it. She's ketch-rigged, fully found, sleeps nine, with bunks for three crew in the forecastle, and she's got a new Budda deisel and a cruising range of 1,600 miles on engine. She's designed by Herreshoff and she'll take you anywhere in the world. She cost $300,000 to build four years ago. You offer the owner $50,000 cash and he'll smother you with kisses. Come aboard and I'll show you what you're buying."

It took me nearly a week to get the papers for the *Vega*, but after a final four-hour session at the Customs House with Tom Riley assisting, I had them in my pocket. The *Vega* had cost me $35,000, not $50,000. The papers were made out in the name of Daniel Andrews, an identity I had had FANG supply me.

Then I set up a meeting with Magardi and Nicosa at the St.

Charles. Since the arrest of the Apalachin Dons and their release on bail, they were not any longer in hiding. They were not making any public appearances, either, but they were available. Nicosa and Magardi were anxious for the conference. I had something to give them, and nobody else was giving them anything but trouble.

We held our meeting in a suite that apparently belonged to Nicosa on the top floor of the hotel. I put the yacht papers in front of them.

"Generally, there are two kinds of people," I said. "There are boat people and land people. I spent my summers as a kid out on Long Island among the boat people and I know a lot about them. They are entirely different from others—they have all sorts of freedoms that land people don't enjoy. The important one for us concerns the United States Customs Service.

"Yachts don't go through customs. They fly a yacht flag when entering a harbor and that's sufficient. There is no examination in any port. Occasionally the Coast Guard will look over their papers, but that's merely for safety regulations. Nobody ever hunts for contraband cargo aboard yachts.

"These are the papers for a sea-going yacht. It cost us $35,000 and we can have her in the water the end of March. She can go anywhere in the world and she can carry a couple of tons of anything down in her bottom. She could be, let us say, in the West Indies in April. She could pick up as much goods as you'd want and she could sail right into any American port with it. Nobody would ask a single question. . . . Do I make myself clear?"

Nicosa had a dreamy look on his face. He said, "You got brains, Danny. Always thinking. Why ain't nobody gone for this racket before?"

"They have," I said, "but they've gone about it wrong. They've tried to smuggle all sorts of stuff on yachts and a lot of them have been caught because they've been careless. They haven't taken the trouble to establish their boats as pleasure craft—to go in and out of harbors on cruises. My idea is to put the *Vega* in the charter boat business—to advertise for charters and conduct a legitimate service. We've got plenty of *mafiosi* who were brought up as fishermen, who know boats. Most Sicilians do. We put our own captain and crew on the *Vega* and we're set."

Magardi looked over the papers and asked me questions. He knew boats, it developed. He seemed satisfied with my answers.

Then Nicosa said, "What's the rest of it, Danny? You got more plan than this."

"Sure," I said. "We go over to the other side with a bundle. All the scratch we can raise. We buy up twenty, thirty, forty kilos of goods. About six or seven hundred grand. We send the goods out by freighter to the West Indies—ports like Ciudad Trujillo, San Juan, Port au Prince; maybe Cuba or Martinique—where the customs guys are for sale for a buck. We send somebody down to look over a port and we set it up.

"Then the *Vega* comes along. We take the goods on board. After we cruise around for a while, the *Vega* comes back to America. She's got to come north for the hurricane season anyway, so it's a routine trip. Now then, here's the real gimmick. Here's how we cash in.

"We don't sell the goods wholesale and uncut. We load a few hundred pounds of sugar on our boat before we go south. We've got a captain and two crew on board and they are experts at cutting H and packaging it for the retail trade. Then we have a ton of it when it's cut. We start around at New Orleans, say, and we distribute it all the way up the coast—to Miami, Charleston, Norfolk, Baltimore, Philly, New York, and Boston. We can even go through the Erie Canal, if you want, and hit the upper New York State towns and Buffalo, Cleveland, Detroit, and Chicago.

"We take maybe a year to get rid of it all. We don't collect just a few millions. We collect more dough than you can count in a month. We have a steady income to take care of everybody, no matter what the Federal courts do."

Nicosa's dreamy look was dreamier. He closed his eyes and sat thinking.

Magardi said, "That's one side of it, Danny-boy. Let's look at the other side. You got all this stuff in one place. You got all your investment tied up in one boat and you got just three guys handling it for you. Maybe one of them makes a mistake. Just a little mistake. Then along come these Angslinger bastards and you lose it all. Every goddamn ounce and every goddamn dollar."

"Sure," I agreed. "That's the chance you always take. You donate plenty the way you do it now, don't you? Pick the right men, Don Magardi, and you won't lose."

"What do you think, Vito?" he asked.

"I like it," replied Nicosa. "It's big thinking. It's what we need. I've got the man for the boat, Aldo Danelli. It's made to order for him. We'll need confirmation, of course. Any deal this size . . ." Then suddenly his face darkened and he shook his head. "We ain't got nobody can go over there now to buy. Who could leave this lousy country? Them bastards got every one of us tied down!"

I waited. There was an answer to that but it was not for me to say at that moment.

Magardi said, "Vince Carmi is over there, if we could get the dough to him."

"I wouldn't trust one of these *contadini* with a nickel!" Nicosa exclaimed angrily. "Who's left? Nobody! Johnny Castle is dead. Joey and Nino and Leo are indicted and can't travel . . ."

Then he looked at me, his eyes boring into mine.

"You want to take a trip?" he demanded.

"I don't mind," I said.

"You got a passport?"

"Yes, I have one."

"You work with Carmi," he said. "You and him do the buying and you make the deal for transportation. I'll write him a letter today. You get this lined up down in the islands. You pick the port, Danny-boy, and get the customs thieves paid off. Let me know when it's set up and I'll have the dough. You'd better have plenty now for the pay-offs."

He reached into his pocket and pulled out a packet of new $1,000 bills. He counted out fifty of them and pushed them across the coffee table towards me.

"You think you can clean it up with fifty grand?" he asked.

I nodded. "That ought to be sufficient."

"O.K. Go home. Wait until I call you—maybe a day or so. Then fly down to the islands and do your business. When you come back we'll fix up the rest of it."

I put the money in my pocket and got up. I shook hands with them and started for the door. Then Magardi said, "You know we ain't found that Templer dame yet?"

"That's what I figured when you didn't call me."

"I can't understand it how somebody like that could disappear."

"That Anti-Mafia gang is hiding her," said Nicosa. "Them sonsofbitches must have a hell of an organization."

"Maybe, but they haven't got us yet," I said.

"They won't," he said, "not so long as you keep using your brain, Danny-boy."

FANG suggested Ciudad Trujillo. I flew down there early in February and bought Colonel Valdez, chief of the customs service, and all of his minions for $10,000 down and the promise of $20,000 more on performance.

There was always the risk that the customs officer, a sharp, shifty little man, would seize the heroin for himself, so I gave another $20,000 to an army general to keep the customs man honest, and I paid out $10,000 more to the chief

165

of police to watch the two of them. I thought I had it pretty well covered.

Then I talked to the Irish captain of a 3,000-ton tramp freighter headed East. He was a big, red-necked thief by the name of Tom O'Hara. He told me he would be in the Mediterranean the end of March and would pick up cargo at both Genoa and Naples. I bought him a case of Irish whisky and told him I would hunt for him and his ship, the *Celeste-Anne*, in Naples and that we might do business. He was avid for business. He wouldn't cost more than five grand.

I flew back to New York and met the captain and crew for the *Vega*, and set up the charter project with the aid of FANG. This Aldo Danelli came from Castellammare and was brought up on his father's fishing boats. He spoke English with a slight accent and he was more personable than most *mafiosi* workmen, without the usual glowering unfriendliness. He was right on the verge of becoming an Ivy Leaguer. The two crew were former Grand Banks fishermen from Massachusetts, Joe Allegri and Sally (Salvatore) Fondi. The three moved out to Oyster Bay and started to work on the *Vega* immediately, getting her in shape for her Spring commissioning.

When I reported to Vito Nicosa, there were just the two of us in his St. Charles suite. He gave me $650,000 neatly packed in a wide money belt. He shook my hand and he spoke his farewell in flowery Sicilian, with emotion.

"You are the savior of the Brotherhood," he said. He extolled my virtues and vices and there were tears in his eyes. He concluded with, "We will never forget you, Danny-boy."

Well . . . I could have told him that.

TWENTY

IT WAS DECIDED THAT AT NOON ON APRIL 24, 1959, THE ruling Dons of the Mafia would be executed. Bloody Friday ... *Sangu lava sangu,* we hoped.

Was it too little time for me? Assuming that all would work out according to plan—that the Patriarch himself would participate in this rich deal—there was still Vincent Carmi, who would never accept me. He had the Sicilian's endowment of hate, of never forgiving. Now he had something tangible to hate me for, the death of Johnny Castle.

I remembered Trina had called Castle a fag. Trina would know. Women of the show world are wise about that. And so, how about Carmi? I had never seen the Professor with a woman, despite the *capo mafiosi* tradition. Carmi and Johnny Castle. There was an erotic possibility!

The Professor would know Castle had been trailing me. He would know of the subway death of Castle's workman, which occurred before he went to Europe. And so, what was I walking into?

There would be no Frankie Magardi or Vito Nicosa to protect me. There would be no FANG on the sidelines to come to my aid. I would be completely on my own. I had training and my wits and my reflexes, and I was strong enough to snap the Professor's neck like a chicken's. I kept adding up these assets and trying to find solace in them. It wasn't much use. Carmi was certainly as smart as I was, probably smarter. And that's what would pay off in the end. Well, there was only one way to find out.

I flew to Rome on T.W.A., then Italian Air Lines to Palermo. I checked into the Monreale Hotel, as arranged by Nicosa, and I waited. This was the last week in March. Sunday, the 28th, was my birthday. I'd be twenty-eight. I was pretty sure of that birthday. It was nice to have something to be sure of. Twenty-nine seemed an unlikely eventuality.

Spring comes early to Palermo. The sun was bright and warm and the streets filled with strollers. I strolled. I went to the huge main square, with its ancient opera house and its stone houses and stores and coffee houses. I walked and

167

drank *cappochino* and walked. I visited the old part of the
city near the harbor, then legged it up the hill to *Il Borgo*
section, a famed stronghold of the Mafia. Was *Il Borgo* the
"hills behind Palermo" or did I have to go further up?

There was no question of sleeping in the mornings. The
early day was made hideous by the bawling of the street
peddlers—the brush sellers, the vegetable vendors, the gla-
ziers, the tinkers, each vying with his competitor in brass-
voiced disharmony, testing his lung-power, imitating the notes
he imagined resounded from the rafters of the opera house.
Noise and more noise. It was Bernard Shaw who said the
intelligence of a people can be judged in inverse ratio to
the din they create. That would put the Sicilians down near
the bottom of the scale. It would account for the connota-
tions of the word *contadini*. It would account for the Mafia,
created by ignorance and nurtured by the viciousness of
small minds.

I admit I am biased about these Palermo Sicilians who
have brought such evil to America with their Brotherhood.
I felt alone among them. I told myself repeatedly that these
were my people, but I couldn't convince myself. The poison
of the Mafia was in my heart.

I waited five days. On the evening of the fifth just after
I returned to my room from a lone dinner, there was a
knock on my door. It was opened immediately before I could
get to it, and I remembered with chagrin that I had neglected
to lock it. I was getting too careless.

The Professor stood in the doorway for a moment, examining me and my lodgings, then he closed the door behind
him and locked it. He strode to me and held out a limp
hand. He was observing the amenities. He chatted about
my trip and about Palermo, sitting on a wood bench at
the window and smoking a cigar.

Then he asked, "You've got the money?"

I nodded. "Sure."

"I'll take it."

"Of course, Don Carmi. You have the goods?"

"Are you crazy? It's not done that way!"

"That's what I thought."

"I don't follow you. Are you being deliberately vague?
I want the money."

"In my vague way I gathered that, Don Carmi. The money
will be paid over when you or I or both of us obtain the
goods. Meanwhile I'll keep it."

"I've given you an order, my boy." He smiled, but it was
a thin smile.

"I received a prior order from Don Nicosa. You want it

canceled, get him to cancel it. You going to try to push some more, Don Carmi?"

I was being deliberately offensive. His face reddened and his hands shook. He spat a *gergo* phrase at me I didn't know. It had the word *lupara* in it and that means to kill a man.

I said, "You can have me killed, just as I can kill you right here and now. But I'll tell you something, Don Carmi, if you do you'll never find the six hundred fifty thousand dollars and you'll choke to death trying to explain that to Don Nicosa and the Patriarch up in the hills."

He sat and smoked and his anger seemed to subside. His hands stopped shaking. He said in a reasonable voice, "You killed Johnny Castle, didn't you?"

"I was home in bed when that happened. I can produce the girl I was in bed with. This girl, by the way, told me that Johnny Castle was a fairy. Are you aware of that, Don Carmi?"

"You have a rather clever way of twisting a conversation around to get on the offensive," he said loftily. "I suppose you've found it effectual in confusing issues. The lawyer's tactic. You are also a part of this Anti-Mafia, I understand."

"What poppycock! You know damned well if there was any basis for such an accusation I'd be dead! Are you trying to goad me, Don Carmi?"

"No. I'm merely putting things together from the perspective of Sicily. There are so many small facts that fall into place, when you observe them from a distance. You were the friend of Trina Templer, as an instance. Nicosa and Magardi don't know that but I do. It was Templer who was the last person seen with Johnny. He was killed and she disappeared. Don't you agree it seems likely that you met them both at the airport and killed Castle?"

"I could have but I didn't. I haven't seen Miss Templer since she left for Las Vegas. I phoned her but she was never friendly. I'm certain Castle told you all that."

"He did, and that brings up another interesting point. You admit you know Johnny was listening to your telephone wooing. It follows that you know he was having you tailed. It follows that you killed this man in the subway at Spring Street. Johnny was certain of that."

I smiled at him. "Your reasoning is sometimes amusing, Don Carmi, but otherwise you bore the hell out of me. Your accusations are not going to help your life expectancy.

His face got hard and his eyes glared. "Don't threaten! You won't get ten feet outside this hotel if I am not accompanying you in robust health!"

"So—what did you come up here for besides the money?"

Again he controlled his anger. He lowered his voice. "Negotiations for the goods start in Naples tomorrow. Since you refuse to be reasonable about the money, you will have to come to Naples with me."

"You trust me that far?"

"I don't. I will be protected."

"You go to Naples and I will meet you there—in my own way and in my own time.

"Impossible! Are you insane?"

I grinned at him. "You will not have the opportunity to get the money and have me knocked off," I said. "I trust you far less than you trust me, Don Carmi. I will make certain neither you nor your associates will be around when the payoff is made, nor will you find me with the money on my person. Is that clear?"

He nodded at me, then got up. "I'll be at the Vesuvio," he said. "Come when you are ready."

He was a good poker player. He knew when to drop his hand and cut his losses. But he wasn't nearly as smart as I'd expected him to be. Not on this play he wasn't. He'd allowed me to get him angry twice. He'd talked too much.

I gave him three minutes, then followed him out. I took the stairs down and arrived at the bottom just as he was going out the front door. I went out and stood in the shadow of the building to the left of the portal.

There was a green Fiat across the street and Carmi was approaching it. There was a man behind the wheel and Carmi stopped and spoke to him. Then he went to the car parked ahead, a black Lancia, and got in and drove off.

The Monreale is in a residential district and the sidewalks were deserted at this hour. I took my knife out of its sheath under my arm and put it up my right sleeve. I crossed the street to the Fiat. I stooped to the open window and put the point of the knife against the driver's throat, not gently.

"Put your hands on top of your head and keep them there," I ordered. I spoke in the *gergo mafioso*, in the harsh voice that accompanies their slang.

He did as he was told.

I fanned his body with my left hand and found a pistol in his belt. Then I opened the car door and told him to move over.

I drove up the hill to *Il Borgo* section, holding the pistol in my lap, and stopped on a deserted street of shuttered stores and tenements. Neither of us had spoken. There was a street light nearby and I could see his face now. A typical *bassa mafioso,* a brother of the Joes and Louies in America. I held the gun in my lap, pointed at him.

"You know me?"

He nodded. "Andradi."

"Don Andradi!" I roared. "You stupid *contadino!*"

"Yes, Don Andradi." He was unperturbed.

"Who ordered you to tail me?"

He looked at me and shrugged. "You know," he said.

"Don Carmi?"

"Who else?"

"That's what I'm asking you, who else?"

He shrugged again.

"You were to follow me until I got the money, then kill me. Is that the deal?"

His head nodded imperceptibly. It might have been an affirmative.

"I've got the money now," I said. I tapped my stomach with my left hand. "It's right here. You want to make a try for it?"

He looked at me with expressionless eyes, the lids half-closed. It was the *mafioso* way of threatening. "I have my orders," he said.

"I've got mine," I replied. "Who do you think you're dealing with, you fathead? Don't you know you're double-crossing the American Elders?"

He sneered at me then, and there was a world of meaning in that sneer. Only one associated with the top would dare sneer at the American Elders.

"Who do you work for?" I demanded.

A mule-stubborn look came over his face. I raised the pistol and pointed it at his forehead.

"Give me a name!" I said. "Give me a name or start praying!"

He turned his head carefully away from me. He was breathing hard. He was frightened. Then suddenly he made a desperate grab for the gun with his right hand and poked me with shattering force in the side with his left elbow.

It was a suicidal thing to do. As he grabbed the gun by the barrel it went off. I couldn't have prevented it, for he pulled the gun against my trigger finger.

I dropped the gun on the seat and got out of the car fast. I gave him a brief glance before I turned and started walking back to the avenue. He had been shot in the neck and blood was spurting from the wound.

People were running and two policemen were peddling hard on bicycles towards the car as I reached the corner. I stood in the darkened doorway of a store for a moment and looked at them, then started walking down the hill, not fast enough to attract attention.

I told the Professor in his room at the top of the Vesuvio in Naples, "You want to call a truce until we make this deal, or you want me to keep knocking off your workmen? You make the choice, Carmi. I'm sick of it and I'm sick of you and your double-dealing."

He was rolling a cigar in his long, thin fingers. He put it in his mouth and lit it carefully, then looked at me through a puff of smoke.

"I can't save you now, Andradi. That wasn't my workman you killed. You've offended a man of great power."

"You tell this man of great power that both you and he have offended me. You tell him that he and his whole bloody Brotherhood can go whistling for the six hundred and fifty thousand dollars. You think Italy is the only place I can buy goods? The Corsicans have it for sale. The Russians have it by the ton. I can get it in Turkey and Syria. Tell him I'll buy elsewhere. I'll wait here in Naples for his reply."

Carmi didn't lose his poise but there was a subtle change in his expression, as of the player who suddenly discovers he has misread his cards—that he holds nothing more threatening than a busted flush.

"I believe you would do it, you vicious sonofabitch."

I reached out, not quickly, and slapped his face with force. "Watch your tongue, Carmi."

He turned white. I'd finally got to him. Just that little slap did it. I'd scared him. Maybe it was the first time any man had ever laid a violent hand on him. We both discovered, he and I, that he had no stomach for the physical. But that didn't forward my situation any. He still had access to the Patriarch and I did not.

I told him, "I came over here for one thing, Carmi, to buy. I'm going to buy. Whether it's from the Brotherhood or somebody else makes no difference to me. I'll be at the Continental for two days. You're out of it. You keep out of my sight. If I see you I'll kill you."

I was keeping it on the level of Mafia understanding. Carmi understood. I left him, feeling embarrassed for him, and went across the Via Partenope and down worn stone steps to the restaurants bordering the bay. I picked one, ignoring the fact that I was being followed, and sat out in the open on the terrace. There was still the money, and only I knew it was around my waist, so I was safe enough. The money would keep me alive.

I ate a luncheon of scaloppini and an excellent gorgonzola

172

and coffee—nothing different from any Italian restaurant in America—and sat there waiting out the afternoon.

Nothing and nobody. I had an aperitif at the same table, then dinner. I was bored, sick of my own company, sick of practicing patience. At 9:00 P.M. I left the restaurant and gave my various shadows the slip, just to keep in practice. Then I picked them all up again at my hotel, which was a block down from the Vesuvio.

The next morning at 10:00 I was back on the terrace of the bayside restaurant eating breakfast and watching my shadows arrange themselves for observation. At 11:42 a small pimp-type Italian in tight pants approached my table and asked me if I would accompany him to see a friend. He used a *gergo mafioso* expression, which was sufficient identification.

I followed him to a taxi waiting with the engine running. I got in beside my escort and we took off, being driven with Italian abandon through a series of narrow streets, always going up and getting steeper as we progressed.

As we got higher the city grew quieter and looked cleaner. Far below was the curving bay, the Mediterranean a deep blue that has inspired so much rhyming. Even in my mood of disparagement I had to admit it was impressive.

We arrived before a small cafe near the top of the hill and the taxi stopped. I followed my escort into a long room with booths lining the sides, a small dance floor in the middle, and a curved bar at the back. There was a bright light halfway down which seemed to be focused upon one of the booths, most of which were occupied.

I was taken to the booth with the light on it and sitting in its glare, apparently oblivious to the brightness, was a well-padded Italian who looked like a successful businessman with a fat portfolio of "interests."

He got up as we approached and extended a hand to me. "Signor Andradi? I am Luigi Gordini. Please join me for luncheon. It is a great honor to meet you, sir."

I finished shaking his hand, which was damp, and sat. The place he indicated on the banquette had the light full in my eyes and I immediately resented its discomfort.

Gordini purred at me, "I know the light is a nuisance, Signor Andradi. I have complained to the patron. He has promised to have it fixed. Please be patient."

He spoke in the Sicilian dialect but he was not too familiar with it. I guessed he was from the north, by the size of him. He was an outgoing and cheerful host, as glib as a Florida real estate salesman, and it took me some time to penetrate beyond his garrulousness and discover what was going on.

173

What was going on was a sort of underworld lineup, staged for the identification of Danny-boy Andradi to the workmen, thieves, jobbers, and assassins occupying the tables.

So now they knew me.

I broke into one of Gordini's more flowery periods and said, "This is a good way to do it, Signor. They know me and I don't know them. But I'll tell you something. If you and your boys want the six hundred and fifty thousand dollars you're going to have to sell me goods. You'll never get it any other way."

He nodded at me cheerfully enough. "We will sell you what you want to buy. I will personally show you a sample in a very few days—as soon as we have made the arrangements."

I ate a hearty lunch and found the place pleasant after the light was turned off. I relaxed. Negotiations were under way and I had a comfortable twenty-one days in which to conclude them. In which to conclude everything.

TWENTY-ONE

Buying narcotics in the Italian market is not only a most secretive activity but it is as highly complicated as devious minds can make it. Added to the normal Latin proclivity towards ceremonial folderol is the underworld proclivity towards deceit. Thus the transaction becomes a charade of misdirection, and in due course the negotiator finds himself bordering on a nervous decline.

I had the money and I wanted to buy, and that ordinarily poses the simplest of economic problems—but not with heroin for export. I was not able to find out who had the heroin and who would sell it to me until weeks of exasperation and broken appointments that chased me from one end of Italy to the other—that enabled a score of persons to misguide me and test my patience, my determination, and my gullibility. An important part of the charade was to try every means to cheat me, all in the friendliest of spirits.

These activities took time, and I saw the days slipping by and my deadline approaching with growing apprehension.

After my first meeting with Gordini I waited for three days until I saw him again. I sat out most of the time in my room at the Continental or on the terrace of the waterside restaurant. I was strongly inclined to the belief, before Gordini's knock came on my door Monday evening, that this was some subtle form of Sicilian revenge devised by Carmi.

"We will have to go north for the samples," he said. "They are not available in Naples—you don't mind a little trip, Signor Andradi?"

"No," I replied. "Where north?"

"You will come with me," he said. "I will show you."

We got a plane that night and flew to Genoa, arriving at midnight. Gordini was his talkative, affable self all the way, but said nothing of importance regarding the purchase. What he said about that, several times, was, "Wait and see."

So I waited and, in a large apartment building overlooking the port, about 1:00 A.M., I saw two men who were introduced as Bennito and Alessandro—Benny and Alex. Then Gordini bade me adieu and I went out with the pair. I thought I was getting some action at last.

175

They had a small Fiat parked a block away and the three of us got in. Alex and I sat in the back and Benny drove. He was short, fat, and bald, an unkempt little man with tobacco-stained teeth and a strong odor of garlic. Alex was a little taller and a little cleaner, but not much improvement. The thing about him that may have been significant was that he carried a gun. It was in a shoulder holster and I would suppose he believed it was not apparent. I had spotted it in the apartment, so I had shifted my own .380 automatic to my right-hand pocket where it would be handier.

We drove west out of Genoa and north on an *autostrade*. There was a sign at the toll booth reading "Milano." That figured, too, because one of the largest opium-refining plants in Italy was in Milan. FANG had once told me that much of the Mafia heroin was smuggled out of this plant and covered by forged records.

The *autostrade* was deserted. A few miles along, high up in the hills, Alex suddenly asked me if I had the money with me.

"No," I said.

"Then we cannot do business," he said. "We will have to go back."

"I can have it in Milan in an hour," I said. "All it needs is a phone call."

"You mean somebody else will bring the money?"

"That's it."

"You trust somebody with that much?"

"Sure. Somebody trusted me with it, didn't they?"

As the Fiat was laboring up a steep grade a car overtook us, then slowed down. I had glanced at it as it drew abreast and saw three men in the car. One of them resembled Gordini. So the plot thickened.

Benny fiddled with the lights just then, turning them off and on. The other car then picked up speed and soon vanished.

I said to Alex, "I have a gun, too, bright boy."

A surprised look came over his face. "Is that a fact?" he said.

It was about 3:00 A.M. when I checked into the Grand Hotel in Milan, waking up the night porter who roused the clerk. Benny and Alex were still with me. They wanted my room number before leaving, so they could see me that afternoon. I gave it to them and Alex assured me he would be back.

All day Tuesday passed and no Alex. At 7:30 P.M. Wednesday there was a knock on my door and grubby Benny pushed past me into the room when I opened it. He waited until I closed the door, then put his finger to his lips.

"We are having trouble," he whispered. "We wait here for an hour, then I will take you."

We waited an hour and he took me. The Fiat was parked at the hotel entrance. Benny and I drove out of the city southeast on a very rough country road, past two small villages clinging precariously to hillsides. We turned into a farm in the middle of a small valley. It was a black night and I could see nothing beyond the perimeter of the headlights. There were no lights from the farmhouse.

Benny turned off the motor and got out. I followed him up the steps of a porch. He banged loudly on a door. Almost immediately it was opened. We entered and a man with a flashlight led us through a living room, a dining room, and into a large kitchen in the rear that was well lighted. There were heavy curtains on two windows. Around a wooden table with the top bleached by years of scrubbing sat five men. Gordini was one of them and Alex was another. The other three made me feel right at home—Sicilian *bassa mafiosi*—Brothers.

I was introduced to a Tony, a Julo and a Carmine and we shook hands. A chair was vacated for me, next to Gordini, and Carmine stood near the door with Benny. Gordini launched into a speech which apparently was designed to impress me with the great difficulties involved in conducting such a business. I interrupted him with a minimum of politeness.

"Pardon me, Signor Gordini, but let's get on with it," I said. "I have very little interest in your problems. You've got something to sell, you say. I've got money to buy. Let's see it."

The three *mafiosi* regarded me with stony-faced disapproval. Gordini frowned, then pushed his chair back a few inches. He reached into his coat pocket and brought out a small package wrapped in white paper and sealed. He put it on the table, broke the seal, and unwrapped it. He made a production of it. Nothing was going to be easy—even unpeeling a package.

"As you wish, Signor Andradi," he said. "This is the finest merchandise to be obtained anywhere in the world. You will examine it yourself.

The last of the wrapping came off. There was a small cardboard box holding about an ounce of white powder. He pushed it towards me.

I dipped my fingers into the powder and rubbed them together. I smelled them. Then I wet the tip of a finger with my

177

tongue and tasted it. I closed the lid on the box and pushed it back to Gordini.

I wasn't angry. Frustrated is the word. I said, "I will give you twenty cents a pound American money for such stuff as that, Signor Gordini. You are a fool if you think I will be so easily cheated."

A look of astonishment came on his face. He picked up the box, opened the lid and looked in. Then he broke into profuse apologies. He hit his forehead with the heel of his hand, called himself an idiot, and produced a package similar to the first from another pocket. It was a fair display of histrionics.

"As you say, you are an idiot," I said. "I am not now interested in what you have in your other package. I will go elsewhere. Do not delude yourself that you have a corner on this market."

That turned the trick. Never were there such protestations of affection and respect, such assurances of bargain prices and honest dealing. Even the three *mafiosi* relaxed their scowling.

I permitted myself to be persuaded. I gave the powder the cursory tests FANG had taught me and it seemed to be high-grade heroin, very slightly diluted.

I pushed the box back to Gordini and shook my head. "You've got to do better than that," I said. "I'm not paying for milk sugar—not one ounce of milk sugar in a kilo, Signor Gordini. Now that you have tried to cheat me, I shall be much more difficult."

More protestations, more apologies, more head pounding. I got up. "All right then, signor, we will continue the negotiations. I will accept your assurances."

I will not detail further the course of the interminable bargaining that went on for the rest of the days left to me up to April 24, that took me from Milan to Rome, then back to Naples, then to Rome again, and finally to Palermo.

Gordini faded out of the picture after Milan, being replaced by a *capo mafioso* named Pete Colangelo who had been deported from America shortly before World War II. Through him I met many of the ex-Americans of the Mafia in Rome and Naples, all deportees and all bitter men against the Federals. After Colangelo came a *capo mafioso* of quite a different type, Don Angelo Ruzzi, who had never been to America and had no desire to go there. He had it made in Sicily and Italy and he didn't need anything or anybody outside the Brotherhood.

After three days of meetings with Ruzzi in various parts

of Rome, apparently with no more reason than to exchange comments on the weather, I became desperate. It was now April 20 and I had only four days to my deadline. Sicily had not been mentioned once, and it appeared at that hour all of my planning had been for nothing. I was becoming convinced that I would never get to the Mafia fountainhead on this narcotics trail.

On this third day Ruzzi took me to a small restaurant, off the Via Appia for lunch and when we were seated, I said, "I have delighted in your company, Don Ruzzi, and I don't want to appear impolite, but we must settle our business today or I shall have to withdraw. I have been talking to a friend of the Russians and I am planning other arrangements."

He was unperturbed. He nodded and said, "That will not be necessary. Our dealings are about concluded."

"We have had no dealings yet," I said.

"Oh, yes. I have been very busy. I know what you want. I have a price for you—a most advantageous price—and the other matters are settled. We can conclude the details today, if you insist."

"The delivery and the payment?" I asked.

"Oh, no! That must wait. That cannot take place in Rome, you know."

"Where?" I asked.

"Ah! I will show you. We will go there together."

"I have a most important appointment on Friday at noon in Palermo and I cannot miss it."

"In Palermo!" he exclaimed. "That is fortunate. We will leave Rome tomorrow morning and by Friday noon the goods will be in your hands and you may keep your appointment."

"Fine," I said. Did he mean we were going to Palermo together? I had to assume so—or there would be no Bloody Friday.

The final price set by Don Ruzzi was slightly under $15,500 per kilo—far below the price paid by Magardi and his syndicate for their last shipment bought in Italy. He had paid nearer $18,000 a kilo. I was getting forty-two kilos for the $650,000, and it did not bother me at all that it was adulterated some three to five per cent. The Mafia would never see it to complain about it.

During my second trip to Naples I had found Captain Tom O'Hara and his tramp freighter *Celeste-Anne* in port and I had concluded the arrangements with him to carry my "suitcase" with him back to Ciudad Trujillo. He was not sailing from Naples until the end of April, so I had plenty of time to get the goods on board. I had given him $2,000 and another case of Irish whisky (which had been no easy thing to find) and had promised him $3,000 more when the bag was delivered.

I met Ruzzi at 8:00 A.M. on April 22 at his hotel. I told him, "I've been wondering if it would be possible for you to put me in touch with Don Carmi. I'd like very much to see him again before we conclude our business."

He looked at me and nodded, smiling the slightest bit. "You are certain to see him in due course, Signor Andradi."

I let it go. We took a cab to the Rome airport, where Don Ruzzi bought two tickets for Palermo.

I checked into the Monreale once more, at Ruzzi's suggestion and got a room just below the one I had occupied before. This was around 1:00 P.M. and he told me he would come back for me after dinner.

"Have the money," he said. "It will be paid over very soon after I pick you up."

"I will have it," I assured him. "But now that we are back in Palermo, time is no longer so pressing. I think I would prefer to conclude our business at a later date. Not tonight, Don Ruzzi."

He looked at me narrowly and for the first time permitted me to see the hardness under his suave exterior.

"I don't understand you," he said.

I shrugged. "I have fallen in with the delaying customs of these negotiations. No, I will not do business tonight. I will see you Friday morning, Don Ruzzi. I should like to conclude this transaction just before noon on Friday. I think that is the most propitious hour for me."

He hesitated, undecided whether to permit his anger to show itself. Then suddenly his face relaxed and he smiled.

"I will see you Friday shortly after eleven," he said.

He had been gone less than a minute when there was a knock on the door. I thought it was he returning for some forgotten instruction. I opened the door and the day porter stood there with a letter in his hand. He held it out to me.

"This came for you during your absence," he said. "We did not have a forwarding address so we held it."

I took it, gave him 100 lira, and closed the door. The envelope was addressed to me in a feminine handwriting I'd never seen before. What possible woman in the world would know I had been at the Monreale in Palermo?

I tore it open and extracted a birthday card. There was a handwritten note under the printed verse. It read: "Hurry home. I miss you. Love, Trina."

I had never seen Trina's handwriting. I looked at it a long time, then examined the envelope closely. It had been mailed in New York on March 28—the day of my birthday. I tried to pull the glued flap open and it stuck fast. I found a minute spot of glue in one corner. There was no doubt the envelope had been opened and re-sealed with glue before it had reached me.

This was no birthday greeting from Trina. This was a clumsy and obvious attempt to link Trina to me—and to link me to the Anti-Mafia. But clumsy and obvious or not, it was diabolically effective. It was, in Palermo, the equivalent of a sentence to death.

TWENTY-TWO

MY PREPARATIONS FOR THE CONCLUSION OF THE NARCOTICS deal were not unreasonable.

I strapped the .380 automatic to my right leg, on the inside of the thigh, with adhesive tape. I cut the tape part way through with a scissors in several places, after the strapping, so a pull outward would free the gun quickly.

I strapped my knife to the inside of my right forearm in the same way, so that it would stay there until I gave it a yank. Then I cut out the two side pockets of my pants so I could reach the gun with either hand.

When I dressed I left off the money belt Nicosa had given me for the first time since leaving New York. I took out the packages of bills and tied them up in a neat bundle covered with wrapping paper. Then I went down to wait in the lobby.

Angelo Ruzzi arrived at the hotel at 11:18 on April 24—forty-two minutes before the execution deadline. It was not much time, certainly. Most likely it was too little. But a few minutes one way or the other wouldn't make any difference, so long as I met the Patriarch at last. All of my certainties about that were back with me. Now I knew where I was going to be taken and who would greet me there. The forged birthday card told me it would be Don Carmi and the Patriarch.

I followed Don Ruzzi out of the hotel to a car parked at the curb. It was a Lancia with a workman behind the wheel. We got in the back and he started off, without instructions.

Don Ruzzi had stopped being affable. When we were in the car, he pointed to the package I carried and asked in a sneering voice, "Is that the money, Andradi?"

"Yes."

"You had it with you all of the time, didn't you?"

"Of course."

"You think you got away with something, eh? You're going to meet Don Carmi this morning."

"Good. Somebody else, too, I hope."

"Yes, somebody else."

"Fine."

We drove up the hill behind Palermo. We drove through the *Il Borgo* section and on up. We climbed steadily for a half-hour and there were twelve minutes left to noon when we swung off the avenue into the driveway of a huge stone villa, box-square, of two stories. On our right, down the hill, was a formal garden of several acres, visible from the driveway, and farther below us was spread Palermo and the bay.

Ruzzi and I got out and I followed him to the door. It was opened as we arrived by a workman dressed in livery. We were in a hallway rising two stories with a mosaic ceiling and tiled floor. There was a wide stairway to the left, curving gracefully to a balcony, and the walls were covered with tapestries depicting scenes of knighthood. I didn't get much chance to examine them; we were approached immediately by two workmen who gave me an expert frisk. One of them discovered the knife up my sleeve and asked me politely to give it to him. I did. The pistol they missed.

Ruzzi said to me with undisguised animosity, "Where's your gun, Andradi? Don't tell me you trust us that far?"

I said, "You're the one who will need the gun, Don Ruzzi."

It was another one of my silly remarks.

I followed Ruzzi and the two workmen followed me to an oaken door, darkened with age, off to the right. Ruzzi knocked, then opened it, and stood aside as we entered.

This room was a combination library and office. There were a couple of tall bookcases, there was a large mahogany desk, and there were four deep, comfortable chairs around a fireplace.

Behind the desk was the imposing head and broad shoulders of a truly superior Sicilian—a man so obviously above all ordinary men that he could have been none other than the great Mafia Patriarch. His hair was iron gray and nicely curled. His lips were full and red and pouting.

Ruzzi came up behind me and said, "Don Mazzarina, this is Andradi. He has come with the money in his hand, as you see, as you have ordered."

I said, "The money is for the purchase of goods, Don Mazzarini. I hope you have them."

In the *gergo mafioso* in which we spoke, the last phrase carried a threat with it. It was literally "I hope you have them" but the connotation was that you'd better have them or else.

The Patriarch looked me over and did not deign to reply. He said to the workman standing at the right, "Get the goods, Carlo."

Carlo went to a cabinet behind the desk, opened it, and

took out a large suitcase. He picked it up and put it at my feet. I hefted it and it seemed to weigh the required eighty-two or eighty-three pounds. I got down on my knee and opened it, unbuckling two straps and unsnapping the lock.

Mazzarini said, "Where do you want it delivered, Andradi?"

I looked up at him. "I will take it with me," I said.

He laughed, a completely humorless sound. "Don't play the fool, Andradi! Don Carmi will show you proof that you are working for this Anti-Mafia—that you are a traitor to the Brotherhood and a violator of *omertà*.

"What proof?" I demanded.

"The birthday card from the Templer woman. He has a photograph of it, Andradi."

I nodded at him. I said, "Then the goods are to be delivered aboard a ship, the *Celeste-Anne*, now in Naples. She will be in Naples until the end of the month. All arrangements are made with the captain and the bag is to be given to him."

He wrote down the name of the ship. "Who is the captain?"

"Tom O'Hara."

He wrote that down. I was still on my knees. I began examining the packages. The lid of the suitcase hid me from him below the shoulders. I got my left hand in my pants pocket and my fingers around the butt of the gun. I gave it a yank and it came free. Ruzzi and the two workmen were slightly behind me. I waited for them to jump me. They didn't.

I slipped the gun under the package of money, on the floor at my right hand. Then I closed the suitcase, buckled the straps, and got up, picking up the money with the gun under it and holding it against my body.

I said, "I am satisfied with the goods, Don Mazzarini."

He told Carlo, "Take the goods out to the car and have them delivered to this ship." He handed the workman the slip of paper upon which he had written my instructions. "Get them out of the house quickly. They have been here too long."

Carlo picked up the bag and left. That left three of them: Don Ruzzi of Rome and Palermo, a workman and Don Lupi Mazzarini, ruler of the Brotherhood, fountainhead of evil.

Mazzarini was the greatest of the *capo mafiosi*, the man whose widom traditionally cemented the Brotherhood into an effective unit, but he was greedy, too, as were all *mafiosi*. He was avaricious enough to have me standing before him on this April twenty-fourth at noon.

I said, "Here is the money, Don Mazzarini." I approached his desk. I glanced down at my watch and saw that it was after twelve—about eight minutes after.

I held the money package with my left hand and got my finger on the trigger of the gun. I moved the safety off with my thumb.

I put the money on Mazzarini's desk and pointed the gun at his head. There were the two at my back, so I didn't have much time for a speech. I said, *"Sangu lava sangu,* Don Mazzarini."

I pulled the trigger. I shot him in the center of his forehead.

Then I whirled and I shot the workman. I shot him because he was drawing his gun. I looked at Ruzzi and wondered how he had been able to keep his composure.

I said, "This is the day of execution, Ruzzi. This is the day Don Mazzarini and all of the rulers of the Mafia in America were killed by the Anti-Mafia. . . . Let us find Don Carmi."

He nodded at me. He said, "You are very able. Don Nicosa warned us. We should have taken greater precautions."

"Where's Carmi?" I demanded.

He seemed not to hear me. He said, "We should have had you killed on the way up here. It is Don Mazzarini's fault. He wanted to have a look at you. He said he would kill you himself after Don Carmi had talked to you. He has a gun in the drawer of his desk, Andradi . . ."

Then Don Carmi's voice came from behind me and I knew why Ruzzi had kept talking. Carmi had come in through a door at the far end of the room. He had been expected.

He said, "Turn around, Andradi. I want you to be looking at me when I kill you."

It was typical of Carmi to say just that and to wait until I had turned around. Any *mafioso* with an ounce of sense would have shot first and talked later.

I turned. I whirled fast and I shot at the same instant and I got Carmi just above the bridge of the nose. But his gun had fired also, at the same split second as mine, and I was knocked to my knees by a heavy-calibre slug high on my left arm.

I swung my gun around to Ruzzi, fighting to keep steady. I got slowly to my feet and said, "Let's get out of here, Ruzzi. You lead the way. Stay close. If you co-operate you'll live."

I fanned him for a gun as he opened the door and took a Browning automatic from his belt. I looked out into the great hall. The liveried workman was standing near the front door with a gun in his hand, looking questioningly at us. Up on the balcony were two others with guns, just standing and

185

looking down. I pulled Ruzzi back into the room and closed the door.

"Show me another way out," I said.

He led me to the far side of the room and to the door by which Carmi had entered. He opened it slowly. I looked down a long hallway and there was nobody in sight.

"Lead on," I said. "Just stay close."

I followed him to the end of the hall and to a glassed-in conservatory overlooking the formal garden. French windows opened onto a lawn and we went out and walked fast towards a graveled path that led down into the garden. We had progressed about twenty feet and were near a hedge when there was a shot from the house.

I jumped to my right and landed on my good arm in a bed of lilies. I rolled behind the hedge and almost did for myself when my weight hit my wounded arm. There were two more quick shots from the house and one of them kicked up dirt inches from my head.

I looked around for Ruzzi. He was lying in the path on his face, his arms spread wide. There was blood in his gray hair.

I crawled down the hill, keeping trees and bushes and the hedge between myself and the house. There were only two more shots, both too close. Somebody had found a rifle.

I was soon out of sight of the house entirely, concealed by heavier growth at the bottom of the garden. My arm had been numb up to then, except when I had rolled on it. Now it began to ache like an ulcerated tooth.

I got down behind a bush and took off my jacket and shirt and examined the wound. The bullet had gouged out a chunk of flesh but apparently had not damaged the bone. It had gone right through and had left a bloody, aching mess. I cut the sleeves from my shirt with a pocket knife and bandaged the wound with them.

There was a wall at the bottom of the garden, about seven feet high. Climbing it was out of the question with my bad arm. I started exploring it to the right and found nothing but wall all the way to the corner, where it took a right-angle turn and started back up the hill. Then I retraced my steps and tried it in the other direction. Still nothing but wall. Those in the house knew all this, of course. So they'd be out hunting me down like a cornered rabbit. That damned Carmi and his lucky shot!

I started back up the hill, following the far wall, moving just a little at a time, examining every bush and every bit of cover. The hunted could also be the hunter. Maybe, if I was lucky, I could discourage them.

186

I made about a hundred yards and was within sight of the house again without encountering anyone. It was far worse than seeing my pursuers; I was certain they were all about me. Then I saw someone and the question was answered. This someone was a policeman. The cops had come.

This policeman was standing where Ruzzi had fallen, looking down at his body. I went back down the garden, hunting for something entirely different this time. I was hunting for a place to hole up until dark. I felt relatively safe now. The *mafiosi* certainly wouldn't tell the police about me. *Omertà* would prevent that. So if the police didn't know, they wouldn't be hunting for me. Yes, I was safe. The only people after me were the *mafiosi*—say about ten per cent of the population of Palermo.

It took me two weeks and most of the money I had—some $7,000—to get out of Sicily. A necessary part of it was getting my wounded arm properly treated, for it soon became infected. I was able to buy antibiotics on the black market and to bribe a couple of doctors not to report me to the police.

These two weeks of flight began with my theft of a police car at the villa on the night of the 24th and ended at Messina on May 9 when I found a small cargo vessel to take me to Tunis.

This concludes my account of Anti-Mafia and the efforts of a group of intelligent and dedicated men to combat the evil of the Brotherhood in America. I have no doubt that all of this bloodshed in which I participated was justified by its results. It is still too early, perhaps to indite an epitaph to the Hoodlum Empire, but there appears to be ample evidence that the Mafia's stranglehold on America has been broken.

The underworld is as powerful as always, and the larceny in the souls of most men support this power in many ways, but without the master organization of the Mafia to guide their manifold evils, the problems of policing and control are once more possible of solution.

Trina and I live on an island and I will tell you that it's in the West Indies. If you want to come down there—if you want to "get" me for my violation of the sacred commandments of *omertà*—you will have difficulty. The island is well guarded by our friends and neighbors—all former FANG people—and on the good days, which are most of the days of the year, we even have air cover, a patrolling seaplane that stops all boats which get too close to our vicinity and urges them elsewhere.

We have a boat and we do a great deal of sailing, always with the seaplane within radio call. Our boat is the *Vega* which I purchased with Mafia money for their use. I think you should know about the *Vega* before I close this account.

FANG had our island picked out long before I arrived in Bermuda to get Trina. Smith, Jones and Judge Williams, all in Bermuda on ostensible vacations, told me that we should go there immediately. It was the last of our councils of Anti-Mafia elders, held on a private beach in the sun, the four of us lying on towels after a swim.

I listened to their proposal for a time, then I made a speech —a not unusual procedure for me.

I said, "Trina and I are going away together—just the two of us. We don't want a lot of neighbors on a small island somewhere. Not yet. We're going to get married, first. I think we'll fly down to Granada and get married there. A friend told me of a church up on a hill overlooking the harbor, and that sounds like a good place.

"Then we're going on a honeymoon—all alone. We'll knock around this island and that, going where the spirit moves, seeing people and places and living like normal honeymooners and tourists. No Mafia and no alarums and no FANG. So long as we keep out of Cuba we'll have no Mafia after us. It's as safe as a Sunday stroll in Central Park—that is, before nightfall. . . . I'm not asking you gentlemen about this. I'm telling you."

Trina had just come out of the water and her beautiful legs gleamed wetly in the sun. She came up to us just in time to hear the tail end of my speech. She frowned at me and said, "Are you being belligerent again, Danny-boy?"

I said, "Can't you wait until we're married to make me over?"

She said, "You apologize to these gentlemen. Go on."

So I apologized. Why argue? Then Judge Williams said, "I suppose it's up to you, Danny. If that's what you want to do, you do it."

I looked at Trina. "O.K.?" I asked.

"O.K.," she said.

So we were married in the church on the hill on the island of Granada, by an old priest who had asthma and had difficulty getting through the ceremony, as I myself did, and then we started our tour. In due course we found ourselves in Ciudad Trujillo, and I must admit none of my danger reflexes were working very well or we never would have gone there. I suppose I was too relaxed.

We checked into the Reforma Hotel on the beach and before we'd been able to make up our minds whether to go to lunch or lie down and rest—I was all for resting—there was a knock on the door.

It was the little customs officer, Colonel Valdez, all dressed up in his Sunday uniform, smiling and affable. He kissed Trina's hand when I introduced him and he shook mine with enthusiastic warmth. He'd come for his $20,000.

I said, "Then everything's come off as scheduled?"

"Oh yes, señor. Your boat is all ready to sail. I told your captain to wait until I had talked to you as soon as I found out you had arrived, in case there were any further instructions. He will call on you shortly."

I didn't have any $20,000. I had only a few hundred. The days of the big Mafia bankrolls were gone forever.

I said, "I will have the money for you this evening, Colonel Valdez. Do you wish to drop by or shall I send it to you?"

He was annoyed. He hid it hardly at all. "I will come by at eight o'clock," he said shortly and left.

"What's that all about?" Trina demanded.

"Some loose ends I forgot to tie up. I owe that man $20,000, it appears. Now we are about to be visited by the *mafiosi*—Aldo Danelli and his two boys."

She laughed. She said, "And you without your gun! Aren't you going to look silly!"

I said, "I'm going to look as silly as a sieve, if they've heard anything. You get out of here. Go on down to the bar and I'll meet you later."

"I should say not! Do you think I'm going to miss this?"

"Look, Trina, this isn't play-acting. These people don't fool around, believe me. They're going to come up here with blood in their eyes if they've heard of the big double-cross. They're—"

There was a knock on the door. I'd wasted too much time arguing. I shooed her into the bedroom. Then I went to the door and opened it. I felt my belly contract, waiting for the blow. I was back again in the fear and violence of the Brotherhood.

Aldo Danelli came in smiling with his hand held out. The two workmen, Joe Allegri and Sally Fondi, came in behind him, not smiling but with their hands extended.

I shook hands all around. Aldo said, "We did not expect you, Don Andradi. This is fine. I have been telling the boys that now maybe you will sail back with us."

I said, "When did you get here?"

"Just last night, Don Andradi. We had a long charter all the way up from Trinidad and we did not get rid of our passengers until day before yesterday. I'm sorry we were so late. . . ."

"You've been sailing all the time for the past few weeks? Since April twenty-fourth?"

"Most of the time. We'd go into ports now and then, but not often."

"You've seen newspapers—listened to the radio?"

He shook his head. "This charter we had, he was real crazy. A writer or something. He wouldn't permit the radio and he hated newspapers. He said all the time the world was going to hell and he didn't want to hear about it."

I let out my breath, which apparently I'd been holding. I said, "O.K., you boys go on back to my boat. Wait for me. I'll figure out something."

Trina came into the room then and I introduced her. Aldo kissed her hand with a flourish and congratulated the both of us. Joe and Sally smiled for the first time and stopped looking like workmen on a job.

Trina said, "Did I hear something about a boat?"

I said, "It's nothing—"

Aldo interrupted, "It's Don Andradi's boat, signora. A beautiful boat. You should come with us when we sail north."

She looked at me. She said, "Your boat, huh? Why didn't you tell me, darling?"

I said, "I wanted it to be a surprise. . . . You men run along. I'll see you later."

I got rid of them. I tried to explain the situation to Trina. I didn't want to mention the heroin, so the rest of it didn't make much sense.

Then she summed it up. "It's all a lot of foolishness, Danny. Those men are charming and they adore you. Anyone can see that. We'll go for a cruise. They can take us to our island, then we'll have the boat. Doesn't that make sense?"

"No," I said.

"O.K. We'll do it anyway—you've pushed me around enough. Now it's my turn. I told you how it was going to be when we got married. You thought I was kidding, eh?"

I said, "No, darling. We'll do it your way. I'll just buy a gun in town here and try to keep the both of us alive long enough for you to see your mistake. Then you can apologize to me with your last breath."

"You're an alarmist, that's what. Those three are darling!"

I got $25,000 in cash from FANG, after a brief argument over the telephone. They had to fly the money to me from New York, but it arrived before 8:00 P.M. I gave $20,000 of it to Colonel Valdez when he called a little after 8:00 and then I took $3,000 and hunted for Captain Tom O'Hara. I found him in a bar where I'd gone with him several times for drinks and I had a last one with him. Then I went back to the hotel and got Trina and we went aboard the *Vega*.

I ordered Aldo to sail immediately and we left the harbor on engine shortly before midnight, going almost due east to our island.

The second night out, when we were off the coast of Puerto Rico, heading into the trade winds and a gentle swell, I told Aldo to bring the suitcase of goods on the deck.

He hesitated. He had an astonished look on his face. "On the deck, Don Andradi?"

"Yes, that's what I said. And stop calling me Don Andradi."

When he had gone below Trina said, "You do have a nasty manner. Why talk to him that way?"

"You'll see, darling. This is something we've got to go through—Aldo, Joe, Sally and myself. You just stand there and look pretty and let me handle it."

"All right—just this once. But don't think I'm abdicating. I'm still the boss."

"O.K., boss."

I kissed her in the moonlight and then Aldo came on deck lugging the suitcase.

"Get Joe and Sally," I said.

Joe was in the wheelhouse on watch. Aldo lashed the wheel and told him to join us, then went below and came back with Sally. When the three of them were lined up by the rail I opened the suitcase and took out one of the packages. I addressed them.

"From now on, no more narcotics. No more Mafia. No more crime. We're all straight, the five of us. We have the boat which we will all share equally, and we have plenty of dough for everything we need. We go to an island about 300 miles east and we live there, off the fat of the land. You can work if you want to but you don't have to. We're pulling out. Do I make myself clear?"

I opened the package of heroin and spilled the white powder over the side.

Sally was the first to speak. He said, "Jeeze!"

Then Aldo said, "They won't let us, Don Andradi."

"Stop calling me Don Andradi—they won't have anything to say about it. We've got protection—the Federals. You get the pitch?"

"If you say so, Don—Mister Andradi. How do we know?"

"You'll have to try it. Mrs. Andradi and I are going to

try it. We're not worried. You've got as much guts as she has, haven't you?"

"Sure," said Aldo. "But—couldn't I have just one of those packages, Mr. Andradi? Just one?"

"No. I told you. We're all straight."

"One of 'em is a fortune!" said Joe. "A fortune!"

I opened a second package and spilled out the powder. Then Aldo sighed, shrugged, and reached for one. He opened it and dumped its contents. Sally joined him. Only Joe held out.

"I couldn't do it," he said simply.

So now we have the ketch *Vega* and the finest captain and crew in the West Indies. We can sail anywhere—that is, almost anywhere—and we live a life that many people would call idyllic, with our FANG friends and our three *mafiosi*. The only bug in the *gribische*, if you want to call it a bug, is a situation that arises occasionally when we board the *Vega* for a cruise. This situation develops from a remark that Trina likes to make.

"Didn't I tell you so?" she says.